▶▶▶ ACCEL·WORLD ⁰8

THE BINARY STARS OF DESTINY

REKI KAWAHARA
ILLUSTRATION BY **HIMA**
DESIGN BY **bee-pee**

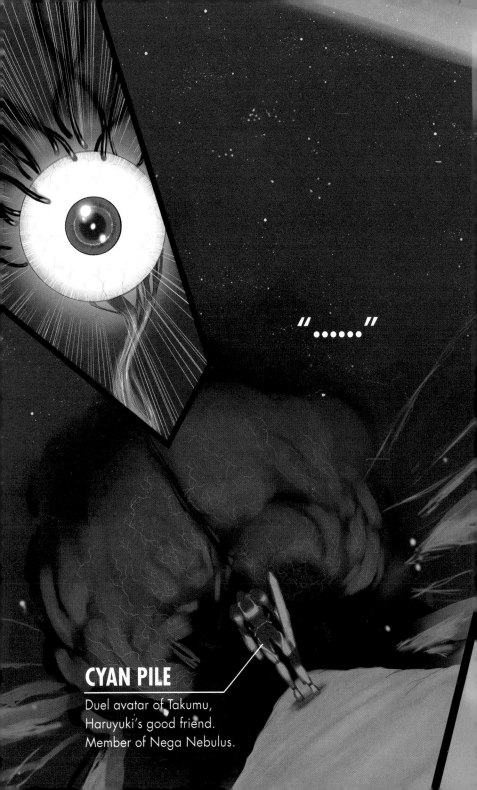

"......"

CYAN PILE
Duel avatar of Takumu,
Haruyuki's good friend.
Member of Nega Nebulus.

CHIYURI

Controls the Nega Nebulus duel avatar Lime Bell. Haruyuki's childhood friend.

"Wh-what are you doing?!"

KUROYUKIHIME

Vice president of the Umesato
Junior High student council.
Controls the "Black King,"
Black Lotus.

"I'm sorry!
W-wi-wipe
it off or it'll
st-st-stain—"

"Mm.
I'll wipe it
off, then."

UTAI SHINOMIYA

Controls the duel avatar Ardor Maiden, a member of the old Nega Nebulus. Grade four student.

"Shi... nomi... ya...?"

"There's no need to feel awkward, Arita. This is most likely out of view of the social cameras."

TRILEAD TETROXIDE

Mysterious, young samurai-type avatar encountered in the Castle.

"Th-that's... I mean, me too, meeting you, Lead..."

"...So that is your true form, then, Crow. I truly am happy to have met you."

WHAT ARE THE SEVEN STARS, THE LEGENDARY EQUIPMENT MODELED AFTER THE BIG DIPPER?

Also known as the Seven Arcs, the Seven Stars are the most powerful Enhanced Armaments in the Accelerated World. In star order of the Big Dipper, they are:

Star No. 1 (alpha): *Tensuu* Arc, the greatsword Impulse
Star No. 2 (beta): *Tensen* Arc, the staff Tempest
Star No. 3 (gamma): *Tenki* Arc, the large shield Strife
Star No. 4 (delta): *Tenken* Arc, the form of which is unknown, named the Luminary
Star No. 5 (epsilon): *Gyokko* Arc, the straight sword Infinity
Star No. 6 (zeta): *Kaiyou* Arc, the full-body armor Destiny
Star No. 7 (eta): *Youkou* Arc, the form of which is unknown, named the Fluctuating Light

Stars one through four, which comprise the cup of the Big Dipper, were enshrined in the very deepest levels of dungeons to the north, south, east, and west of the Castle. These dungeons lie in Shiba Park, Tokyo Dome, the Shinjuku government building, and below Tokyo Station, respectively.

Currently, the greatsword Impulse (from the dungeon in the Shinjuku government building) belongs to the Blue King, Blue Knight; the staff Tempest (from the dungeon below Tokyo Station) belongs to the Purple King, Purple Thorn; while the large shield Strife (from the Tokyo Dome dungeon) belongs to the Green King, Green Grandé. The ownership of the Luminary (from the enormous maze in Shiba Park) is unknown.

Stars five through seven, which make up the handle of the Big Dipper, were enshrined within the Castle. The straight sword Infinity is owned by Trilead Tetroxide, while the full-body armor Destiny came into the possession of Silver Crow after it changed form. As of now, only the Fluctuating Light remains on its pedestal unclaimed, in the innermost part of the Castle.

Star No. 2 (beta)
Tensen, the staff Tempest

Star No. 3 (gamma)
Tenki, the large shield Strife

Star No. 1 (alpha)
Tensuu, the greatsword Impulse

Star No. 4 (delta)
Tenken, form unknown, the Luminary

Star No. 5 (epsilon)
Gyokko, the straight sword Infinity

Star No. 6 (zeta)
Kaiyou, the full-body armor Destiny

Star No. 7 (eta)
Youkou, form unknown, the Fluctuating Light

▶▶▶*ACCEL·WORLD*
THE BINARY STARS OF DESTINY

Reki Kawahara
Illustrations: HIMA
Design: bee-pee

NEW YORK

■ Kuroyukihime = Umesato Junior High School student council vice president. Trim and clever girl who has it all. Her background is shrouded in mystery. Her in-school avatar is a spangle butterfly she programmed herself. Her duel avatar is the Black King, Black Lotus (level nine).

■ Haruyuki = Haruyuki Arita. Eighth grader at Umesato Junior High School. Bullied, on the pudgy side. He's good at games, but shy. His in-school avatar is a pink pig. His duel avatar is Silver Crow (level five).

■ Chiyuri = Chiyuri Kurashima. Haruyuki's childhood friend. Meddling, energetic girl. Her in-school avatar is a silver cat. Her duel avatar is Lime Bell (level four).

■ Takumu = Takumu Mayuzumi. A boy Haruyuki and Chiyuri have known since childhood. Good at kendo. His duel avatar is Cyan Pile (level five).

■ Fuko = Fuko Kurasaki. Burst Linker belonging to the old Nega Nebulus. One of the Four Elements. Lived as a recluse due to certain circumstances, but is persuaded by Kuroyukihime and Haruyuki to come back to the battlefront. Taught Haruyuki about the Incarnate System. Her duel avatar is Sky Raker (level eight).

■ Uiui = Utai Shinomiya. Burst Linker belonging to the old Nega Nebulus. One of the Four Elements. Fourth-grade student in the elementary division of Matsunogi Academy. Not only can she use the advanced curse removal command "Purify," she is also skilled at long-range attacks. Her duel avatar is Ardor Maiden (level seven).

■ Neurolinker = A portable Internet terminal that connects with the brain via a wireless quantum connection and enhances all five senses with images, sounds, and other stimuli.

■ Brain Burst = Neurolinker application sent to Haruyuki by Kuroyukihime.

■ Duel avatar = Player's virtual self, operated when fighting in Brain Burst.

■ Legion = Groups composed of many duel avatars with the objective of expanding occupied areas and securing rights. There are seven main Legions, each led by one of the Seven Kings of Pure Color.

■ Normal Duel Field = The field where normal Brain Burst battles (one-on-one) are carried out. Although the specs do possess elements of reality, the system is essentially on the level of an old-school fighting game.

■ Unlimited Neutral Field = Field for high-level players where only duel avatars at levels four and up are allowed. The game system is of a wholly

■ Movement Control System = System in charge of avatar control. Normally, this system handles all avatar movement.

■ Image Control System = System in which the player creates a strong image in their mind to operate the avatar. The mechanism is very different from the normal movement control system, and very few players can use it. Key component of the Incarnate System.

■ Incarnate System = Technique allowing players to interfere with the Brain Burst program's Image Control System to bring about a reality outside of the game's framework. Also referred to as "overwriting" game phenomena.

■ Acceleration Research Society = Mysterious Burst Linker group. They do not think of Brain Burst as a simple fighting game and are planning something. Black Vise and Rust Jigsaw are members.

■ Armor of Catastrophe = Enhanced Armament, also called Chrome Disaster. Equipped with this, an avatar can use powerful abilities such as Drain, which absorbs the HP of the Enemy avatar, and Divination, which calculates enemy attacks in advance to evade them. However, the spirit of the wearer is polluted by Chrome Disaster, which comes to rule the wearer completely.

■ ISS kit = Abbreviation for "IS mode study kit." IS mode is "Incarnate System mode." The kit allows any duel avatar who uses it to make use of the Incarnate System. While using it, a red "eye" is attached to some part of the avatar, and a black aura overlay—the staple of Incarnate attacks—is emitted from the eye.

■ Seven Arcs = The seven strongest Enhanced Armaments in the Accelerated World. They are the greatsword Impulse, the staff Tempest, the large shield Strife, the Luminary (form unknown), the straight sword Infinity, the full-body armor Destiny, and the Fluctuating Light (form unknown).

▶▶▶*ACCEL·WORLD*

1

"Equip…the Destiny."

Haruyuki's voice command made the bone-dry air of the Scorched Earth stage ripple and shake ever so slightly. As if a switch had been flipped, the distant roar of the wind, the alarm sounded by his nearly empty HP gauge, the crash of his opponent smashing through one thick wall after another in his relentless march toward Haruyuki—all of it disappeared.

Haruyuki stood in the center of a large, scorched-concrete room, blanketed by heavy silence. And then sensation exploded from a single point within him.

Intense pain.

Like a molten lance piercing deep between his shoulder blades. His vision was haloed in white while an infinite shower of sparks scattered across his brain. His virtual breath stopped. Even his thoughts broke into countless fragments and shot off in all directions.

"…Ngh…Hnk…Aaaah!!" His entire body jerked backward like a bow after its arrow, and a hoarse scream leaked out of his mouth. But even so, a voice abruptly echoed toward him from far, far away—though perhaps it was closer than anything else.

*   *   *

It's useless.

I can no longer be separated from my vessel.

Due to our overwhelming rage, grief, and despair, the armor derived from the Destiny cannot be changed. We desire nothing but blood. Only endless slaughter. Only an eternal parade of catastrophe.

Before his snowy vision, several image fragments flashed in succession, like a "suggested videos" screen had taken over. At the center of them all was a knight-type duel avatar, body covered in heavy blackish-silver armor. But the design was different each time that image flashed.

Innumerable teeth growing from the edge of a hood-shaped helmet.

Tentacles of some sort twisting out from the entire face area.

Long silver hair hanging from the bottom of the helmet down to the feet.

Crimson flames shooting up from the head, dragon's breath.

And a sinister greatsword brandished below a sharply tapered visor that came low over the eyes.

Haruyuki knew instinctively that they were the successive generations of Chrome Disaster. The forms might have been different, but the color of the armor, the aura of darkness, and the frenzied fighting style were exactly the same. In the fragments he saw, these knights swung swords, slashed with talons, and stabbed with teeth as if compelled by an unseen force. They were howling, wailing in excitement as they slaughtered entire groups of duel avatars, avatars who were nowhere near a match for their might.

As the images faded, the voice echoed in his head once more:

Smash. And devour. That is what you desire.

Eat, take, become infinitely strong. Until you alone are left in the wastelands of the Accelerated World.

Until the demise of this world.

From the center of his spine—the exact position of the wire hook that the fifth Disaster had pierced him with—a pain like pale lightning radiated outward, stabbing into his extremities. But Haruyuki gritted his teeth to keep from screaming. If he lost to the destructive impulses now, all this would be for nothing.

The sadness of Niko forced to condemn Cherry Rook, her parent and closest friend, in order to perform her duty as a king.

The love of Chiyuri, who pulled Haruyuki back from the edge after he began to run wild on Hermes' Cord by returning the armor to a seed state for him.

The desire of Kuroyukihime, who reached out to the Haruyuki hiding in the depths of the local net and gave him wings called hope.

And the prayers of a single girl lodged in a corner of the armor, waiting for such a long time…

The pain simply kept growing, endlessly, surpassing the domain of physical sensation to become a storm of energy that overwhelmed, attempting to shred Haruyuki's consciousness. It would all go away if he just called the name "Disaster." He knew that, but he mustered the last of his mental energy and endured the onslaught with everything he had.

At that moment, from the distance of the incandescent world far, far away, another voice came to him.

Believe.

It's all right. I know you can do it, you of all people. You're the one I've been waiting for all this time…

The voice was without a doubt that of the golden girl who appeared before him earlier like a vision. Haruyuki used what little remaining focus he had to give a brief reply.

I'm sorry. I'm not the special person you've been waiting for. I have a ton of problems. I worry all the time. All I do is mess up. I can't trust people, so I run away, even though I can't even walk straight by myself. I'm pathetic.

But I do have one thing I'm proud of now.

I know how to like people again. And lots of them, so many people. I still don't like myself or believe in myself, but even still, I can keep fighting for them. I know that now. It's not much, but I want to do whatever I can to protect our warm place...

These thoughts of Haruyuki's, a torch on the verge of burning out, were answered by that kind voice.

That's more than enough. After all, that—that all by itself—is proof of strength.

Inside Haruyuki, there came the faint but definite sound of something cracking. But not the echo of collapse. The sound of something bouncing off the inside of a shell of hard, hard seed. The sound of *birth*.

A clear silver the temperature of snowmelt spilled out, *gushed out* of him, pushing away the luminescent pain. Haruyuki opened his eyes wide.

Glittering armor was smoothly generating from the fingertips of his remaining right arm. An even more pure, true silver than Silver Crow's own covering—the armor.

The design was powerful, but there was nothing sinister about it. From the palm of his hand to his wrist, up to his elbow, then his upper arm, the armor equipped itself with a light metallic *clink*. Each time he felt another bit of reassuring weight add itself, a vitality twice as great as the armor was heavy filled him, and his body actually seemed to lighten.

Instinctively, Haruyuki understood that this silver Enhanced Armament was the original form of "the Disaster," the Armor of Catastrophe: "the Destiny." The theta star of the Seven Arcs, enshrined alongside the epsilon—the straight sword Infinity—was the armor covering him now.

A long, long time ago, someone had successfully made it into the Castle and obtained the Destiny. But after that, something—many sadnesses, the golden-yellow girl had said—happened, and the form of the armor was distorted to become the Disaster. When Fuko Kurasaki and Utai Shinomiya spoke of the "four confirmed Arcs," they were referring to the Blue King's greatsword Impulse, the Green King's large shield Strife, and the Purple King's staff

Tempest, with the last one being the Disaster Haruyuki himself owned.

Once he knew this, the incredible power hidden within the Armor of Catastrophe made sense. When he considered the fact that it was one of the Seven Arcs and that the epsilon star was effectively sealed away with the eta star still untouched, it was no exaggeration to say that this was the strongest Enhanced Armament in the Accelerated World.

At that moment, Haruyuki was, by calling the armor's true name, attempting to summon the original from before its transformation. If he succeeded, there should be no mental interference when he equipped it. And although the future-prediction function that had allowed him to effortlessly slaughter the powerful enemy Rust Jigsaw would no longer exist, he didn't need that sort of power in this fight.

He didn't want to beat the IS-equipped Cyan Pile.

Takumu couldn't stop blaming himself for past crimes, and now that he was finally caught on the edge of despair, Haruyuki simply wanted to tell him. Tell him how much he, Haruyuki Arita, trusted, relied on, and needed this person, Takumu Mayuzumi. He wanted to be able to deliver a punch with all these feelings in it, a final blow. He wanted to borrow the power to smash through that aura of darkness, with the very little that was left in his HP gauge.

As if in response to Haruyuki's prayers, the pure silver armor continued to appear before his eyes. A large elbow pad, and then the light stretched out from there to his upper arm.

However.

Just as the armor was about to reach his shoulder, he abruptly felt a fierce resistance. A ferocious roar thundered faintly in his ears, and he realized it was the voice of the spirit housed in the arm, the voice of the beast, the Disaster. The beast refused to disappear. Enraged that only the Destiny, the Enhanced Armament it possessed, was being summoned, it was trying to interfere with the creation of the object.

Kreee! A fierce creaking sound ripped through him, and the silver armor stopped where it had covered half of Silver Crow's right shoulder. In the left of his field of view, a string of text in the system font was flashing irregularly. YOU EQUIPPED AN ENHANCED ARMAMENT: THE...He could read it up to there, but after that, only the blurry forms of the letters D, S, and T floated up.

All the voices and pain receded until they were finally gone.

For a moment, silence—so characteristic of the Scorched Earth stage—filled the charred space, the first floor of his real-world condo's B wing. In the center of the dark room he was currently in, Haruyuki raised his right arm, covered in the new armor, and squeezed his hand into a fist.

And then the front wall crumbled into tiny pieces, a large silhouette appearing from the other side.

The dark aura blanketing Cyan Pile—Takumu—had grown even thicker. The true light-blue coloring of his armor was hidden; only the crimson eye of the ISS kit lodged in the Pile Driver, the Enhanced Armament of his right arm, glittered vividly. Even the eye lenses behind his mask's narrow slits had changed from their old light blue to a sharp purple. Those eyes stared hard at Haruyuki.

Finally, a quiet voice: "Is that the original form of the Armor of Catastrophe?"

Even propelled by destructive, ruinous urges, Takumu had apparently not lost his power of insight.

Haruyuki looked down at his right arm, covered in its new armor, and nodded. "Yeah. Although I couldn't summon anything more than one arm..."

"That alone is seriously impressive. You're probably the first of all those Burst Linkers the armor has swallowed to resist its power." Takumu's voice was gentle but nearly inflectionless; it rang hollow. "You're strong, Haru. You know, if you just gave in to the temptation of the armor, you could have tens, hundreds of times the power you have now, but you can still fight it. If it had parasitized me, it would have taken me over immediately.

I'd probably have bared my fangs at you and Chii, and even Master..."

"No way. Taku, you'd be able to summon more than one arm of the Destiny for sure. You'd get the whole thing. I really believe that," Haruyuki asserted immediately, staring at Cyan Pile's face mask.

But Takumu hung his head low, perhaps to escape that stare and those words. "You still don't understand, Haru?" he murmured, voice slightly quavering. "I...I'm not the kind of person you can say things like that about. I just put on this show. The truth is, inside, I'm jealous of other people. I hate them. I don't want people to be happy; I pray for them to be *un*happy. I laugh in the shadows when my rival gets bad grades; I feel good when the guy I'm up against for a regular spot on the team gets hurt. When my two best friends stopped talking, the people most important to me, people I'd been with basically since I was born? I pretended to be worried, but I was secretly relieved."

From eye slits now devoid of any light, several white particles spilled out. "That's me. That's the real Takumu Mayuzumi!" He'd shouted like he was spitting blood, and the black aura jetting up from his body increased in strength, reaching up almost to the ceiling.

Thud. Cyan Pile took a step forward, and the charred, burned ground of the stage cracked beneath his foot. A pressure charged forward at Haruyuki, threatening to send him flying back if he stopped concentrating for even a second, but he resisted that power and opened his mouth once more.

"Taku. I'm basically exactly the same." He worked hard to keep his voice from shaking and began to quietly tell his story. "If we're comparing the number of people we've cursed in our hearts, I'm definitely ten times worse than you. You think I haven't been jealous of you, that I haven't envied you? The only reason I can manage to resist the temptation of the armor is because my insides are as black as it is."

Takumu was silent then, the jet-black storm around him subsiding the slightest bit. His shoulders shook minutely.

"Heh. Heh-heh. The way you talk hasn't changed since we were kids. Right…You've always done this. You've always managed to control the dark parts of your heart. Not like me, always trying to put up a front—"

"We're no different! You and me, we're the same! We get lost, we worry, and just when we think we've taken a step forward, we smash into a wall. But even with all that, the reason I've made it this far is because you were right there with me! So I know you can fight this black power, too! You can fight it and break it and move forward again! You can, Taku!!" Haruyuki cried earnestly, and he felt like Takumu smiled faintly beneath his mask.

"Thanks. Thanks, Haru. You saying that to me now…maybe becoming a Burst Linker, fighting like this—it wasn't a waste of time. But, you know…that's exactly why I want to use my power until the end—for you, for the Legion. The control of…this ISS kit is overwhelming…I'm practically bursting with the urge to destroy right now. But how much of that is me and how much of it is the kit making me feel that…I don't know anymore." The voice murmuring this was quiet. But that quiet was a seed, ripe with omen.

Brandishing the pulsing, blood-colored eye affixed to the Pile Driver of his right arm, Takumu continued, tense, "This parasite was probably put together by some king-level experts, fusing their abilities and special attacks and wills. The more you fight, the more Enemies you devour, the greater the power it generates. And then at some point, it divides and makes a child—I mean, a clone."

"…A clone…" Haruyuki shuddered. Something that deliberately dirtied the parent-child system that was the foundation of Brain Burst…

Takumu lowered his arm before opening his mouth again, and Haruyuki felt even more strongly that his friend was fiercely enduring something he couldn't see. "The terrifying part is…the kit clones are connected by the medium of negative imagination. When Burst Linkers with clones of the same cluster cultivate their hatred and malice and rage inside the kit, the kits of the parent and child display even greater power. So the more clones you disseminate, the stronger you, too, can become."

"Th-that's…So you mean Burst Linkers who have kits compete to spread their own clones…?" Haruyuki asked hoarsely.

"Yeah." Takumu nodded gravely. "While we're here doing this, I can feel the black emotions pouring in from the Burst Linker Magenta Scissor, who gave me this kit in Setagaya, as well as Bush Utan and Olive Grab and the others who have her first-generation clones. And at the same time, the darkness I've cultivated is strengthening them."

In other words.

The network of ISS kit clones was a malicious copy of both the parent and Legion systems that were the proper Brain Burst. If parents and Legions were joined by positive bonds of love and friendship, then the ISS kit clones were connected by the negative chains seeking power and profit.

Haruyuki was speechless. But Takumu's voice came to him, creaking like glass on the verge of breaking.

"R-right now…if we don't do something right away, the kit will blanket the Accelerated World in the blink of an eye, like a terrifying epidemic. We don't have the luxury of waiting for the meeting of the Seven Kings four days from now and whatever decision they come to. I can get the names of the people behind this from Magenta Scissor. I think she's really close to the source of the kits. We might have to do a little sparring, but I intend to get some information about the kit. I don't know the motives or objectives of whoever's behind this, but anyone planning something as big as this has to have some way of controlling the situation…"

Thud.

Takumu took another step forward and looked down on Haruyuki, a mere two meters away. "The rest is up to you, Haru. Even if I do end up losing all my points fighting the people behind this, before my memory's cut out, I'll tell you whatever I've learned, somehow. So you have to go and save this world. I know you can…You're the only one who can. I believe that."

"…Taku." Haruyuki managed to call his friend's name in a voice almost inaudible. He couldn't get out any other words of substance.

Resolve.

Right now, the fact that Takumu was able to resist the terrifying control of the ISS kit—albeit just barely—was no doubt because of the massive boulder that was his own resolve. He had already decided. On the place of his own death. On his own final battle.

But.

The source of that resolve was despair at himself. The fact that he lost to the temptation of the ISS kit. The fact that he slaughtered the PK group Supernova Remnant in his rage. The fact that he set up the backdoor program in Chiyuri and attacked Kuroyukihime. And the fact that a long time ago, he had broken the circle of three childhood friends. He had made up his mind that these sins were absolutely unforgivable and changed that despair into resolve to face his final battle.

"I can't. Let you go," Haruyuki said, his voice shaking like a child trying to keep from weeping. "There's absolutely no way I'm going to just say, 'Got it. Leave the rest to me.' I can't leave you to sacrifice yourself and still go on being a Burst Linker myself."

"Heh-heh. Stubborn right down to the bone." Takumu chuckled, smiling as if he were truly happy. "I guess I wanted to hear you say that, so I forced you into this direct duel…but it's enough already. Thanks, Haru. Your feelings give me energy. I feel like I can stay myself a little bit longer. So, okay. I guess it's about time we finished this."

He raised his sturdy left hand and rolled his fingers in from the littlest up to his thumb. The concentrated black aura made even the stage itself shake faintly.

As if in response, Haruyuki faced him, again tightly clenching the fist covered in silver Armament. He lifted his chin and nodded slowly. "Yeah. We've already said everything we can say in words."

Right.

If they didn't meet fist with fist, nothing would start, and nothing would end, either. They had both dived into this final battle stage to do exactly that; Brain Burst existed for only this purpose.

Haruyuki mustered up every ounce of willpower his duel avatar had, body now missing both left arm and wing, and concentrated it in his right fist. The silver overlay ripped through the pulsating, wild darkness and pushed it back.

He had managed to summon just one arm of the Destiny, theta of the Seven Arcs, which should have offered nowhere near the total performance of the Disaster. This Enhanced Armament had neither the vast wealth of battle data built up over long years nor a will inscribed with the rage and hatred of those who had worn the armor in the past.

But the Destiny had exactly one thing the Disaster did not.

Hope. A single shining hope, glittering like a star, protected for many long years by the mysterious golden-yellow girl avatar lodged in one corner of the armor. He still didn't know who she was, why her consciousness lived in the armor, or what she wanted, but that faint warmth gave Haruyuki courage. It didn't spur him into battle like the Disaster had, but rather supported and encouraged him.

Now that I think about it, someone's always been there to support me. During the Hospital Battle right at the start, in the fight after that against the fifth Chrome Disaster, the fight against Dusk Taker, the race at Hermes' Cord, the God Suzaku protecting the gate...Kuroyukihime, Chiyu, Master Raker, Ash, Niko, Pard, Mei, and of course Taku—they were always there to protect me, to cheer me on. There's basically not a single fight I've won on my own.

But that's okay. Because those connections...those bonds are the true power of a Burst Linker. I want Taku to know that. I want him to understand there are a ton of people besides me who are thinking about him, who need him.

So please lend me the strength to do that.

He could hear no answering voice to this cry in his heart. But he felt heat thump to life in the center of his fist, and then an even more dazzling white light gushed out.

Takumu slowly drew back his left fist and lowered his stance. Haruyuki lifted his right hand and sharply pointed his fingers. As the two spoke their technique names simultaneously, their voices held a quiet resolve, as though trying to console each other.

"Dark Blow."
"Laser Sword."

The instant the ink-dark and silver-white attack trajectories crossed each other, their current battleground of B wing followed in the steps of the already destroyed A wing, to be transformed into innumerable clumps that exploded in all directions.

When Takumu had hit him with the same Incarnate technique minutes earlier, Haruyuki had been sent flying dozens of meters backward, unable to resist the enormous force of impact for even a second. He should have been smashed to bits right then and there.

But this time, although the Dark Blow did indeed at first smash into him, Haruyuki braced himself and pushed back on Takumu's fist, however slightly. Outstretched arms—separated by a mere ten centimeters—struggled for supremacy, sparks shooting from the gap between them as light and dark fought with surprising ferocity.

The divine protection of the Destiny Arc was awe-inspiring. Its defense alone was even more powerful than the Disaster, which had shifted a great deal of its potential to offense.

But there was no point in simply sitting here and struggling against each other like this. Haruyuki had to pierce the storm of raging darkness and tell Takumu. He had to tell him that there was not a single crime for which he could not be forgiven. That everyone in the Legion needed him. And that no matter how deep in the dark night he might be, if he looked up at the sky, there would always be the light of the stars shining on the path ahead.

Reach him.

Reach him!!
Body and soul, Haruyuki prayed—and thereby gave form to his will.

Rrrrring! A crisp echo, like a bell ringing, joined his prayer. Overlay, pure and white, spread out across the silver armor that covered his right arm. At the same time, from the tips of his fingers, his sword of light began to grow longer, bit by bit by bit.

Haruyuki's Laser Sword was a range-expansion Incarnate technique. The source of its power was the desire to reach out to a place that was not normally reachable. For a long time, Haruyuki thought this meant he wanted to run away from things. Run away from his ugly, cowering self. Run away from the kids who bullied that self. Run away from his mother's gaze, which looked at him like he was just another hassle in her life. Run away from the memory of his father claiming not to want him. Run, run, stretch out this hand to some place where he wasn't…

But a place where he wasn't didn't exist. Wherever he might try to go, he would be there. That hand reaching out would always be connected to his own self. So reaching out his hand was an active gesture, one that tied him to what he wished to grasp.

Which is why this silver light has to connect me and Taku. It will bring my feelings to him, my heart. It will overwrite the digital defense and attack power calculations of the Brain Burst system and make a tiny miracle happen.

Reach…him…!

The cry from Haruyuki's heart rang out across the field with a powerful echo.

His pure, glittering silver light melted the superconcentrated darkness, pierced it, and pushed forward bit by bit. It was no longer a sword. It was Haruyuki's own flesh-and-blood arm reaching out from Silver Crow's.

Taku!! I need you…!!

Beyond the end of his outstretched arm, he suddenly saw something on the other side of the pitch-black darkness.

A pale left hand, just like his own, with no armor of any kind.

Takumu's hand, fingers callused from swinging a sword every day. The fingers, curled up into a tight ball, twitched. Slowly, tentatively, they opened up, then pulled back, shaking. But they reached out hesitantly once more and moved toward Haruyuki's hand.

At that moment.

Countless spikes of light the color of dark blood exploded between them.

"Ngh?!" Pulled from the vision guiding the imagination circuit and back into the duel field, Haruyuki saw an unexpected sight.

The Pile Driver of Cyan Pile's right arm was held up before his chest, as the eyeball-shaped ISS kit parasitizing the surface opened its eye so wide it threatened to fall out. It bathed them in concentrated light the shade of fresh blood. Black tissue like blood vessels reached out from around the eyeball and came together about ten centimeters away to form a round protuberance.

The lump immediately grew to the same size as the eyeball next to it, and then the surface of the black lump split lengthwise. One piece went upward, the other downward, and then the eyelids opened to reveal another eyeball.

On the surface of Takumu's arm, the two adjacent eyeballs of the ISS kit gazed at Haruyuki from extremely close range. In them, Haruyuki felt the definite will of someone else. A bottomless hunger. The urge to destroy. The craving to multiply. And hatred.

"Wh-why—!" Takumu cried out, still struggling with Haruyuki's Incarnate with his left fist. Apparently he hadn't expected anything like this, either. "I didn't give the command! So why did a clone…?!"

Haruyuki grasped the meaning of this at basically the same time as ten—or maybe more—thin black tentacles stretched out from around the second eyeball to plunge into Silver Crow's chest.

Cold.

No, hot.

Abnormal signals raced through his entire nervous system. It was almost as if ice water had been injected directly into his blood vessels with a needle. The herd of capillaries, strangely like microwires, drove deeper and deeper into his body. They wrapped around his heart, tangled through his lungs, climbed up his spine, and entered his head.

Haruyuki couldn't move. He couldn't speak.

And although the many tentacles had pierced deep into the chest of his avatar, his HP gauge, with only a few percent remaining, did not decrease a single dot. But that itself showed the abnormality of the phenomenon. The silver overlay flowing from his right arm shuddered and flickered; the Laser Sword that had extended from there also melted and crumbled away like snow flurries.

Normally, the equilibrium between their two Incarnates would have been destroyed, and Cyan Pile's Dark Blow would have easily dispatched Silver Crow.

However, that did not happen. As Haruyuki's Incarnate flickered, Takumu pulled back his left hand and screamed, "Don't you touch Haruuuuuuuu!!"

Veiled in the obsidian aura, he used his left hand to grab hold of the bundle of black wires that had come out of his own right arm and were piercing Haruyuki's chest. He twisted his entire body in an effort to rip them out, yanking as hard as he could. But the wires shuddered like some kind of living creature and fought to keep from being removed.

Paralyzed, unable to move a muscle, Haruyuki met Takumu's eyes as his friend yanked and tugged at the black tentacles.

Takumu smiled thinly. Or that's what it felt like. In that smile was none of the emptiness, the deep resignation of the other smiles he had given Haruyuki any number of times over the course of the fight. It was the reliable, warm smile that had always been there when Haruyuki looked to his side during their days of fighting alongside each other in their Legion.

Cyan Pile put the barrel of his Pile Driver against his own throat.

"…T-Taku…," Haruyuki struggled to say.

But at that exact moment, Takumu firmly called out the technique name: "Lightning Cyan Spark!!"

From the gap between the thick armor and the barrel glued to it, a pale light jetted out. Then, a beam of lightning shot up from the nape of Cyan Pile's neck, higher and higher into the sky of the Scorched Earth stage.

Having launched his special attack into the vital spot of his own avatar, Takumu staggered backward and caught himself just as he was about to fall. His HP gauge, at nearly 40 percent before the self-inflicted blow, was dyed entirely red and dropped precipitously from the right side until it hit zero.

The movement of the black fibers, digging deep into Haruyuki's body, very close to reaching the center of his head, stopped. They wilted and slid out of his chest before melting into the air and disappearing.

The second eyeball also closed its lids, looked vexed somehow, and disappeared as if absorbed into the first.

Standing there, dumbfounded, Haruyuki's ears picked up his friend's soft whisper. "…Thank goodness…"

Leaving just those two words, Cyan Pile and his enormous blue body, black aura completely gone, shattered into shards of glass and scattered in all directions.

Thus Haruyuki was left alone in the center of an enormous crater in the Scorched Earth stage, the area scarred and burned. The silver Enhanced Armament was released, dissembling into the air off his right arm.

As if to escape the flaming proclamation You win! displayed in the center of his field of view, Haruyuki looked up at the darkening evening sky.

A vortex of feeling he couldn't put a name to filled his chest and spilled out from both eyes, blurring the reddish purple of the sky. The duel was over, and until the moment he was pulled out of the Accelerated World, Haruyuki simply stood there, the shoulders of his avatar shaking quietly.

The instant he returned to the real world and opened his eyes, Haruyuki felt a single drop of water bounce off his cheek. It was the tear Takumu had shed immediately before the direct duel started. Having burst out at roughly the same time, Takumu was still holding down Haruyuki's shoulder with his left hand, pinning him flat on the bed, while gripping the direct cable with his right, both eyes open wide. On the other side of his glasses, new droplets were born and dripped down onto the lenses.

"...I..." Takumu's lips trembled slightly as a hoarse voice slid out of his throat. But instead of saying anything further, he slowly lowered his body and fell over to Haruyuki's right with a *thud*.

Silent for a while, the two friends lay side by side on the wide single bed, at a diagonal. Their eyes rested on an A2-size poster, printed on thin polyfilm and plastered to the ceiling of Takumu's room.

It featured an adult kendo player. Judging from the fact that there was no text of any kind on it, it was probably a photo Takumu had found and printed out himself. The composition had the player positioned at a diagonal, on the verge of launching a mask strike, the tip of the bamboo shinai sword plainly blurred. It was nothing more than a 2-D photo, but it held an intensity great enough to rouse passion just by viewing it.

"Is that player your teacher? An older student?" Haruyuki asked cautiously in neurospeak, through the direct cable that still connected their Neurolinkers.

After a while, a quiet reply came back to him. *"No. He was a kendo player fifty years ago."*

"So then...he's someone you want to be like?"

"...It's more like...respect, maybe? I mean, it's ridiculous to think I could be like him. In the nineteen nineties, he won the national

kendo championships six times. And that record hasn't been broken even now, fifty years later."

"So…what's the second-place record?"

"Three times. And even that is a seriously nice piece of work."

In which case, the player in the photo was the best kendo practitioner in real-world Japan—no, in the entire real world. The instant the thought crossed his mind, Haruyuki murmured, *"Wonder what it's like to be that strong. Like maybe you wouldn't worry about stuff or not knowing what to do, you know?"*

"In an interview he did after he retired from competition, when he was working as an instructor, he said, 'I haven't gotten a hold on anything yet. I'm still dawdling at the entrance of a pitch-black tunnel.'"

"Huh…Really?" Haruyuki sighed unconsciously before voicing his thoughts as they came. *"But, like, if it's pitch-black, how can you tell if it's the entrance or not? Maybe the exit's just up ahead."*

He paused for a second before continuing. *"It's not actually ridiculous to compare yourself to him. I-I've thought that, too, so many times—that I'm in the middle of a tunnel without an exit. But there was an exit. There always was. And the next tunnel will…come along again soon, but…even still…"*

Earnestly fumbling for words, Haruyuki turned his face to the left and looked at Takumu's profile, less than a meter away. Eyes still blurred by tiny droplets, the frames of his glasses cutting across his pale cheeks, he stared intently at the poster on the ceiling.

Haruyuki steadied his resolve and opened his mouth to speak the heart of the matter in his real voice. "Taku, before, you stopped your Incarnate attack—Dark Blow—for me. To save me, you resisted the ISS kit and used your special attack on yourself. That action shows your true nature—that's what I believe. Even if you did accept the kit and use its dark power this one time…you cut down that temptation and made it out of the tunnel. That's what I believe."

He couldn't say the words before, out of fear that when the

conversation was over, Takumu would stand up, say good-bye, and leave the room—to go and fight Magenta Scissor and the Acceleration Research Society.

Even after Haruyuki closed his mouth, Takumu continued to stare silently up at the ceiling for a while. After ten seconds or so, his friend asked him an entirely unexpected question in his real voice. "Haru, yesterday, in the solo song presentation in music class, you sang 'Wings Please,' right?"

"Uh, uh-huh." Haruyuki nodded, perplexed.

Takumu glanced at him, smiling faintly as he continued. "The teacher gave us a bunch of other choices. Why'd you pick that one? You've always hated that song."

"Yeah...that's true." The enormous anxiety blocking his chest receded just a little as Haruyuki smiled a light, wry smile. "Well, it wasn't like I had any real reason for hating it, either, you know. I dunno, I've always thought the song had 'wishes that won't come true' as its basic premise."

Looking out the corner of his eye at Takumu wordlessly encouraging him to continue, Haruyuki added, "It's also because I'm pretty cynical, right? I always felt like right before the first line of the song—'If I could have one wish come true right now, I'd ask for wings'—there was actually another line: 'I know that I can't, but...' And, like, that was just too close to how I actually felt. So I could never manage to like that song."

He turned his gaze back to the ceiling and gently raised his right hand. With his fingertips, he caressed the sky that lay beyond the wallpaper and concrete.

"But, like, when I listened to it again in the reference sound files we got for homework last week, I could kinda think...*maybe not*, you know? Umm...Umm..."

Explaining his own mental state in words was the thing Haruyuki was worst at in all the world. But as he moved his upturned palm like a bird, he worked to get it all out. "That song, maybe it's not so important whether it comes true or not. I was thinking it's maybe a song about wanting to go there sometime. 'Up into the free sky, where there is no sadness,' while always walking along on the ground one step at a time. I mean, like, what's important is…"

Here, his language-processing faculties ran up against their limit, and he was stuck simply opening and closing his mouth.

"Not the result, but the process," Takumu muttered softly, on his behalf. "The really important thing is that ongoing process."

"R-right. That's it." Haruyuki clenched his right hand, still up in the air, and passionately said, "Like, Kuroyukihime is always telling me strength's not a word that's just about winning. And Shinomiya said so, too. True strength is moving forward without giving up, no matter if you lose, or fall down, or fail…And when I started thinking that maybe that song's trying to say the same thing, I felt kinda bad for hating it all this time. Or, you know, maybe it's just because I can fly in the Accelerated World that I can forgive it now."

As he pulled down his arm and stuck it behind his head, Haruyuki added with a wry smile, "Either way, my singing was really awful. Thank God recording's not allowed at school."

"It wasn't that bad, Haru."

Haruyuki turned his head then and saw Takumu smiling as he stared up at the ceiling.

Takumu closed his eyes gently. "You probably didn't notice, but Chii was secretly crying," he murmured, as if remembering the lesson the day before. "While listening to you singing your heart out with that piece."

"Huh." Haruyuki was speechless.

His friend continued gently, smile still in place. "The me of a little while ago would have probably been torn up with jealousy and self-loathing seeing Chii like that. But…but, you know, I was happy then, too. I was happy watching you sing that song so proudly and Chii crying while she listened to it. That moment… In just that moment…the circle of the three of us…was like it used to be…" Takumu's voice suddenly trembled, and from his tightly closed eyelids, transparent droplets once again flowed silently.

Struck with emotion, Haruyuki clenched his teeth. But he soon turned over toward Takumu, propping himself up on one elbow as he started speaking. "Not 'like it used to be.' Like it *is*. This *is* us now. Taku, Chiyu and I need you now just as ever!"

For a moment, Takumu turned his face away, as though trying to escape from the declaration.

But Haruyuki was certain his words would reach his best friend's heart. They had gone up against each other with everything they had in the Accelerated World, and, fist on fist, they had spoken.

A few seconds later, Takumu turned back to him with damp eyes. "Haru," he whispered in a shaky voice. "I…Maybe I can change like you. Maybe I can keep fighting the black emotions in my heart and aim for the 'sky.' Maybe I can keep walking forward."

"O-of course you can, Taku! I mean, you're always changing. The way you shot yourself with that Lightning Spike at the end of the battle just now is proof of that."

Haruyuki inched a little closer to Takumu and gripped his friend's shoulder. He looked hard past the blue glasses, damp with tears. "Taku, give me just a little more time. Tomorrow, Thursday…at seven tomorrow night, I'm definitely coming back alive from the Castle with Shinomiya. She should be able to purify your ISS kit, too. One more day. Hold on against the temptation of the kit for one more day, Taku."

Takumu lowered his eyes against Haruyuki's earnest plea without immediately responding. "Last night, I got the kit from Magenta Scissor in the Setagaya area," he finally squeezed out in a strained voice. "It was still in the sealed card state. But…after I got home and ate and took a bath, when I was falling asleep in bed…it started talking to me. Not in words—in feelings. Rage, hatred, jealousy, all kinds of negative emotions poured into me. And when this was happening, I *wasn't wearing* my Neurolinker. All night, I had this long, long nightmare. When I woke up, my heart was full of black things…"

Haruyuki could feel through the palm of his hand Takumu's sturdy frame shaking.

"Haru," his friend whispered weakly, lowering his face even farther, as if he were a child again. "I'm scared. It's not in the realm of Neurolinker memory anymore, it's inside my *head*. Now that I've broken the seal, what will it show me tonight? Can I make it to tomorrow morning as the same me I am now? I'm so scared of it, I can hardly stand it. I mean, already—I didn't even hesitate to hurt you so badly in the battle."

Interference from the Accelerated World even when his Neurolinker was not equipped. In principle, it was impossible. However, it was a phenomenon that Haruyuki himself had experienced. He had, more than once in the past, heard the voice of the Armor of Catastrophe in an unaccelerated state or when he wasn't wearing his Neurolinker.

But thinking about it, the acceleration of thought the Brain Burst program pulled off as a matter of course was itself an extraordinary phenomenon. And that wasn't all. Two months earlier, Haruyuki had witnessed an actual Burst Linker lose Brain Burst and have his memory tinkered with therein, to the point that memory of the program was ultimately erased.

Which meant the program had the power to interfere with human consciousness—with the soul itself. In which case, anything could happen. Accept it and fight. That was all they could do.

"So then, Taku, come stay at my place today," Haruyuki said, gripping Takumu's trembling shoulder even more tightly.

"...What?"

It was quite unexpected, after all. Faced with the dumbfounded expression on Takumu's face, Haruyuki began rattling on at high speed.

"If we fall asleep in a heap, playing games like we used to, you won't have time for scary dreams or anything. Although I guess you can't call it a heap with only two people. So then let's get Chiyu to come, too. If we say the three of us are gonna do homework or something, her parents'll let her. And I mean, we actually do have math and Japanese homework, right? So then, you take care of the math, Chiyu does the Japanese, and I'll get the tea. And did you know? If you open homework files in the initial accelerated space, that stupid stingy protection doesn't work, so you can copy-paste answers!"

As the tidal wave of Haruyuki's argument crashing over him, Takumu opened both eyes wide and stared. But finally, after staring at his friend's chattering mouth for a while, Takumu sighed in resignation, a wry smile crossing his lips.

"You always used to do this to me: get so carried away that I get caught up, too, and then you'd convince me to do all sorts of things. I used to get into so much trouble, you know."

"Did I? I don't remember that." Releasing the shoulder he had been clutching, Haruyuki scratched his own head pointedly.

The wryness gradually disappeared from the smile on his face, though, and Takumu soon removed his glasses and wiped his eyes roughly. "I guess that's that, then. I can't let exhaustion from doing homework affect the Castle escape mission tomorrow. I'll come over and help you. But as senior Burst Linker here, I can't let you use a point and accelerate just to copy-paste homework answers. I'll teach you the concepts, but you have to do the calculations yourself."

"Whaaat…" Pursing his lips, Haruyuki blinked several times and cleared away what threatened to blur his vision.

The ISS kit lodged inside Takumu still existed. Even as they lay there, it was watching vigilantly for its next chance. Just like the Armor of Catastrophe inside Haruyuki.

But Haruyuki had been able to push back against the armor's control and summon the original Destiny, albeit just once and only one arm of it. But it was proof that Takumu should be able to do it, too. To keep resisting the temptation of the kit for just another twenty-four hours, until Ardor Maiden, the "purifying shrine maiden," came back alive from within the Castle walls. Because Takumu had already stepped back from the brink of despair once and was trying to walk away from it.

"Okay! Now that that's decided, let's head over to my place! On the way, we can stop at the mall downstairs for food. Or no, wait. If we call Chiyu, maybe she'll come with a bonus item."

Haruyuki fell into thought, and Takumu lightly jabbed at his chest, laughing.

"You don't want to call Chii. What you really want is to invite the dinner her mom'll make us."

"N-no! I mean, the two are just kind of indivisible. Like, mention Chiyu, you get provisions. Mention provisions, get Chiyu."

"Uh-huh. Go ahead and try saying that to Chii."

"N-no way! O-okay, I'm gonna mail her, so you go get your mom to say yes."

Making like he hadn't said the offending line in the first place, Haruyuki stood up from the bed.

Just when he was about to casually pull out the XSB cable still plugged into his Neurolinker, the faintest neurovoice reverberated gently, deep within his brain, like a droplet falling on the surface of a pond.

"Thanks, Haru. I'm so glad...we can still be friends."

Back still turned to his good friend, Haruyuki reflected heavily on this before returning in the same tender neurospeak:

"Me too, Taku."

2

Naturally, there were a few hurdles in making this impromptu sleepover actually happen.

Getting permission from Takumu's parents, who definitely did not harbor any particular goodwill toward Haruyuki.

The right and wrong of Chiyu staying at the Arita house when they would be fourteen that year, regardless of the fact that they were childhood friends.

And, of course, Haruyuki's mother.

Unexpectedly, the easiest of the three to take care of was the last. Haruyuki timidly typed out a brief mail to his mother, who was still at work, asking if it would be okay if he had two friends stay over. The response he got was brief: "If you make a mess, clean it up. I won't be home tonight, so take care of things."

It wasn't clear if she had already planned not to be home or if she was taking the opportunity to go out on the town herself, or if she was actually being considerate of her son and clearing out of the house when his friends stayed over, but if his mother wasn't going to be home, they could use the living room the whole night.

The next hurdle cleared was the first one: permission from Takumu's parents. The simple sentence "we're going to do homework" worked wonders.

The issue was the second hurdle. Wondering exactly how

Chiyu herself and her parents would come down on the matter, Takumu and Haruyuki crossed the connecting bridge on the twentieth floor of the condo and rang the bell of the Kurashima home at 2108 of B wing. But...

"My goodness, Haru! And Taku! It's been ages. Oh, Taku, you've gotten so big! How tall are you now...Oh my! A hundred and seventy-five centimeters?! You're taller than my dear hubby now. You kids these days are really something! So why are the three of you going to do the tough homework? Oh, that's right, you're all in the same class this year, for the first time, hmm? When I heard you transferred to Umesato, Taku, honey, I was pleased as punch! But now things are going to be tougher for our Chiyu finally. If only both of you could marry her..."

It had been a while, and so Haruyuki and Takumu simply listened, baffled, at the stream-of-consciousness chatter that was Chiyuri's mother's specialty. However, here the lone daughter in question poked her head out from the kitchen and shouted, her face a raging conflagration, "Mom! You don't have to say everything in your head! The pot's boiling over!"

"Ooh! Goodness! Don't let it! Turn it off! No, don't turn it off, turn the heat down! Down!" As Chiyuri's mother hurried into the kitchen, Chiyuri strode out into the hallway to take her place and glared down at them from the entryway's step.

"Those faces aren't *we're going to get up to something*. Those faces say you've already gotten up to it," she remarked. She did have a keen eye. And as two boys who had already gotten up to one fight, all they could do was cock their heads with a half laugh.

The mail Haruyuki sent before they came over had simply said, "Would you like to stay over tonight with Taku?" but Chiyuri was quick to whip aside that curtain in no time flat and see through to the heart of things. She had apparently showered at school after practice; her hair was half-dried as she stood there in a plain T-shirt, hands planted on her hips as she glared at them.

But eventually, she snorted softly. "Well, whatever. I'll hang out," she said quickly.

"Huh? R-really?" Without thinking, Haruyuki went for confirmation…stupidly.

"Weren't you the one who invited me?!" As the corners of her eyes turned up sharply once more in irritation, he hurried to bow deeply along with Takumu.

Twenty minutes later, with a basket full of supper forced on them by Chiyuri's mother, Haruyuki and his friends moved to the Arita home. He could never come home alone to the large, deserted, sparsely furnished three-bedroom condo in the evenings without feeling a chill, but returning with his two childhood friends, he didn't have the time to think about things like that.

He went and dropped his bag in his bedroom, and after changing into more comfortable clothes, he launched his mailer before heading back out into the living room.

Fuko Kurasaki and Utai Shinomiya had told him about Takumu (Cyan Pile) being attacked by and then turning the tables on the PK group Supernova Remnant in the Unlimited Neutral Field, but Kuroyukihime probably also knew by now. No doubt they were all worried deeply, too. He needed to update them on the situation, but he'd never be able to explain in a mail the full details of the ISS kit and the fight between them.

So he simply wrote, "Takumu is okay. I'll explain everything during the Castle escape mission tomorrow," and sent the message. All three quickly responded that they understood, and in those concise replies, Haruyuki felt keenly their thoughtfulness.

Kuroyukihime, Fuko, and Utai had to have sensed long ago that something momentous, something that couldn't be neatly tied up in the word *okay* had happened. However, there wasn't the slightest hint of question in their replies. Kuroyukihime and the others implicitly communicated their intention to leave everything to the judgment of Haruyuki and Takumu.

But at the same time, if something Haruyuki and Takumu

couldn't take back happened, the responsibility would also sit squarely on their shoulders.

Twenty-four more hours. The two of them—no, three of them with Chiyuri—had to make it through this one night so that Takumu didn't lose himself again in the interference from the ISS kit. They could do it. The three of them had been on countless adventures together since they were little.

Having thought things through this far, Haruyuki suddenly realized something and his fingers froze.

He hadn't had any specific purpose in inviting Chiyuri to their impromptu sleepover party. It had been simply the expectation, the near *conviction* that the three of them could get through it somehow.

However. A certain power Chiyuri possessed...If they used that, then could they maybe remove through the system itself the parasite causing Takumu so much agony? Given the utter irregularity of the situation, he couldn't even count on the possibility, but still, it was worth a try.

"Kuroyukihime, Master, Mei..." Haruyuki softly called to his three missing companions. "I know, I just know we'll manage something. Because Taku and Chiyu...they're my best friends."

Taking large strides, Haruyuki yanked open the door to the living room, where something smelled delicious.

What Chiyuri's mother had prepared for them in a mere half hour was a soupy curry with plenty of summer vegetables. All they had to do was heat up some of the rice stockpiled in the Arita freezer and set out some iced jasmine tea, and then, just like that, a splendid, ample dining table appeared before them.

After a hearty "Let's eat!" the threesome chowed down wordlessly. Even Takumu, who hadn't eaten anything since the morning, seemed to have managed to get back some of his appetite somehow. Or maybe it was the power of Chiyuri's mother's cooking, which was impossible to resist, especially when you were carrying around a heavy emotional burden.

"Aah! Eggplant's totally different when you fry it up," Haruyuki proclaimed, a blissful expression on his face as he stuffed his cheeks full with eggplant slices that had been fried in olive oil before being gently simmered in the curry sauce.

"Fried and boiled eggplant's always delicious!" Chiyuri cried out in reprimand.

"No, but unfried eggplant's basically a sponge you can eat. Deep-fried eggplant, though, that's the food of the gods."

"Oh, come on! You have the taste of a child! You don't even get the magical delight of eggplant roasted and peeled and then eaten with some ginger and soy sauce!"

After watching the back-and-forth between his friends, Takumu cleared his throat. "Okay, okay, you two. Fried eggplant and roasted eggplant are both delicious, but the best is when it's pickled. That bright blue, pickled in brine—*that* is the taste of summer."

At this very un-teenager-like declaration, Chiyuri and Haruyuki exchanged a look and let out a long "Whoooooaaaa" at the same time.

"Sorry to say this, Taku, but for me, pickled eggplant's a bit… *that's* when it's like a sponge."

"Yeah, me, too. I know you're a blue type, Taku, but that you'd look for blue even in pickles…"

"Wh-what? This has nothing to do with my avatar's color!" Takumu looked genuinely hurt, and Chiyuri patted his shoulder, grinning.

"Ah-ha-ha! Sorry! Sorry! To make up for it, I'll ask Mom to do some eggplant, too, the next time she makes her famous pickles!"

As they chattered lightly, Haruyuki was aware in a part of his mind that it had been a fairly long time since just the three of them had had supper together like this.

The circle that bound Haruyuki, Chiyuri, and Takumu at the

moment was maintained by an incredibly subtle balance. The relationship between Takumu and Chiyuri, who started dating in the winter of fifth grade, had been reset with the backdoor program incident last fall, and they had been estranged for a while after that. But Takumu transferred to Umesato Junior High in the third term of last year, and then, in the first term of eighth grade, Chiyuri ended up becoming a Burst Linker, too, so the distance between them as friends, including Haruyuki, had begun to close once more, albeit awkwardly at times. And going through the difficult fight with the Twilight Marauder, Dusk Taker, when he attacked them not long after that, once again cemented the circle that connected them. Or that's what it had seemed like.

But that relationship was built on being Burst Linkers, on being members of the Legion Nega Nebulus. If, hypothetically, one of them was to lose all their burst points and all memories of the Accelerated World, would the three of them be able to maintain this bond? Haruyuki didn't know.

The one sure thing was that this was not the time to cower before hypothetical dangers. They had to charge toward all obstacles head-on, break through, and race toward their sole and ultimate goal. Toward the horizon that was level ten, the objective of their Legion Master, Kuroyukihime.

As he reaffirmed his resolve, Haruyuki went to reach his fork out toward the nearly empty curry bowl. But just as he was about to—

"Haru, since you like them so much, you can have my eggplant! In exchange, I'll be taking this little lovely!" Chiyuri said, grinning as she dropped a slice of eggplant onto his plate and picked up a large chunk of chicken on her way back out.

"Ah! Aaaah! You! My precious, precious baby that I raised—I mean, kept aside…!"

"Huh? You shaid behore that ehhplan was a hundred times hetter than hicken."

"I did not! Spit that out and give it back!" Tearing up, he fought valiantly, but the soft, stewed, juicy chicken meat was chewed up in Chiyuri's mouth before his eyes.

"Ah, sho *hood*. To make this delicious flavor last longer, I'd even use the 'acceleration' command."

"D-dammit!" As Haruyuki stamped his feet against his chair in frustration, Takumu watched with a slightly exasperated look, but eventually...

"Pft! Ha-ha! Ah-ha-ha!" He laughed cheerfully out loud.

Chiyuri and Haruyuki were quick to join in. And the threesome kept laughing and laughing, forks in hand.

After they worked together to clear the table and do the dishes, it was homework time as advertised.

They moved to the sofa set on the west side of the living room, huddled together, and launched the homework app. In the specialized software, developed by the major education corporation that was the managing parent organization of Umesato Junior High, the specifications were utterly inflexible to the point where no copying and pasting of answers whatsoever was permitted, and it was also impossible to view another person's screen, even if connected through an ad hoc or direct wired connection. If you used the "Burst Link" command to dive into the blue world of the initial acceleration space, those restrictions were all rendered null and void, but unless it was at school five minutes before homeroom started, they couldn't allow themselves the luxury of accelerating to take care of their homework.

And so the three friends shared information with one another using the rather dated method of spreading out A3-size electronic paper on the glass coffee table and then writing by hand. But, in the end, it took care of their math and Japanese homework in just forty minutes. If it had been Haruyuki working alone, the whole thing would have taken twice as long.

They looked at the clock and saw that it wasn't even eight yet, so the evening turned into an old game tournament, featuring selections from Haruyuki's collection, something else they hadn't done in a very long time. They connected the hardware—over thirty years old, so that if it broke, even the manufacturer couldn't repair it anymore—to the flat-screen TV on the wall, and, enjoying even the roughness of the resolution (1080p), they got entirely and gleefully carried away by games replete with violence almost never seen in modern games.

Once the hands of the clock had swung past nine thirty, the three took turns in the bath—naturally, they couldn't get in together anymore like they used to way, way back—changed into their pajamas, and came together once more in the living room. They put away the game console and then laid out three bouncy folding mattresses, pillows, and blankets on the floor.

"Okay, then." Chiyuri, in light-green pajamas with a small cat print on them, looked at Haruyuki and Takumu in turn and said, grinning, "Both of you, sit down there."

"Huh?"

"O-okay."

They hurriedly drank down the iced tea they had poured after getting out of the bath and sat down alongside each other on the mattress in front of Chiyuri, who was still standing. The fact that they were both sitting in the formal style on their knees was perhaps because of the knowledge etched into their brains and hearts since childhood that when all was said and done, they were Chiyuri's subordinates.

The smile still on her face, arms crossed tightly before her chest, Chiyuri continued speaking. "Now, perhaps you could explain this all to me again? What exactly did you two do this time, and what terrible position has it put us in?"

Whoa, she's figured it out already. While he was deeply impressed, Haruyuki's thoughts went into high gear in the back of his mind.

The biggest reason he had dragged Chiyuri into this impromptu sleepover party was because he had hoped that her presence—to be more precise, this situation with the three childhood friends huddled together like they used to be—would interrupt the interference from the ISS kit saved somewhere inside Takumu. He hadn't thought it through to the point where they spilled everything about the current state of affairs to her. Because *that* would be the same as revealing the deep scars Takumu carried within him, right up to the feelings of guilt that he was the one who'd smashed the circle the three of them had once made.

But Chiyuri had already guessed at the situation to a certain extent—to a place fairly near the heart of the matter, actually. And if they were going to try erasing the kit's power, then either way, they couldn't hide the truth.

Haruyuki glanced at Takumu, off to his left. His friend, hair freshly washed, met his eyes dead-on for about a second before turning back to Chiyuri.

"Chii, I'm pretty sure you've heard the rumors by now at least," he said. "About the ISS kit problem that's been seriously affecting the Accelerated World for just over a week now..." And then Takumu told her everything, taking about twenty minutes to do so.

About how he'd gone to the empty area of Setagaya by himself the night before, and the Burst Linker Magenta Scissor he'd encountered had handed him an ISS kit in a sealed state. How after he'd returned home and gone to bed, he'd had dreams that were clearly interference from the kit even though he had taken off his Neurolinker. How he'd had a slight fever when he'd woken up, so he'd taken the opportunity of his parents sending him to see the family doctor to collect information in the Shinjuku area. How his old Legion companion had sold his information, and he'd been attacked in the real by the PK group Supernova Remnant.

Takumu had dived with them into the Unlimited Neutral Field and summoned the ISS kit there to press all the members of Remnant into total point loss with the dark Incarnate. As a result, although he'd managed to keep Brain Burst, the kit had eaten into his mind all that much more. Believing he would end up hurting his friends in Nega Nebulus, he'd resolved to fight Magenta Scissor, determine the source of the kit distribution, and gather information while ready to strike out at any enemies—all while he could still control the dark power, which was, already, just barely.

However, immediately before that, he'd ended up in a direct duel with Haruyuki, who had raced to Takumu's house from Umesato Junior High, and the two of them had fought, throwing all the power and suppressed emotion they had in them at each other. And at the end of the intense battle, he had succeeded in pushing back against the interference from the kit to a certain extent. However...

"It's still inside me." Finishing up the long story, Takumu grabbed his blue Neurolinker, which he had taken off before getting in the bath, in both hands and summed up in a half whisper, "The kit is hiding somewhere in this Neurolinker—and maybe part of it is somewhere in my head. It's steadily absorbing power from the other kits it's linked to, getting stronger with every passing second, even now, while we're sitting here like this. Tonight... if I have that nightmare again, I might call up that black thing in my heart. So Haru's trying to stop that by having the three of us spend the night together like this. That's why he invited you over out of the blue. All of it...my own foolish conceit brought all this on." Here, Takumu closed his mouth and hung his head.

Chiyuri had listened to the entire long story still standing, not moving a muscle, and now she abruptly dropped to her knees before Takumu. She stretched out a pale hand from the elbow-length sleeve of her pajamas to, with a gentle finger, wipe away the wetness from the left side of Takumu's glasses. "I'm sorry, Taku."

"Huh?" He lifted his face, eyes open wide.

Chiyuri began speaking softly. "I've known for a long time that you...you're a kind person who is maybe as easily hurt as Haru is. But...all this time, I was spoiled by that kindness of yours."

Her eyes, always shining brightly like a cat's, were slowly lowered. Chiyuri brought down her hand and seated herself more formally, like her friends, before lifting her gaze and speaking in a resolute tone.

"When I was little, I believed so hard that no matter how many years went by, the three of us would be close, we'd always be able to laugh together. But the truth is, that's impossible, isn't it? We can't stop the flow of time. We can't rewind it, either. Even though I *knew* that somewhere in my head…I've been wishing all this time for just a little longer. For us to be like this just a little longer."

She took a deep breath. Looking at Haruyuki and Takumu in turn, Chiyuri suddenly gave voice to something wholly unexpected. "Haru, Taku. We haven't told anyone outside my family this, but…Okay. My dad might not live very long."

As though the words went in through Haruyuki's ears up into his brain to dam it up somewhere, he couldn't identify the meaning in them for a while. Apparently having the same reaction, Takumu wasn't even breathing, much less moving.

With both her friends gazing at her, Chiyuri opened her mouth to continue, the gentle expression on her face still perfectly intact. "You already know why I could meet the first condition of being a Burst Linker, right?"

"Yeah." As Haruyuki nodded, a part of his mind started thinking.

To become a Burst Linker—i.e., to install the Brain Burst program in your Neurolinker—there were two conditions. The first was that you had to have been wearing a Neurolinker continuously since soon after you were born. The second was to have a high-level affinity for the quantum connection.

The second could be met through long-term full-dive experience and active training—like Chiyuri herself had done. But there was nothing a person could do at this stage about the first condition. In other words, Burst Linker affinity could be said to be half-inherent.

The majority of reasons for equipping a newborn with a

Neurolinker could be boiled down to making child-rearing easier or gifted infant education. Haruyuki had been given an infant Neurolinker immediately after he was born for the former reason, Takumu for the latter.

But neither of these applied to Chiyuri.

Just before she was born, her father had developed an illness in his throat and had his vocal cords removed, making conversation with his real voice problematic. However, Chiyuri's parents wanted to bring up their beloved daughter hearing both of their voices somehow, so they decided to use the neurospeak function of the Neurolinker. And so, Chiyuri had been raised from the time she was a baby hearing her father's voice through her Neurolinker.

As if waiting for Haruyuki and Takumu to imagine their way to this point, Chiyuri said slowly, "So the disease that made Dad lose his voice was hypopharyngeal cancer."

At their panicked faces, Chiyuri shook her head lightly to reassure her once again speechless friends.

"It's okay. None of this is immediate or anything. I mean, cancer itself isn't the scary disease it used to be anymore, with all the advances in radiation therapy micromachines…But, you know, I guess even the technology now can't completely get rid of the cancer cells once they start moving and spread throughout the body. And in the last ten years, Dad's had it show up again, once in his esophagus and once in his lungs. Both times, they managed to push it back with anticancer drugs and MM treatment, but…I guess now the doctor's saying that if it recurs somewhere, the prognosis won't be so great."

As she continued talking, the strong smile stayed on her face, but Haruyuki noticed her large eyes blurring over.

"Mom and Dad try to make sure I don't worry, of course, but still, I know. We've been doing this family thing for a while now, after all. When Dad was in treatment, the side effects were really hard on him. And Mom would wake up over and over during the night to touch Dad. So once the treatment was over and he was better again, I prayed to God from the bottom of my heart. 'Please let us stay the way we are now. Dad and Mom and me, and you guys, all of us healthy and close the way we are now.' That was…in fourth grade. For me…it's like this time wrapped in a golden light. We had so much fun every day."

Here, Chiyuri closed her mouth and turned her eyes up to the ceiling to keep her tears from spilling out.

Still unable to actually say anything, Haruyuki had a vision of Chiyuri's father pop up in the back of his mind. When they were in third or fourth grade and they came home exhausted from playing outside, he would go to the Kurashimas' basically every day and eat supper with them, even taking his nighttime bath there. He regularly saw Chiyuri's father, but he hadn't let Haruyuki see the slightest hint of the fact that he had been struggling fiercely with cancer for years. He always had a bright smile on his thin face, and he even joined in their games sometimes.

"Chiyu…I didn't…"

I didn't notice anything.

As Haruyuki tried to give voice to these words, Chiyuri turned her smile on him once more and shook her head in short bursts.

"I told you, it's not like anything's going to happen right away or something. It's just if the cancer comes back again, then maybe. Which is why I really shouldn't just be freaking out about the future. But I've pretended that I couldn't see anything changing. I didn't even try to understand how you feel, Taku…Now could turn into then, and I'd still be trying to go back there. It was only natural you'd try to figure out how I really felt last fall, Taku. I mean, even though I was right there beside you, even in dive calls, I was never really looking at the Taku in front of me."

"No." Having been silent up to that point, Takumu clenched his hands into fists on his knees and shook his head fiercely from side to side. "Chii, you're wrong. I'm the one to blame here for not being able to trust you. I'm the one who didn't even notice anything about what you were carrying around. I just kept pushing you with my own selfish wish, for you to look at me, to look *only* at me. And in the end…I…Your Neurolinker, I…"

The voice he tried to squeeze out of his throat sounded very much like the cry of anguish when he'd fought Haruyuki earlier.

But Haruyuki believed that the Takumu speaking his heart now was not simply coming from backward-looking self-reproach or self-hatred.

Believe. He forced himself to swallow the word.

Takumu clenched his hands one final time, almost to the point of creaking, and then released them before he continued hoarsely, "But…" He lifted his head and looked directly at Haruyuki, and then at Chiyuri. "But I've changed, Chii. I promise. It's only a little at a time, but I'm getting stronger. Someday I'll pay for all my crimes, so that this time for sure, I can take your hand and pull you toward the future."

"Uh-huh." Chiyuri nodded, a tear spilling from her eyes. "Me, too. I'm going to stop just looking at the past. Right now…I'm too scared to look ahead at what's coming. But still, I'm going to treasure this moment. I mean, I'm having fun now. Moving toward the same goal with you and Haru and Kuroyukihime and Big Sister and Ui, it's fun, I'm happy. So…" She took a deep breath, straightened her back, and, after wiping roughly at her eyes, she said with her voice clear, "So I'm not going to let this ISS kit or whatever it's called do whatever it wants with you, Taku. I'll protect you. Me and Haru, we'll protect you, Taku."

3

Haruyuki was prone to forgetting this fact, but it had been only two months since Chiyuri had become a Burst Linker. A very short period of time comparatively, a fourth of Haruyuki's time, and only a seventh of that of her "parent," Takumu.

However, once she had heard all the details about the ISS kit from the two more experienced Burst Linkers, after thinking about it for mere seconds, Chiyuri screwed her face up in an exaggerated fashion. "Could it be...those guys again? The Acceleration Research Society."

Unconsciously, Haruyuki and Takumu looked at each other, and when they turned their gazes back to Chiyuri—who was flopped over on the last of the three mattresses pushed together—they nodded simultaneously.

"Y-yeah, we were thinking the same thing..."

"Y-you're amazing, Chii. It took me and Haru way more time to get to that conclusion, even though we had two heads working on it."

"But, I mean, you know..." Face still puckered up, Chiyuri lowered her voice a bit. "It's really the same as the way *he* did things. Like, they don't attack straight on, they sort of eat into things from all sides."

The "he" Chiyuri was referring to was Dusk Taker, a former

member of the Acceleration Research Society, now banished from the Accelerated World. By the time he appeared before Haruyuki and named himself, he had already dug up all the information on Nega Nebulus and held Haruyuki's fatal weakness in his hand.

And now, the kits had started circulating from the so-called empty areas of Setagaya, Ota, and Edogawa. There was most likely a large number of people among the Burst Linkers who made their home in the city center who still didn't know what was happening.

The matter of the kits would very likely be taken up on the agenda at the meeting of the Seven Kings scheduled to take place four days from now, on Sunday, but there was at least the possibility that the situation would have already progressed at that point to a pandemic state impossible to get under control.

Forcing himself to swallow such stinging anxieties, Haruyuki tightened his crossed arms and legs and opened his mouth.

"So, like, in the Accelerated World, there's something like a formula, right? Built into powerful techniques and items is always a risk or a weak point to balance them out. I mean, all the other abilities of my avatar have basically been sacrificed for my flight, and with Taku's Pile Driver or Master's Gale Thruster, once they use them, they can't use them again until they recharge."

"That's..." Chiyuri nodded. "You're right. The activation movement for my Citron Call is huge, and since there's no homing function, you can avoid it pretty easily."

"Even the Incarnate System, which is technically outside the game system, is the same," Takumu followed, pushing up his glasses. "You basically can't learn Incarnate that goes against your avatar's affinities, and if you use it too often, there's the risk that your heart'll be swallowed up by darkness and you won't be able to control the power. Oh, right, so what you're trying to say, Haru, is..."

"Yeah. I have no idea right now how they came up with the principles of the ISS kit, but at the very least, from what the Brain

Burst program will allow, in exchange for that terrifying power and boundless infectiousness…I think it has some massive vulnerability. So big that if we push down on it, the entire network it's built up will just crumble."

"True. That's really plausible." His usual intellectual gleam back in his narrowed eyes, if only temporarily, Takumu continued, gradually picking up speed as he spoke. "The creator of the kit—probably someone near the top of the Acceleration Research Society—I thought they must have included some kind of suicide program. I was going to die fighting for any details I could get. But it is possible that some vulnerability had to have been part of the kits right from the start…In which case, if we can find out that secret, we might be able to force the kits to self-destruct even if we don't have any kind of activation key." Here, he yanked his face up and took a deep breath, mouth about to open again.

"No, Taku." Chiyuri thrust the index finger of her right hand out before him.

"Huh?"

"You were totally thinking you could use yourself as a test subject and get Kuroyukihime and Big Sister to investigate the weak points of the kit."

"Oh…Well, y-yeah…but, I mean, Master and the others would be able to shut me down before I lost control or some—"

"Noooo! Our Legion totally does not let anyone sacrifice themselves and suffer all alone to achieve whatever goal!" Having made this blunt declaration, Chiyuri looked at her friends once more. She knew what she was talking about; she had, in fact, sacrificed herself and suffered to save both of them when they went up against Dusk Taker.

But she was basically saying she'd already forgiven them for the whole thing as she shut down Takumu, and after thinking for a moment, she opened her mouth again. "Hey, Taku? Maybe I can get rid of that…the ISS kit that's possessing you with my Citron Call Mode Two?"

Haruyuki inhaled sharply the instant he heard this. Her

proposal was the very idea he himself had been warming to for the past several hours.

Citron Call, the special attack of Chiyuri's avatar, Lime Bell, had the rather impressive effect of rewinding time for the targeted avatar. It also had two different modes, depending on the motion and the amount of her special-attack gauge she used.

Mode I, which used half her gauge, rewound the receiving avatar a few seconds. It was a powerful technique to replenish HP and special-attack gauges, which in reality allowed her to fulfill a Healer role, one of very few in the Accelerated World.

And Mode II, which used up her entire gauge, was even more impressive. This technique rewound the condition of the target avatar, in increments of status changes. Status changes mainly referred to equipping and removing Enhanced Armament, losing parts, and—in the case of transforming avatars—transformations. Equipping Enhanced Armament left an avatar open to attack during the process, and a lot of equipment could be summoned only once in a duel, so if it was forcibly removed during battle with this technique, all the opponent could do was retreat.

However, the preposterousness of this Mode II was the fact that even the obtainment of Enhanced Armament was canceled. Status couldn't be rewound infinitely—at present, Chiyuri was up to four steps back—so the phenomenon was essentially limited to immediately after the item was obtained, but when the timing was just right like this, Mode II canceled even a direct handover of Enhanced Armament, while Armament bought with hard-earned points popped back up in the storefront because of this enforced cooling-off period. Although, naturally, in that case, the points spent would also be returned.

With all this information popping into his head, Haruyuki counted the status changes that Takumu had been through.

His innate Enhanced Armament Pile Driver was always equipped, so there was no need to count that. And the transformation of the Pile Driver into Cyan Blade was Incarnate and therefore outside the system, so he didn't include that, either.

Which meant that Takumu shouting the command to activate IS mode and equipping the ISS kit in the fight before was one step. And he would have done the same thing in the battle with the PK group Supernova Remnant, so that was two. Before that, he had the bout the previous night with Magenta Scissor in the Setagaya area and accepted the ISS kit in that fight in a sealed state. That made three steps. The maximum Citron Call Mode II could rewind was four, so they could still make it.

"Taku," Haruyuki called to his friend quietly, knowing that Takumu had also traced out the same line of thinking as he just had.

His friend turned to look at him, a faint light of hope in his eyes. But then he quickly lowered his gaze and slowly shook his head. "No...It's true I've had fewer than four status changes, but it's probably impossible to remove that thing with Citron Call."

"Wh-why, Taku?! We'll smash that thing to pieces and send it back to Magenta Scissor, COD!"

Takumu smiled slightly at Chiyuri's threatening declaration. But he soon shook his head once more and spoke calmly, as though admonishing her. "Chii. That thing...part of that thing, or maybe the *main* part of it, is already in not just my Neurolinker, but in my head. The only thing that could possibly allow that to happen is the Incarnate System. Remember? When you tried to bring back Raker's legs with Citron Call?"

Both Takumu and Chiyuri lightly bit their bottom lips.

"Raker's 'part loss' was still within four status changes," Takumu continued, "but her legs didn't come back. Because she had been rejecting her own legs through an unconscious Incarnate. I'm pretty sure the ISS kit will always refuse to be removed through its own Incarnate."

"Then! Then me, too!" Chiyuri shouted, looking at both Haruyuki and Takumu. "I'll train in the Incarnate System, too! However many years it takes in the Unlimited Neutral Field, I will get the power to at least remove the ISS kit from Taku!"

"You can't, Chii!" Takumu shouted instantly.

"Why not?!" Chiyuri shouted back without a moment's hesitation. "Kuroyukihime and Big Sister said the time would come when I'd find my own Incarnate and nurture it! So why can't that be now?!"

Takumu started to open his mouth to keep fighting, but cut himself off.

Having a pretty good idea of what Takumu had been about to say and why he'd stopped himself, Haruyuki leaned forward and placed a gentle hand on Chiyuri's slender left arm.

"Chiyu." He stared into the large catlike eyes she turned on him and spoke slowly. "Chiyu, your Citron Call is an incredible technique. In a certain sense, it may be the strongest power in Nega Nebulus. But, like, it's definitely…the power of longing for the past. I don't know if you noticed this, but the sound of the bells you can hear when you activate the technique…it's exactly the same as the sound of the after-school bell at the elementary school we went to."

She had probably noticed this, too. Her eyes opened wide, and she quickly lowered her face.

As she sank into silence, Haruyuki kept talking. "Of course, my Incarnate attack and Taku's are both strongly tied to our past memories. But Taku's at least is the materialization of his will to cut away from the past and move forward. Which is why I—and I'm sure Taku's the same—want you to look to the future when you train in the Incarnate System. I don't know what kind of power it'll end up being, but…I just think it'd be pretty great if it was a power that came totally from you stretching out your hands toward the future."

For a while, no one moved a muscle, much less opened their mouths. Only the slender hands of the wall clock moved along smoothly, marking their approach to ten o'clock. The built-in air conditioner hummed softly on dehumidifier mode, while on the other side of the noise-reduction windows, the faint sound of EV tires coming and going on the nighttime Kannana reached them.

Finally, Chiyuri slumped back with a heavy sigh and smiled gently, eyes still wet. "I guess so," she whispered, nodded once, and then moved her lips again. "I guess. I mean, a technique set by the system's one thing. But a technique I find and cultivate in my own heart...something that comes from a hand stretched out toward hope is better, right? Like yours, Taku. And like yours, Haru."

"Oh no, my Incarnate attack's not a big deal like that."

"Nuh-uh. I love Laser Sword just as much as Cyan Blade." Smiling broadly, Chiyuri continued in her usual cheerful voice, "Oh, I got it! Maybe I'll do some kind of sword so we can all match! A really great one that could knock you both flying!"

"Uh..." The two boys met each other's eyes again. The truth was, they didn't know the depths of Lime Bell's potential yet. It wasn't impossible for her to awaken an Incarnate technique that would easily surpass either of theirs.

"G-go easy on us," Haruyuki said, and now it was time for Chiyuri and Takumu to exchange looks before bursting out in laughter together.

Of course they had school the next day, and the mission to get out of the Castle was waiting for them after that, so they decided it was about time they went to sleep. They lay down on the three springy mattresses laid out on the floor in order of Haruyuki, Takumu, and Chiyuri, from east to west. Ever since they were little, whenever they napped together at any of their houses, Chiyuri was always in the middle, but the star tonight was Takumu.

If interference from the ISS kit while Takumu was asleep was that much of a concern, then they would all stay up all night. They had examined this possibility, but Takumu had rejected it immediately, since it would affect the Castle escape mission the next day. The kit was an urgent problem, but Haruyuki's other self, his duel avatar Silver Crow, was sealed away in the Unlimited Neutral Field. If he didn't somehow manage to escape with Ardor Maiden, who held the power of purification, and get her to purify him of the Armor of Catastrophe before the meeting of the Seven Kings on Sunday, he would end up with the biggest bounty in the Accelerated World slapped on his head.

"It's okay. If you guys are right here next to me, I'll be able to relax, and sleep until morning," Takumu said, head resting on his pillow.

"Hey, if you do feel like you're going to have scary dreams or something, say so," Haruyuki replied. "I'll hit you and wake you up."

"I appreciate that, but if I'm sleeping, how am I supposed to tell you?"

"Uh, umm…sleep-talk?"

Haruyuki felt his eyelids growing heavier and heavier as they chatted, until Chiyuri, on the other side of Takumu, snapped her fingers.

"I got it! So, like, if you can't avoid the interference if you take off your Neurolinker, how about we go to sleep directing with one another?"

"Huh?!" Haruyuki blinked hard.

Chiyuri popped her head up before continuing. "If we're directing, then we'll be able to talk in neurospeak even when we're sleeping, right? If something's weird with Taku, we might be able to notice it."

"Ohh…right, I didn't think of that." Takumu sounded impressed, and after a momentary exchange of looks, the threesome agreed to give it a try.

They got up and put on their Neurolinkers, which were in the middle of wireless charging on the coffee table. After pulling out two XSB cables, they lay down again, this time with Haruyuki in the middle because Haruyuki's Neurolinker was the only one equipped with two direct terminals.

Direct connection with Chiyuri on the left terminal and Takumu on the right. The second wired connection warning disappeared, leaving only the small CONNECTED icon in his field of view.

Pulling the blankets up to his neck, Haruyuki felt a mysterious sensation.

A direct connection, no matter who it was with, always brought with it varying degrees of nervousness. The feeling of defenselessness, at deliberately removing the protective walls of his Neurolinker, and of immorality, from physically connecting consciousness itself—it always made his heart pound.

But at that moment, Haruyuki simply felt nothing more than a quiet peace. The sensation that he and his childhood friends, the people he had spent more time with than anyone else, were protecting and being protected by one another. It was almost as if, through the two cables, their sense of security was pouring into him and filling his own heart.

At some point, he had closed his eyes. The AI of his home server detected that its owner had gone to sleep and automatically dimmed the panel lights. From the other side of the gentle darkness that visited him came two voices.

Night.

Good night.

Unable to tell whether their voices were real or neurospeak, Haruyuki also mumbled, "*Night...*"

4

......Haru.

...Hey, wake up, Haru.

Haruyuki slowly lifted his eyelids, prodded by the sense that someone was calling him. The world around him was a dense charcoal color. Beyond it, a hazy human figure.

"...It's still dark out...Let me sleep a little longer," he mumbled, and started to go back to sleep.

But then someone was shaking his shoulders. "Wake up, Haru."

The voice contained an urgency of a sort, and this poked at his cotton-ball consciousness. He reluctantly opened his eyes once more. It was indeed still dark. Given the season, it was probably still barely four o'clock.

"...What's wrong, Chiyu...?" he asked hoarsely, blinking hard and then forcing his eyes open again.

It was indeed Chiyuri before him, hand on his right shoulder as he lay there. Slender silhouette sitting firm, short hair with a large pointed hat on top, entire body encased in a semitransparent light-green armor. On her left hand, a large bell–shaped Enhanced Armament...

"—Huh?!"

His brain finally more than half-awake, Haruyuki sprang up out of bed. His own body immediately *screeched* and *clanged*. Rather than striped, short-sleeved pajamas, he saw shining, mirrored silver armor. Hurriedly, he looked at his hands and touched his face. He didn't need to feel the smooth mask beneath his fingertips to know that this was his duel avatar, Silver Crow. And the yellow-green avatar before him was Chiyuri's Lime Bell.

Why? Did I challenge Chiyuri in my sleep or something?

That being his first thought, he turned his gaze upward to check the health gauges and countdown timer that should have been in the upper part of his field of view. But there was nothing. No green bar, no numbers ticking down from 1,800 seconds, no other display of any kind.

But that wasn't possible. If they were duel avatars—if they were in a full dive in a duel stage—he would definitely be able to see his own health gauge at least, Normal Duel Field or Unlimited Neutral Field; you couldn't get rid of that in the settings.

In which case, this was a dream.

Still sitting with his legs splayed out before him, Haruyuki tried to pinch his own cheek with his right hand. But his hard helmet got in the way, and he couldn't touch it. His brain still half-asleep, he started to stretch out a hand to the avatar sitting immediately to his left, thinking to use Chiyuri's cheek instead—only to remember that the face masks of all duel avatars were hard. So what else could he pinch? Now that he was thinking about it, what were the breasts of the female-shaped avatars like anyway?

Random thoughts drifting through his brain, Haruyuki brought an index finger toward the round swelling peeking out from beneath Lime Bell's cloak armor.

Squoosh was the sensation that traveled back to him through his fingertip. A half second later:

"Wh-what are you doing?!" Simultaneous with the shriek was a loud *clang* and an enormous impact to the top of his head. Lime

Bell had slammed the Enhanced Armament of her left hand, Choir Chime, into Silver Crow as hard as she could.

"Hnngh!" Tiny yellow chicks flapped around his head for a while before Haruyuki finally fully woke up and lifted his face with a gasp.

Taking a quick look around, he saw that they were no longer in the living room of the Arita house but rather a dim, tube-shaped space. To the right was an immediate dead end, but the narrow tunnel to the left looked like it continued twisting along.

This was not a dream. But it wasn't a normal duel, either. Through some irregular phenomenon, he and Chiyuri had dived into some unknown space while they were asleep.

Just the two of them?

"Wh-where's Taku?!" Haruyuki checked his surroundings again, but Cyan Pile's bulk was nowhere to be found. He turned his eyes back to Chiyuri, and her fresh green avatar glared at him, hands hiding her chest, as her face resumed its worried expression.

"Dunno." She shook her large pointed hat lightly. "I just woke up a minute ago. And when I opened my eyes, I was my duel avatar, and you were sleeping beside me, and Taku was gone."

"He was?" Haruyuki thought for a minute below his helmet.

They had both been transformed into their duel avatars, but given that there was no timer nor any health or special-attack gauges, they were clearly not in a Normal Duel Field. Unconsciously, he tried to deploy the wings on his back, but they didn't even twitch, despite his normally being able to at least open them when his gauge was zero. Apparently, their abilities had been deactivated.

So then he could think of only one thing. This strange phenomenon was probably—no, definitely caused by the ISS kit parasitizing Takumu. And Haruyuki and Chiyuri, asleep while directing with him, had been pulled in through the XSB cable. In other words, in a certain sense, the two of them were currently inside Takumu's dream.

In which case, Takumu had to exist around here somewhere. The fact that they couldn't see him was no doubt because he had moved…into that dark tunnel that extended who knew how far to their right.

"Let's go, Chiyu. We have to find Taku."

"Right," Chiyuri assented immediately, apparently reaching the same conclusion at essentially the same time as he did.

Haruyuki jumped vertically up from his seated position, an impossible move with his real body, and offered Chiyuri his hand to pull her to her feet.

Rather than letting go after she stood, Lime Bell squeezed his hand. He squeezed back lightly, testing one of the tunnel's walls with his free hand. The light-gray material wasn't earth or cement; it was soft, with a strange elasticity. The faint warmth and the thin rings of the walls were almost like the insides of a living creature—or maybe exactly like.

The pair looked at each other and nodded before starting off briskly down into the tunnel, hand in hand.

Before he knew it, he had lost all sense of time and distance.

To begin with, it wasn't entirely clear if they were currently accelerated or not. If they were unaccelerated, then the alarm in his home server, set for seven in the morning, would wake them up at some point. But if they were accelerated, time had basically stopped for them. They might be able to use the "burst out" command to escape from this strange place, but they were uneasy leaving Takumu. If they were accelerated, then in the few seconds it would take to rouse him in the real world, an immense amount of time would pass here.

Most likely, Takumu had had this dream the night before as well. And in it, something had interfered with his mind and poured something black into it. So right then in that moment, the same thing might be happening. And maybe what Takumu had finally begun to get back through the direct duel with Haruyuki was being stolen from him once more.

A sense of urgency quickened his pace, and before he knew it, Haruyuki was running and pulling Chiyuri along behind him. Probably feeling the same way, Chiyuri didn't protest but intently followed the speed-type Silver Crow. The two avatars ran and ran and ran in the dark tunnel that twisted and turned before them.

If only they could use the wings on his back to fly, but for whatever reason, he apparently couldn't use his flight ability in this place. No matter how he turned his attention to the folded-up metal fins, they didn't move.

When it felt to him like they had gone more than five kilometers, he finally made out a faint light ahead of them.

"An exit?" Chiyuri wondered.

He nodded in reply and quickened his pace further, dashing the last few dozen meters. When they at last broke out of the tunnel, a completely unexpected scene abruptly appeared before them.

Outer space.

Although, technically, it was not quite outer space. But the inky, dark expanse seemed to spread out infinitely, adorned with countless points of light. As they stood there dumbfounded, a group of lights clustered together far above their heads, glittering beautifully like a spherical galaxy. Unlike the starry sky, however, these lights were in constant, trembling motion. One mobile light would collide with a stationary one, and then *that* light would begin to move and hit the next. This chain reaction continued endlessly across the galaxy. Like an enormous three-dimensional game of billiards—or a kind of network.

He couldn't get a sense of the distances involved, so he had no real idea of the size of the shuddering galaxy. But Haruyuki intuitively knew that if he could get right up alongside them, this group of lights would spread out on a galactic scale.

While Haruyuki and Chiyuri took in the scene, the tunnel they had come out of continued to exist, a hole in space itself. A narrow bridge about two meters wide stretched out from the tunnel and continued off in a downward direction through the inky black space. They were standing at the foot of this bridge.

Haruyuki turned his gaze back to the group of resplendent stars and stood motionless, still holding Chiyuri's right hand in his left, when he heard a faint whisper to his left.

"...Wow..."

Haruyuki nodded at this and murmured hoarsely, "What... is it...?"

"Main Visualizer," someone responded quickly from his *right* side.

"Huh?!"

"Who—"

Crying out in surprise at the same time as Chiyuri, Haruyuki turned to his right. Standing gracefully near the edge of the narrow path was a slender silhouette that definitely hadn't been there before.

It wasn't Takumu—Cyan Pile. And of course, it wasn't any of the other Legion members. It was a female-type duel avatar with an all-over flower-petal motif. Her armor color was a warm golden yellow, reminiscent of the sun in spring.

The instant he saw her, Haruyuki dropped his guard and whispered to Chiyuri, "It's okay, Chiyu. She's not an enemy."

"Huh? You know her? So then how is she here? Isn't this Taku's dream?"

"Umm." Haruyuki had a hard time finding an answer to give her. But still, he struggled to put everything he knew into an easy-to-understand form. "She's not inside Taku—she's in me. Or, more accurately, inside the Enhanced Armament Destiny that I have. That's...right, isn't it?" He had already given Chiyu a rough overview that evening of the Destiny Arc he'd summoned.

"I think so." The golden avatar cocked her head slightly. "Although you could also say that's not quite it. It's true that I exist inside the Destiny, but the Destiny itself is inscribed in this world."

"Huh? What does that…And what you said before, 'Main…Visualizer'?"

Questions led to questions, and the mysterious girl came back with an even more surprising answer.

"In your words, it's the Brain Burst central server."

Shocked to his core, Haruyuki froze in place alongside Chiyuri.

The Brain Burst central server was the so-called true form of the Accelerated World, located in some unknown place. The central server recorded all the data in Brain Burst, including the statuses of every single Burst Linker; calculated every single change; and moved all the Enemies—the very heart of the world.

And this central server—which rebuffed any and all unlawful interference, a place players weren't even permitted to imagine the existence of—was before his eyes at this very moment. Or rather, the golden avatar was saying that the three of them were actually *inside* it.

"B-but how can that—? I mean, the BB server's completely impenetrable. Even the oldest veterans say so," he murmured in a trembling voice, and the girl smiled faintly. Or so he felt.

"That is true. But we were given just one way to allow us to touch the truth of this world. You should already know what that is."

"Touch…the truth of this world?" Haruyuki parroted back, before opening his eyes wide with a gasp. "The Incarnate System? 'The power of the image'…Overwriting phenomenon using imagination circuits."

"Exactly." The girl nodded. "A very strong and sad power."

And this sparked a memory: This was not the first time he'd encountered the golden-yellow avatar. That had been earlier that day—actually, it was probably the day before by now—at the end of the direct duel he'd had with Takumu in his room. After being knocked flying by Takumu's Dark Blow, he had lost the power to even get up again when she had appeared from inside him. At the

time, she had indeed said, "*The central system circuits were temporarily activated, and I'm able to talk to you like this.*"

That central system was, in other words, the BB server, what she called the Main Visualizer. And the circuits were imagination circuits. The foundation of the Incarnate System, the path by which the power of an image was transmitted into the logic of the world.

"But...we're not using the Incarnate System?" Having stood slightly behind Haruyuki up to that point, Chiyuri took a step forward as she spoke. "I don't even really get what Incarnate is yet. And to begin with, we're sleeping, both of us."

Haruyuki looked at both avatars again and noted that, although the colors of the armor of Lime Bell and the mysterious golden-yellow avatar were totally different, the lines of their bodies were alike. Not just in the common factor of external leaf and flower-petal motifs; it was something deeper and more essential.

Turning her gaze toward Chiyuri, the girl slowly nodded and pointed at the long, dark tunnel they had come through. "That tunnel is itself an imagination circuit. You followed the circuit of the mind of your friend you are connected with and came to this place."

"Huh? T-Taku?!"

"So then...Taku's activating the Incarnate System right now?"

They both spoke at the same time, and the girl gently shook her head.

"This image doesn't belong to him. The black power that's slipped inside him made that tunnel. There."

The girl raised her right hand to indicate the circuit that stretched out from the tunnel and disappeared into the black expanse. The floating bridge, twisting and turning along its length, appeared to be heading down to the deepest depths of the space, as if trying to escape the enormous glittering galaxy shining in the sky above.

Haruyuki stared intently and, far ahead in the unobstructed darkness, he could just barely see an avatar trudging forward, one step after another, large body pitched forward, head hanging low. He didn't need to see the heavy blue armor or the Enhanced Armament on the right arm to know exactly who it was.

"T-Taku!!"

"Taku!!"

The two friends half screamed his name in unison, ready to start running. But a golden-yellow arm swept down in front of them to block their way.

"No. If you approach carelessly, you'll attract *its* attention."

"I-it?"

Barely holding back his impatience, Haruyuki instinctively focused his gaze on what lay ahead of Takumu. In a few seconds, almost as though his eyes had gotten used to the dark, *something* rose hazily into view.

Enormous was really the only word to describe it. If he had to say further, maybe a lump of black biological tissue. The amorphous, squirming flesh was enclosed in a web of countless blood vessels, pulsing. *Babump. Babump.* The blood vessels stretched out, branching into the surrounding space, the slender tips wriggling like tentacles.

The black lump of flesh, convulsing in a fixed rhythm, somehow resembled the galaxy of light in the sky above. However, the impression was the polar opposite. Chaos versus order. Dark versus light.

"Wh-what is that…Why is something like that in the central server?" Chiyuri asked, voice trembling.

"That…is not something the system created," the girl replied, voice also hushed. "It's something a BB player sowed the seeds for and slowly, carefully cultivated over many long years. The so-called contamination."

"Spread the seeds…and cultivated…," Haruyuki whispered, and a shudder ran through his body. He groaned in a voice that was barely audible. "I-it can't be…the Armor of Catastrophe? Is that the true form of the armor?"

"No, that's not it. The armor is one of the Seven Arcs, a part of the system. Destiny is over there. Look."

The golden arm pointed somewhere near the center of the galaxy glittering in the sky far above. Following it, he saw a group of stars noticeably larger and shinier than the surrounding points of light, all lined up in the shape of a dipper. As if falling into resonance with them, Haruyuki's eyes were pulled to the sixth star from the left.

Unlike the five that came before it, this star alone appeared to be following a small, dark companion star. If, as the girl had said, the sixth star was the true form of the Destiny, then the dark companion star next to it was the will for destruction that lived in the armor.

Haruyuki felt a strange sadness in the odd pair of stars, and he shifted his gaze to the right. The seventh star—the final Arc, Chinese name Youkou, aka the Fluctuating Light—should have been there. And indeed, he could see a massive golden point of light flickering—it looked to Haruyuki like the center of the galaxy itself.

What did that mean, then? Whatever enormous power it might hold, the Arc was supposedly, in the end, Enhanced Armament, a simple item to equip. Was this what existed at the center of the Brain Burst program itself?

Haruyuki soon threw off this momentary question. Now was not the time for considering the structure of the Accelerated World. In a few more minutes, Cyan Pile, head hanging, would walk right into that black lump of flesh. He knew that the amorphous lump was not the Armor of Catastrophe. In which case, what—

"Oh! H-Haru, look! It's not just Taku!" Chiyuri shouted abruptly, pointing a little to Cyan Pile's left.

Obediently, he stared hard, and could indeed make out a slender floating bridge just like the one they were standing on, complete with another avatar walking along on it.

A small duel avatar, and a form he had seen before. Sturdy arms hung down, almost dragging on the bridge, while the large upper body was pitched forward. The armor was grass green.

"B-Bush Utan!"

There was no mistake. That was Bush Utan, member of the Green Legion, little brother to Ash Roller. Only a few days earlier, he had fought Haruyuki in the Suginami area and flung around the terrifying dark Incarnate attack like he was an old hand at it.

Seemingly paying no notice to Haruyuki's shout, Utan was also trudging toward the black lump.

And he wasn't the end of it. Beyond him. And above, below. Countless floating bridges, hidden in the deep darkness until that point, popped up in Haruyuki's field of view.

On every one of them, without exception, there was a single duel avatar, all moving forward lifelessly. At a rough count, there were maybe thirty—no, fifty bridges reaching out concentrically from the lump of flesh.

And then Haruyuki finally understood what the black organism was.

The true form of the mysterious Enhanced Armament, the ISS kit. Hadn't Takumu said so himself? That all the ISS kits were mutually linked? That when one kit got stronger, the surrounding kits also got stronger? The sight before them was precisely that "link." Every night when they went to bed, they were lured into this world through the Brain Burst imagination circuit and connected to one another through the lump of flesh that was the kits' true form.

Several of the duel avatars had actually already reached the lump of flesh and were kneeling before it. Black blood vessels reached out from the lump to crawl over their bodies and appeared to be exchanging some kind of fluid, or information, pulsing all the while.

"No...no..." Chiyuri knew less about the kits than Haruyuki did, but perhaps intuitively guessing at what the scene before them meant, she murmured hoarsely, "It's awful. It's sucking something important out of them all…and pouring in something bad instead."

"Yeah. It is. That…that lump is making Taku feel lost. He was finally starting to get himself back after fighting me, but now, like this, he'll…"

Haruyuki groaned quietly before turning back to the golden-yellow avatar standing to his right. "How can we stop this?!" he shouted. "That's our friend down there! And everyone, all of them out there, is playing the same game—playing Brain Burst with us! If we…If we destroy that black lump, we can stop them. Right?! We can, right?!"

And then without waiting for an answer, Haruyuki took a step to run after Takumu, and once again, the girl swiftly raised an arm to hold him back.

It wasn't hitting her arm that made Haruyuki stop. It was the fact that he slipped right through it. Silver Crow passed soundlessly through the girl's right arm as though it were a video with no physical substance. Surprise brought Haruyuki's feet to a stop. Stunned, he turned around to look at her. He'd been holding Lime Bell's hand the whole time, so it couldn't be that there was a rule against touching in this world.

The girl smiled a little sadly. "I told you, didn't I? I'm…a memory. A souvenir of a BB player who disappeared from this world many long days ago. The echoes of a consciousness."

"M-memory? But you're here talking with us like this," Chiyuri murmured.

The girl nodded slightly. "All data is saved here in the Main Visualizer in the same form as the person's memory. So an object with a strong will…with a prayer or a wish carved into it, has a kind of pseudo thinking. And that's me."

"Strong…wish…" A memory flickered to life in one corner of Haruyuki's brain.

When they first met in the middle of the battle with Takumu, the girl had said she was waiting for the person who could remove the curse of the armor, the person who could heal *his* fury and sadness. Him. Haruyuki didn't know who that person was. But that wish had kept her alive in the Accelerated World all this time.

"In this place, only the will has any actual power." The girl nodded, as if reading Haruyuki's thoughts. "That black lump is a solidified mass of enormous malice. If you get any closer, you'll both be pulled into it, too."

"B-but, I mean, Taku's—!" Frustrated, he looked at the end of the floating bridge again. There were only a few dozen meters now between Cyan Pile walking with his face turned to the ground and the main body of the ISS kit. In less than a minute, Takumu would be caught by the black blood vessels and have something precious stolen from him once more.

And then—

"You have the power," the girl said curtly.

"P-power?"

"Exactly. The power to reach a hand out far into the distance."

Reflexively, Haruyuki looked at his own right hand, wrapped in silver armor. Five slender, tapered fingers. A hand that was afraid of touching anything, afraid of connecting with anyone, a hand that had stayed hidden in his pocket for a long time. Then he looked at his left hand. But that hand was holding on tightly to Lime Bell—Chiyuri's hand—without any fear.

Before he became a Burst Linker, he could never have done anything like this, even as avatars in the middle of a full dive. But ever since that day eight months earlier, so many people had reached out a hand to him; they'd encouraged him and shared their courage with him.

I'm not the me I was back then, staring at the ground when I walked. I don't have these hands just so they can break into a cold sweat and then get hidden behind me. They're here to hold the hands offered to me—no, for me to hold someone else's hand.

"You can do it." As if in perfect harmony with Haruyuki's

thoughts, Chiyuri raised his left hand and squeezed it tightly. "You of all people can do it, Haru. Your hand—your feelings can reach Taku."

"Yeah," Haruyuki said, nodding and squeezing hard in return. "I'm going to reach him. As if I'm going to let that mass of meat take Taku!"

The golden-yellow avatar said that the only power in this world was the will. In other words, that meant he could use only the Incarnate System. Put another way, normal techniques had no power at all. That was the reason Silver Crow couldn't fly in this world.

Haruyuki's sole Incarnate technique was a basic range-expansion technique. That said, the most distance he'd added to his bare hand was barely two meters. In contrast, there were roughly fifty meters from him to Takumu and the black mass of flesh just ahead of his walk.

However, in this world, apparent distances probably meant nothing. If you fired, thinking you'd never make the shot, then even the largest missile wouldn't reach your target. And if you made your shot believing you'd get a hit—even Haruyuki's underdeveloped Incarnate would definitely get there.

Still holding Chiyuri's hand, Haruyuki crouched down and spread out his legs in a runner's stance. He brought the fingers of his right hand to a point.

"You get one chance, one moment," the girl whispered, immediately to his right. "But I know you can do it. Believe. In the power that connects you, your heart with so many people."

And then the girl—her avatar—faded abruptly, and her figure was overlaid onto his, almost as if she were melting into him. And then she disappeared completely.

Haruyuki still had so many things he wanted to ask her. But they'd have the chance to meet again. Right now, he had to focus on getting Takumu back.

He intuitively understood what she meant when she said he'd

get one chance at this. That mass of flesh would expose some fragile part in order to connect with Takumu. He had to aim for that. As he focused his awareness into his right hand, a dazzling silver light was born in his fingertips and soon covered his arm up to his elbow.

Perhaps in reaction to this light, the mass of flesh in the distance began waving the blood vessels that reached out from all over its body. The tips moved exactly like tentacles, seeming to search the area. Just as the girl had said, if he had gone any closer, those tentacles would have noticed him and tried to pull him in. Like the kit when it split at the end of the battle with Takumu.

Vweeeen. The high-pitched hum of vibration echoed. The silver light of his right hand extended several dozen centimeters into a sharp sword shape. As he started to chamber his spear hand at his hip in the usual Laser Sword build-up motion, Haruyuki and his arm both froze.

He suddenly knew he'd never reach with the same technique, the same Incarnate as the one he'd used up to now. He'd already put his Incarnate up against the aura generated by the ISS kit in the duel the previous evening. To penetrate that terrifyingly concentrated darkness, he would need a much, much stronger image.

As if guided, he raised his right hand to shoulder level. He twisted his body, his arm, to pull back as far as he could. The movement his teacher and parent, Kuroyukihime—Black Lotus—had shown him any number of times with her miraculous long-distance attack, Vorpal Strike. That Incarnate attack was most likely the ultimate range/power expansion technique. He wouldn't be able to simply up and use the same technique, but he should definitely be able to overlay the image of it at least. He had to.

Because of the unfamiliar preparatory motion, the image flickered, and the overlay lodged in his right arm blinked irregularly.

"Haru." A whisper. His left hand was clenched even more tightly. "I can't use Incarnate, but I feel the same as you. I want to get Taku back. And not for the past we had, but so the three of us can start walking toward the future. Even if…even if someday, the road ahead of us splits." Her voice was trembling, shaking slightly, but Chiyuri's words were a firm declaration.

Abruptly, Lime Bell's body was covered in a faint light-green shine. The vivid light flowed into Haruyuki through their joined hands and steadied the overlay of his right hand, and more—made it stronger.

"This is the power of Incarnate, Chiyu," Haruyuki replied in a voice that was nearly inaudible. "Pray. Pray that my hand reaches Taku."

"I am."

Vweeeeeen. The sound of resonance, like the lingering ringing of a bell, increased in volume again. The black lump flailed its herd of tentacles in what appeared to be annoyance. But it couldn't quite find Haruyuki and Chiyuri.

At that moment, Cyan Pile finally reached the lump of flesh and stopped. He dropped to his knees like the string holding him up had been cut, his head hanging deeply. On the surface of the Pile Driver of Takumu's right arm, a small black sphere popped up. Opening an eye the color of wet blood, it flicked back and forth from side to side to check its surroundings before the entire sphere plucked itself off, up into the air.

A mass of thin blood vessels still connected to Takumu's arm, the black sphere slowly extended snail-like feelers upward. At the same time, a bundle of thick blood vessels reached out from the black lump of flesh to meet the feelers.

Just as they were about to touch—

Having pulled back his right arm as far as it would go above his shoulder, Haruyuki thrust it forward as hard as he could. At the same time, he shouted the words that rose up in his mind.

"Laser…Lance!!"

With a fierce metallic sound, a thin, concentrated lance of light shot forward from his right hand, growing longer and longer as it did, piercing the darkness lurking around the main body of the ISS kit. Twenty meters, thirty, and still it showed no signs of weakening.

However, at this point, Haruyuki felt a heavy resistance in his arm. *That feeling.* The icy incandescence from when he was first hit with Bush Utan's Dark Blow.

Reach!

Reach him!

Haruyuki's and Chiyuri's simultaneous but soundless shouts rang out. The overlay blanketing their avatars shone dazzlingly bright, melted into each other, and flowed into the lance of light to blow off the thick film of darkness.

Takumu's ISS kit, about to make contact with the group of blood vessels stretching out from the main body, looked back in a motion that was very much that of a living creature and stared at the lance. The black eyelids opened as far as they could go. The kit immediately tried to return to the site it was parasitizing on Cyan Pile's arm, but a fraction of a second before it could, the tip of the Incarnate lance plunged deep into the pupil of the crimson eye.

Pshkt! With a terrifying sound, the eye burst, black liquid spraying everywhere. Instantly, Haruyuki felt the enormous lump of flesh—the main body of the kit—emitting violent waves of rage.

The countless tentacles that stretched out from the lump, so reminiscent of a brain somehow, whirled about searching for the intruder. Directly below it, Cyan Pile jerked his head up.

"T-Taku! Over here!!" Haruyuki roared, as loudly as he humanly could.

Takumu looked back to see Haruyuki and Chiyuri. Beyond the slits carved into his face mask, his pale-blue eyes opened wide; he was apparently wide-awake now.

"Taku! Run!!" Chiyuri shrieked.

Takumu stood up his large avatar and moved toward the two of them. He had run a few steps on the narrow, floating bridge

before he stopped suddenly, perhaps having thought of something, and whirled back around toward the lump of flesh.

The main body of the kit twisted the bulk of its appendages into a single massive tentacle and tried to grab hold of Cyan Pile once more. If it swallowed him up again, Takumu would probably be parasitized with a new kit.

"Taku, run..." Halfway through, Haruyuki swallowed the words he was shouting.

And that was because Takumu suddenly grabbed hold of the Pile Driver's tip with his free hand. That was—that movement, the Incarnate technique Takumu had mastered, the attack power expansion...

"Cyan Blade!!"

His voice triumphantly called out the attack name. His Enhanced Armament pulled apart, and a blue overlay enveloped the now-freestanding spike. By the time he shifted smoothly to firmly hold the blade in both hands, the Armament had already transformed into a large, two-handed sword.

Without flinching at the mass of tentacles rushing toward him, Takumu brandished the shining blue sword above his head.

"Cheeeeeaaaaah!!"

A powerful battle cry. The space itself rippled and shook, and leftover waves of incredible power made it to the two friends frozen in place.

The double-handed sword swung down directly before Cyan Pile, a beam like lightning jetting out of it. The herd of tentacles was cut in half, and the sword dug deeply into the flesh of the main kit body.

A soundless shriek. The entire lump of flesh shuddered violently over and over, and the several dozen Burst Linkers connected to it by those blood vessels also shuddered and shook. Some woke up and stared absently at their surroundings. Blue light radiated outward from around the two-handed sword buried in the mass, and fine fissures raced outward.

Then the kit's main body, ten meters in diameter, exploded from the inside, and massive amounts of black fluid and vapor gushed out in all directions. The circuit on which Takumu, Haruyuki, and Chiyuri stood began to crumble and fall from where it was attached. Losing their support, the avatars were released helplessly into the bottomless expanse of outer space.

Or so it seemed, until the next instant—

5

"Aaah! W-we're gonna fall!" Haruyuki shouted, bolting upright into a sitting position. As he did, something tugged on both sides of his neck. "Huh? What?"

His heart pounding at top speed, he looked around several times. The off-white wallpaper. The extremely thin flat-screen TV. The large dining table and the kitchen counter beyond it. It was the familiar living/dining room combination of his own house. He was sleeping there on a mattress spread out on the floor.

The home server detected him sitting up and turned on the light panel on the ceiling to shed a dim illumination. Looking down in the weak gray light to see what was pulling at his neck, he found two XSB cables stretching out from his still-equipped Neurolinker. With his eyes, he followed the cable on the left to land on the face of his childhood friend Chiyuri Kurashima, sleeping a mere fifty centimeters away, blankets tossed off, stomach peeking out from the bottom of her pajama top.

No way. It was all a dream?

Turning into a duel avatar in a mysterious place, passing through the long tunnel, seeing the galaxy of light, meeting that golden-yellow girl there again…all of it, just a dream?

Just as Haruyuki was seized by doubt, Chiyuri's eyelids flew open with an audible *snap*. She met his eyes for a mere second before shouting hoarsely, "Haru! What about Taku?! Did he make it out okay?!"

Her words showed that she and Haruyuki had shared the same experience.

Right, it couldn't have been just a dream. Everything they had seen and heard in the world, everything that had happened was all real. They had passed through an imagination circuit into the central server of Brain Burst, discovered a strange lump of black flesh—the main body of the ISS kit—and Haruyuki had "awakened" Takumu with an Incarnate technique just as the lump was trying to connect with his friend. And then...

"Taku!" Crying out, Haruyuki twisted his body toward the mattress laid out to his right.

In the gloom, Takumu Mayuzumi was, in contrast with Chiyuri, in a proper sleeping position facing directly upward, eyes closed.

"Taku!" Chiyuri cried out weakly, and jumped over Haruyuki's legs to stand on her knees immediately beside Takumu. Her hand reached out to touch his shoulder, and the young man's eyes popped open.

Hearts in their throats, Chiyuri and Haruyuki watched as his brown eyes took in each of them in turn. His left hand snaked out from under the blanket and touched the Neurolinker on his own neck, at the cable extending from his XSB terminal to Haruyuki's.

"It...wasn't a dream, was it?" Haruyuki's childhood friend said finally, in a clear voice that couldn't be mistaken for sleep-talking. "Or wait. It was a nightmare, and you guys smashed it for me. That's it." And then the exact same gentle smile as always spread across his lips.

Instantly, Haruyuki reached out and gripped his friend's shoulder tightly. "Taku!" he shouted. "Y-you...When I tell you to run, you run! You can't usually counterattack on the spot like that, you know!"

"Exactly! What did you intend to do if those creepy tentacles got ahold of you again?!" Chiyuri also raised a shrill voice, leaning in so far toward him that she threatened to fall on him.

Rebuked for launching a counterattack with his Incarnate rather than running from the rage-crazed main body—after he had broken free of the mind control thanks to Haruyuki's Incarnate attack—Takumu's smile changed into something more apologetic.

"I-it's just, I suddenly got the idea. That that thing was the bad guy, that it was the root of all evil. In which case, I felt like I had to at least send one shot back at it."

"W-well, yeah, I mean, I wanted to get in there and send it to the hospital if I could have." Nodding unconsciously, Haruyuki suddenly lifted his face with a gasp and hurried to ask, "R-right, more importantly...how is it? That thing inside you?"

In the "dream," with his new Incarnate technique Laser Lance, Haruyuki had pierced and destroyed the ISS kit that had separated from Takumu's right arm. But even if it hadn't all been an actual dream, it was still something that had happened in the world of imagination, so he didn't know how much of an impact it would have on reality.

Takumu lowered his eyes and then closed them tightly. He raised his hand and pressed it to his forehead, his furrowed brow trembling a little. He stayed like this for a while, before finally bringing down his hand and opening his eyes again. Takumu looked directly at Chiyuri and Haruyuki in turn.

"It's gone." His voice was quiet.

"Huh?"

"It's gone, Haru. That thing that's been sitting somewhere deep inside my head since last night, constantly whispering to me... it's gone."

The home server, having decided that its master was awake now, turned the lights up further. The daytime color of the panel lighting shone on Takumu's smiling face. It was his best friend's usual smile, the grin that was always there whenever he looked over as they devoted themselves to playing; the look that had been there ever since they became the two forwards of Nega Nebulus—no, ever since they were little kids.

It's Taku. He's back. He broke away from the temptation of the power of darkness and climbed out of the deep hole in his heart and came back to us again. To my side. To a place I can reach if I stretch out my hand.

The instant he felt it sincerely, Takumu's smiling face was covered and blurred in a boisterous dance of white light. As soon as he realized what was spilling hotly out of his own eyes, Haruyuki was so embarrassed he slammed his forehead into Takumu's broad chest.

"M-making us worry!" Shouting with a deliberate roughness, he tried intently to rein in his tears, but they only kept coming, one after another. He clenched his teeth and something like a child's sobs slipped out from his throat. "Unh...Ngh...Huuunh!"

Unable to hold anything back now, Haruyuki wept, shoulders shaking, while a large, warm hand patted his back gently.

"H-hey, Haru! I'm the one who should be doing that!" Chiyuri's exasperated voice also sounded choked. And then she bumped her own body up against Haruyuki's shoulder.

Feeling the warmth of his two childhood friends, Haruyuki continued to simply spill hot tears.

Thank goodness. Abruptly, he heard a faint voice deep in his own head. *You managed to save your friend.*

No mistake, it was the voice of the mysterious golden girl avatar. Stifling his sobs, Haruyuki thought back to her:

Thanks. It's all thanks to you.

Hee-hee. I didn't do anything. The light of your heart shone through the darkness. I want you to keep walking ahead on this road you believe in. If you keep collecting all these lights, I'm sure the time will come when even his deep despair will be healed.

He didn't really understand the meaning of those words at that moment, but Haruyuki murmured, as if guided by something, *Yeah. I promise. I'm definitely going to release you—you and him from the cycle of Catastrophe.*

…Thank you. I believe in you…

The voice receded and disappeared.

Finally getting himself under control, Haruyuki wiped away his tears with the sleeve of his pajamas and lifted his chin, shouting forcefully to hide his embarrassment. "W-we ran until we practically died, and now I'm starving. I'm gonna go check if there's anything in the fridge." He pulled out the direct cable, stood up, and padded quickly into the kitchen.

"Hey now!" Chiyuri's exasperated voice chased him. "We might have been running, but it was actually in a dream, you know!"

Which was followed by Takumu's laughter.

"Ha-ha-ha! Haru, bring me something, too!"

Haruyuki warmed up frozen cubes of clam chowder for three, divided it evenly into soup cups, and then carried these out to the dining room table.

A glance at the wall clock revealed that it was already nearly six in the morning. If he canceled the shade mode on the window glass, the morning sun would come pouring in from the east. It was an hour earlier than he usually got up, but he figured he might as well stay up now. Haruyuki let out a long yawn.

After putting away their bedding and sitting down at the table, the three friends took a sip of the steaming soup. They all let out a sigh and looked at one another.

"Taku." The first to speak was Chiyuri, her face quite serious. "Umm, so I guess we can assume the ISS kit is completely gone now?"

"Yeah, I think so. I don't have any data or anything to back it up, but that's what my gut's telling me." There was no hesitation or doubt in Takumu's immediate reply.

"Rather than breaking down endurance in the duel stage," Haruyuki started thinking out loud, "it's like, um, like you smashed the saved data in the server itself. And it's actually surprising you managed to survive that."

"'Server.' Haru, are you saying that place was Brain Burst's...?"

"Yeah." He nodded lightly at Takumu's question. "The Brain Burst central server. That's what she said."

Takumu had woken up only when they were on the verge of escaping that world, so Haruyuki and Chiyuri took turns explaining what they had experienced there. The long, dark tunnel and the infinite expanse beyond it. The galaxy of shuddering lights, the inky black of the lump of flesh. And the mysterious golden-yellow avatar who had appeared from within Haruyuki to teach them so many things.

"Right." Glasses still off, Takumu fell silent for a while, the look on his face indicating he was in his usual "full professor" mode. After a few seconds of fiercely racking his brain, he lifted his head and spoke crisply. "Haru, do you remember? Last night, before we went to sleep, we talked about the vulnerability of the ISS kit."

"V-vulnerability...Right, we did talk about how, if it has this kind of terrifying power, then it has to have a vulnerability to match, right?"

"Right. You definitely got to the heart of that vulnerability before. The ISS kit automatically opens an imagination circuit while the person who has it equipped is sleeping at night, which connects the wearer's consciousness directly to the central server. Then it does this parallel-processing-of-evil kind of thing with the other wearers, to strengthen the kit's main body and its terminals."

Takumu's words sent a shiver through the other two.

"Th-this is seriously serious," Chiyuri murmured. "Isn't that beyond what a player could actually do, though?"

"Yeah." Takumu bit his lip lightly. "To be honest, I have no idea what kind of logic could create an Enhanced Armament with such an ability. But…if there's one thing I can say, it's that the Brain Burst program had this function right from the start. To open the imagination circuit as a dream and connect to the central server."

"Huh? That's…?"

"Haru, you remember, right? What happened the night after you installed Brain Burst?"

"Oh!" he cried out and met Chiyuri's eyes before bobbing his head up and down.

There was no way he could forget. After getting the program from Kuroyukihime the previous fall, Haruyuki had had a long, long nightmare, although he couldn't remember the details. The program had picked through this dream and created Haruyuki's other self, the duel avatar Silver Crow. His avatar data would have been registered in the central server at the same time—or rather, it was only natural to think this process happened within the central server.

So that night, Haruyuki had indeed been in communication with the server while he slept. It was basically the same as what had happened to Takumu now.

"So then the parallel processing every night is the key to the strength of the ISS kits," Takumu continued, still thinking it through as he sipped his soup. "But at the same time, it's a massive opening. I mean, however you look at it, that means calling the Burst Linkers right up to the main body. It's not a problem if everyone's under the control of the kit like I was, but…"

Takumu lifted his head and smiled meaningfully, and Haruyuki returned his grin. "The guys who made the kits probably never imagined their victims would be directing with another Burst Linker while they slept."

"And even more, that that Burst Linker would be able to use a range-expansion Incarnate technique to attack from outside the range of the main body."

The two boys laughed together, and, watching them, Chiyuri shook her head in mock exasperation but soon spoke in a half-smiling, half-grumbling way. "So then the bond between us was the winner! Right! Aah, honestly, I just want to meet whoever's pulling the strings right now and say, 'Take that!'"

She drained the rest of her soup in one gulp and slammed the cup back down onto the table before shaking a head of short, tousled hair and opening her mouth again. "Hey, Taku? At the end of that dream, you cut down the kit's main body with Cyan Blade, right? Did that destroy the kit?"

"...No." Takumu's face grew serious again, and he shook his head slowly. "Unfortunately, I didn't get any feedback to indicate that I destroyed it completely. But I definitely damaged the accumulated 'evil will' and the circuit it was using to transmit that. The clones in the same cluster as me probably lost a fair bit of power."

The cluster Takumu was talking about was the group of Burst Linkers with the same ISS kit origin—in Takumu's case, Magenta Scissor—or people who got copies of it later. If he hadn't stopped the kit when it split off from him and tried to parasitize Haruyuki at the end of the battle the previous evening, Haruyuki would have become a member of that cluster as well.

"So, then, if we were thinking of freeing Bush Utan and Olive Grab from the kit, now would be the time," Haruyuki muttered, remembering the figure of the dark-green avatar walking beside Takumu in the nightmare.

"Yeah. Right now, you wouldn't have to go into the central server. You could probably destroy the kits in a normal duel. Of course, regular techniques wouldn't work, but I think it'd be possible with Incarnate techniques."

"Got it. I'll pass the info along to his 'big brother.' I wish we could do something ourselves, but we can't move today."

Chiyuri and Takumu looked up at the clock on the wall. The date and time it showed was six thirty AM, Thursday, June 20, 2047.

At seven that evening—a little over twelve hours from that moment—Haruyuki would have to take on a mission of the highest level of difficulty: escape from the Castle.

His other self, Silver Crow, was currently trapped in the depths of the Castle in the center of the Unlimited Neutral Field, along with Ardor Maiden, who had the power of purification. Unless they managed to make it past the fearsome attacks of the God Suzaku one more time, Haruyuki had no future as a Burst Linker. Because, if he couldn't purify himself of the Armor of Catastrophe that lurked deep within his avatar, a bounty of the highest order would be placed on his head at the next meeting of the Seven Kings.

Although he had gone on an unexpected adventure the night before a mission where he really needed to have a solid sleep behind him, Haruyuki actually felt unusually full of energy. He had the real sense that the duel with the infected Takumu and the experience in the central server after that had given him a certain something.

Turning their faces back from the clock, the three nodded firmly. With a smile on her face, Chiyuri slapped Haruyuki hard on the back.

"Haru, you go and cut down that stupid bird and hurry home already!"

"Right, Haru! Compared to fighting me in IS mode, it should be a breeze, right?"

"Oh! You said it, Professor Mayuzumi!"

And with the grins the two boys exchanged once more, the impromptu sleepover party came to an end.

The brave warrior Chiyuri, still in her pajamas, was the first to turn toward the front door in a bid to return to her home two floors below, soon followed by Takumu in his sweats. As he stood at the entryway seeing them off, Haruyuki suddenly noticed Takumu make a small gesture.

He raised his right hand and gently held his left arm around his wrist. The very place where the ISS kit had parasitized him.

Haruyuki took a step forward. "Taku," he said quietly. "I have to apologize. I wrecked your power."

His friend turned and grinned, but Haruyuki felt a certain

faint melancholy behind it. Still, Takumu shook his head from side to side.

"It's true I'd be lying if I said I didn't miss that incredible power," he said in an untroubled voice. "But I really have to thank you from the bottom of my heart. I'd rather be how I am, you know? No matter how much I worry or how lost I am."

"...Taku..."

"And I got something way bigger than that power. Which is why you totally don't need to apologize to me."

"Huh?" Haruyuki blinked several times and then asked, head cocked, "So, like, some kind of amazing special attack?"

Before Takumu could answer, Chiyuri, having put on her shoes, whirled around and shouted, "Aaah! Come on! How can you be so thick!! Taku's trying to say—" For some reason, she cut herself off there and grinned. "Actually, you think about it. It's your homework for tomorrow!"

Haruyuki put the living room back the way it had been before the sleepover and scarfed down a breakfast of cereal and milk before changing into his school uniform and leaving for the day.

As he rode down in the elevator, he typed out a short text message to his mother. The gist of it was a report that he had gotten up and gone to school, and he wrote a thank-you for letting Takumu and Chiyuri stay over the night before. Now that he was thinking about it, all the members of his Legion would be coming together at the Arita house that evening, but the meeting would end before his mother came home, so he left that part out. He sent it as the elevator reached the ground floor.

The reply that came a few seconds later simply said "Understood," but a money code for five hundred yen was attached. Unthinkingly, Haruyuki grinned and happily charged his account with it.

His mother, Saya Arita, was a mysterious woman, even seen through the eyes of her own child. The fact that she was thirty-seven that year meant she had given birth to Haruyuki at twenty-three. She had never told him the details of that time-line herself, but she would have been a student doing her graduate studies at a university within the city at the time. While there, she had married a man three years her senior working in a network-related company and borne a child. But the particulars of this time were unknown, and there had been no wedding, either. And apparently, this was the reason they were estranged from his mother's family in Yamagata.

When she finished her master's course while raising a baby— regardless of the fact that she was relying on the Neurolinker for some of that rearing—and received her MBA, she was hired by a Japanese investment bank with its head office in the United States. She had distinguished herself as a member of the trading department and, through her work on several large cases, gotten promoted in recent years to an associate.

Haruyuki had actually heard all this from Chiyuri's mother, Momoe. She and Haruyuki's mother had apparently been friends since back then. But Momoe also didn't tell him about a certain incident—about why Haruyuki's parents had gotten divorced.

The divorce was finalized seven years earlier. His mother had been thirty, his father thirty-three, and Haruyuki seven. He barely remembered it. But there was one scene burned into one corner of his memory that would never disappear.

One night, hearing voices, little Haruyuki woke up. When he listened closely, he could definitely hear a conversation on the other side of the door. He didn't fall back to sleep right away because of the sharp edges in those two voices. Instead, he got out of bed and quietly opened the door. At the time, he didn't sleep in the larger room he had now but rather a smaller room on the other side of the living room. At the end of the dark hall-way, hazy light shone through the glass dividing door. Haruyuki moved without making a sound and crouched down next to the door.

Although his parents' voices as he eavesdropped were forcibly hushed, they were clearly having heated words. They were arguing fiercely about something. He could catch bits and pieces like "take care of," "promised," and "used," but he didn't understand what they meant. However, young Haruyuki instinctively knew that his parents were fighting about him.

And there his memory ended abruptly, as though slamming into a wall, and Haruyuki absently raised his face.

Before he knew it, he had crossed the large courtyard of his condo and arrived at the edge of Kannana Street. He shook his head lightly and set his thoughts on a new track. He wasn't particularly fond of remembering the past.

At any rate, this Saya Arita was a woman who moved relentlessly forward as though possessed. Never showing anyone the depths of her heart, without even looking at her feet...

He may have at some point thought it was sad, but it didn't particularly bother him now. She didn't hassle him about his grades, she never forgot to give him five hundred yen for lunch, and she let his friends stay over. Complaining about that was an invitation to disaster.

He took a deep breath and then replaced the air built up in his lungs as he glanced at the AR display on his virtual desktop.

The weather forecast for the day was cloudy, with light rain in the afternoon that would stop toward evening. He didn't see any warning message that he'd forgotten anything, and thanks to the fact that he had left the house much earlier than usual, his scheduled arrival time at school was a full thirty minutes before the first bell. He had a little time to spare for a mission before school started.

Stepping out into the crosswalk of the ring road, Haruyuki shifted his bag onto his back and started out toward the south at a brisk pace.

Where he would normally turn right at the intersection under the Chuo Line, he went straight. He climbed the hill of south

Koenji and rode up the escalator to the pedestrian bridge crossing Oume Kaido. At the top, he turned left and then stopped directly above the wide, eight-lane highway. As he looked down on the stream of EVs flowing back and forth, he murmured under his breath, "Burst Link."

Skreeeeee!! Thunder ripped through the air, and the world froze blue. Immediately, he clicked on the flaming B icon at the bottom left of his virtual desktop. From the menu that popped up, he opened the matching list for Suginami Area No. 2 and touched a name in the middle of the list of avatars, which could hardly be said to be lengthy. Without hesitating, he tapped the DUEL button that appeared in a small pop-up window.

The transformation began in the initial accelerated space, and the clear blue world creaked and groaned. The road turned into a dead valley full of debris, the buildings reddish-brown rocky mountains, the sky a dirty pale yellow. A Wasteland stage.

Checking that the guide cursor was pointing south on Kannana, Haruyuki sent his body, in duel avatar form now, over the edge of the pedestrian bridge. He landed with a *thud* and waited for the roar of the gasoline engine approaching from a distance.

Just the other morning, Haruyuki had challenged the exact same opponent at the exact same time in this very place. So his opponent had no doubt guessed his intention—that he wanted to talk rather than fight. Having made this judgment, he raised a hand at the silhouette that came into view.

"Oh, hi! Good morn…" Haruyuki started to offer a greeting, but his words changed midway into a scream. "…eaaaooooh?!"

He barely managed to throw himself to the right and avoid the iron monster charging at him at top speed—a large American motorcycle from the previous century.

Before Haruyuki's eyes, the motorcycle spun around, a shower of sparks jetting off from the front and rear disc brakes, and came to a stop, leaving the smell of burning and a groove dug out of the gravel road.

Haruyuki jumped to his feet and turned toward the rider of the vehicle, shouting in a panic. "Uh, um, sorry! I wanted to talk again in closed mode—"

But the rider—member of the Green Legion, Great Wall, level-five Burst Linker Ash Roller—flicked the fingers of his right hand dismissively, interrupting Haruyuki. "Totally compredés that. I know, so mighty me's starting things off today with a wicked turn!"

"Ah...huh." Overwhelmed, Haruyuki nodded.

"Then listen up, you little crow!" Ash Roller snapped the index fingers of both hands at him. "Today you doo-bappity-du*el* my righteous self for reals! If I lose, I'll listen to what you have to say. But, 'ey, *I* win, and you grant me one wish! That's totally mega even terms, a'ight!"

"Sorry? A w-wish?!"

"Two duels in a row of nada, and the pretty little boys and girls in the Gallery who went to all the trouble of registering me are gonna be mega bummed and blue!"

Cheers like "Yeah! That's right!" and "Show us something hot today!" came one after another at this declaration from beneath the skull–emblazoned face shield of Ash's helmet. Hurriedly looking around, Haruyuki saw the silhouettes of the audience dotting the rooftops of the buildings along Kannana.

There wasn't a ton of people, but it did look like pretty much everyone registered on the matching list had shown up in the stage. Many of the Burst Linkers who made their home in Shinjuku or farther west knew Silver Crow and Ash Roller as fated rivals. Their fights tended to be rather spectacular because both of their avatars had very flashy performance—and they were both level five—so a fight between them was seen as a pretty fun event.

Haruyuki glanced up at the timer, already down sixty seconds, and thought over the situation quickly.

Unlike the day before, when they had talked for very nearly the full thirty minutes, all he had to say to Ash Roller that day was the simple message "if you're going to remove Bush Utan's

ISS kit, now's your chance." That wouldn't even take three minutes. In which case, it wouldn't be a bad idea to make good use of the burst point he'd gone and spent, and take on Ash Roller in a practice match. And he couldn't rule out the possibility that, depending on how the mission to escape the Castle that night and the meeting of the Seven Kings on Sunday went, this might be his last duel.

"Understood." Haruyuki nodded deeply. "I'll accept your terms. If I win, you sit down and listen to meeooowhoa!"

Before he could finish speaking, however, his sentence turned into a shout once more, and he flew off to his left—because Ash Roller's massive bike had suddenly and ferociously charged him.

"Ah! That's dangerous, you know! I was still talk—"

"Shut it. Shut yer yaaaaap! Duel's started, booooyyyy! Boo-hoo to you, 'cos I'm gonna victorize totes gigacooooooool!" Ash Roller shouted, and spun his bike around once more.

Haruyuki made a mental note that the turn radius was much tighter than when they'd first met, as he flung back his own bravado. "I-I'm the one who's gonna pull off a teragorgeous perfect win! But, like, the terms are not even at all. I mean, I win and you listen. You win, and I grant—"

"Suuuuuucks! Not my style to get all worked up over details!"

Exhaust jetting from the fat muffler, the American motorcycle rushed Haruyuki for the third time.

Ash Roller was an irregular Burst Linker, having poured the majority of his duel avatar's potential into the Enhanced Armament that was his bike.

The rider himself had basically no fighting power, close-up or long-range. Instead, the motorcycle had both serious mobility and serious stamina. A vehicle Enhanced Armament was in and of itself rare, but even among the ones that existed, the performance of this one was likely at the top of the class.

If pressed to list its weak points, Haruyuki would have to say that it wasn't as maneuverable as a flesh-and-blood avatar and that it lacked the element of surprise because of its sheer size.

To attack the latter weakness, a concentrated long-distance fire-power attack was effective, but Haruyuki had essentially none of the attack power endemic in red-type avatars.

Thus, if he was fighting Ash Roller on the ground, he ended up risking his life on close-range attacks. Specifically, when he dodged to one side as the charging vehicle was a hairbreadth away and then showered counterattacks on Ash himself or the motorcycle engine.

The best thing was to use Silver Crow's nimble agility to jump straight up into the air and aim for the rider's head, but his opponent was well aware of this strategy. The instant Haruyuki assumed a posture to leap upward, his opponent would no doubt pull up into a wheelie and bring out the "antiaerial attack," front wheel spinning at high speed. The jump attack and the antiaerial attack were mutually incompatible, a game of rock, paper, scissors, and if he took that hit, he wouldn't be able to avoid serious damage. An unstrategic leap was suicide.

"Eeeeeyaaaaaah!"

Together with a high-pitched battle cry from its rider, the bike charged toward Haruyuki, and he concentrated all his mental energies on its enormous front wheel.

His opponent was also no doubt assuming Haruyuki would dodge and was ready to make tiny adjustments to his trajectory one way or the other immediately before Haruyuki could jump. Which was fine if Ash plunged ahead on the opposite side, but Haruyuki was just another jumper on a busy train line if he dodged in the same direction.

Which way...right or left...Don't look at the tire, watch the angle of the bike itself...

Haruyuki activated the hyperpowers of concentration—limited to game play and nothing else—he had polished long before he became a Burst Linker and focused every inch of his mind on the behavior of the entire motorcycle.

Then.

The turn signal on the bike's side, the right from Haruyuki's perspective, began flashing orange.

"Huh." The sound slipped out of him as he reflexively flew to the left.

But at the same time, the bike also angled to the left, and the tough, charcoal-colored tire pressed in on him.

An incredible impact like being hit with an enormous hammer. The entirety of the stage spun round and round. Or rather, Haruyuki himself spun round and round. In a magnificent display that outshone even the more silly anime programs of the day, Silver Crow flew dozens of meters head over heels at top speed through the air before smashing headfirst into one of the rocky mountains along the east side of Kannana Street.

After blacking out for a minute, he braced his hands on the stony face of the mountain and yanked his helmet free. The moment he leapt back to his feet, he shouted indignantly, "Y-y-you turned the opposite way of your signal! That's a traffic violation! Fine of two hundred million yen!!"

"Heeyah-ha-ha-haaaaa!" The skull-faced rider laughed long and loud at this, even as he turned to follow Haruyuki and rush him once more. "Mighty Ash right here! Just me existing's a traffic violation, you knoooooow!"

That was true. In the present day, bringing something that burned fossil fuels onto public roads and generated even a cubic centimeter of carbon dioxide was basically asking to be immediately arrested. And the noise coming from the muffler easily tore through standards for public order; the bike didn't even have a license plate on the back. But of course, in this Accelerated World, there were also no white bikes to pull him over.

Instead of sirens, they were showered in the enthusiastic cheers erupting from the Gallery all around them, as Ash Roller plunged forward to send Haruyuki flying again.

"Damn him!" Cursing, Haruyuki glanced to the top left of his field of view. Silver Crow's health gauge had dropped nearly

20 percent from that hit. In contrast, his special-attack gauge was charged 30 percent, but he still couldn't be sure he could win this if he activated his flying ability.

He'd fly after going up against Ash one more time on the ground. Having resolved this, Haruyuki dropped his stance and waited for the assault. He'd never seen the feint with the turn signal before, so he'd unconsciously fallen for it, but he wouldn't make the same mistake twice. This time, he shouted in his heart, he'd dodge the charge at the very last moment and pummel Ash with a fierce counterattack.

But it seemed that Ash Roller also didn't think the same feint would work a second time. Rather than flicking on his turn signal—

"Huuuup!" he called out as he jumped straight up on the vehicle and stood, using the seat and the handlebars as footholds. He plunged ahead, riding the motorcycle like a surfboard. Ash Roller's so-called secret technique, the V-Twin Punch.

Seemingly a joke in both name and appearance, the technique in fact held a power that couldn't be so easily dismissed. Haruyuki could dodge the front tire of the bike, but then the rider's kick would come flying at him, so it was hard to find the timing for a counterattack. Although he had come up against the V-Twin Punch several times already, he still hadn't been able to find an effective countermeasure to it.

"Yaaahooooooooo!"

Haruyuki glared intently at the motorcycle, slaloming lightly left and right as it pressed in on him, and at the rider shouting on top of it. It was possible for him to evade the attack with a large jump, but then he wouldn't be able to counter. Ash's teacher and parent, Sky Raker, had taken down the V-Twin Punch with the superhuman feat of dashing backward while clutching the motorcycle's brake lever, but that was still beyond Haruyuki's abilities.

Some other weak point, somewhere, somehow—

"Ngh!" A light went on abruptly.

Could Ash Roller still make the bike do a wheelie in that position? No, it was probably impossible. If he did a wheelie, he'd fall off the bike himself. So then where Haruyuki needed to aim was—

"Up!"

The instant the massive tire filled his field of view, Haruyuki bent forward and kicked off the ground as hard as he could to fly up into the air.

"Hungaah?!"

The rider let out a strange sound as Haruyuki crashed into him and clung to him for dear life. The pair fell away from the motorcycle and hit the ground with a thud. Having lost its master, the American bike raced off north on Kannana.

"You! This! Hold me tight—No way, lemme go, dude!" Ash Roller howled, kicking and flailing, while Haruyuki tried with all his might to hold him down. He couldn't let this chance get away from him.

"Nope! You without your bike is like soy sauce pickles without curry!"

"The hell! When it comes to curry, I'm totally on the pickled leeks team!"

The Gallery erupted once more at the two wrestling on the road. But when it came down to actual fisticuffs, Ash Roller simply didn't have the power to pierce Silver Crow's metal armor. Regardless of the punches landing on his face and chest, Haruyuki pushed his way behind Ash Roller and held his chest with both arms.

"Gah! Hey! D-d-d-d-d-d-don't go hugging me, man!"

"I-it's not like I want to be hugging you!"

"Don't say you're hugging me! Dammit, dude!"

"You're the one who said it…first!!" Haruyuki shouted back at Ash Roller, as he deployed the silver wings on his back. His special-attack gauge had been charged a further 10 percent in this ground scuffle, and he used it to deploy the ten metal fins with everything he had.

Vwwmp! Silver Crow and Ash Roller took off directly up into the air like a rocket.

"Ngaaaaah! Wh-what the hell?! Fly hiiiiigh!"

Ash Roller continued his nonsensical yelling, but Haruyuki was done responding; he simply ascended at full power. In an instant, they passed the stony mountains the members of the Gallery stood on, reaching an altitude of one hundred meters, two hundred, three.

"N-noooooo! Heights are no good, no way, no thank you—" The high-pitched cry was abruptly cut off. The body flailing frantically in Haruyuki's arms stiffened, and Ash Roller asked hoarsely, "Uh, um, Crow? Mighty me's not actually? Like a falling star in the night sky?"

"Yes. Like space debris falling out of orbit." Nodding, Haruyuki moved to release his hands, merciless.

He had worked out a number of battle strategies to make use of Silver Crow's flying ability in an actual duel. The one he had been using since the early days was a super-high-speed kick or a punch from a high altitude—his dive attack. And lately, he had been practicing the Aerial Combo technique, which used momentary thrust from his wings in close-range battle on the ground.

But there was a way of using his wings that was more reliable and effective than either of these. He pinned down his duel opponent, carried them high up into the sky, and then released them from serious altitudes for drop damage. It was hard to use on large avatars, and he couldn't manage to even pin down opponents with real fighting abilities, but the moment he got an enemy in the air, real damage was basically assured. The reason Haruyuki didn't use the technique that much was because the second his opponent saw that he was coming in close, they tended to make him eat a painful counterattack. Plus, more than a few avatars were resistant to being dropped even if they couldn't fly, so he couldn't count on a situation like this one, where all the different factors happened to come together. Given that Ash Roller had very weak armor and no hovering or three-dimensional movement abilities, if he was dropped from this height, the maximum value for fall damage would probably be applied.

Haruyuki had gotten swept up in his impending victory and completely forgotten his initial objective, but Ash was not the sort of gallant opponent who could simply keep his mouth shut, even when faced with a stalemate like this.

Before Haruyuki could remove his hands, Ash Roller grabbed on to them tightly and shouted, "Then my mighty self and you are riding tandem straight into hellllllll! Flyyyying Knucklehead!!"

A special attack?! Unconsciously, Haruyuki stiffened up. He hadn't even imagined that Ash Roller's body had a special attack.

But a few seconds passed, and still nothing happened. Deciding that it had been a bluff to buy time, Haruyuki opened his mouth to complain about how his opponent just did not know when to give up, but his words quickly turned into a shout of surprise.

"Come on, Ash! There are limits even fowaaaaaaaah?!"

What had stunned Haruyuki so was not Ash still held in his arms, but rather two spots of light racing toward him from directly below. Long, thin cylindrical bodies closing in, jetting orange flames. Four small wings near the tails and red lenses at the heads. No matter how he looked at them—

"M-m-missiles?!" he screamed as he shot upward in the sky.

But the two missiles were apparently equipped with a homing function and followed him with unerring precision. No matter how he zigged and zagged, he couldn't break away from them.

Now that he was thinking about it, Ash Roller had said something before about getting missiles on his motorcycle. Which meant the launcher of these missiles was that American bike, which had probably fallen over somewhere along Kannana. Which meant that voice commands were still possible even when separated from the Enhanced Armament. However,

"Y-y-you're gonna get blown up, too, though!"

"Ha! Way better than just getting dropped, booooyyyy!"

That was definitely true. Haruyuki tried earnestly to dispose of his burden, but Ash, looking for a draw, had wrapped both arms and legs around him and was clinging to him tightly. Because of this, Haruyuki couldn't manage to produce more than half his usual speed, which meant the missiles would be reaching for the tips of his toes in a few seconds.

"Key shooooooop!" At the same time as Ash Roller shouted this incomprehensible cry, there was a magnificent explosion.

The really terrifying part of explosive attacks—although this naturally depended on the power and range of the explosion—was that when you were hit, you didn't know which way was up for a while. Falling from a height of three hundred meters upside down, head spinning, Haruyuki just barely managed to collect himself before he plunged headfirst into the earth and spread both wings to apply the emergency brakes.

Still tangled up with Ash Roller, he landed in the middle of the intersection of the original Kannana and Oume Kaido. He peeled off the clinging Ash Roller and pushed him half a meter or so away before asking in a groan, "Hey, Ash. What was that 'key shop' thing before?"

Apparently recovering his senses a little more slowly, the motorcycle rider shook his skull helmet lightly back and forth as he whispered in reply, "Okay, so, like...when you set off fireworks, you shout out *tamaya* or *kagiya*, right? I just figured I'd translate that into English...Would 'ball shop' be more compredés for you?"

For once, Ash had translated them correctly, albeit entirely too literally to make any sense. "I'm telling you from the bottom of my heart, either is fine. Which is to say they're both incomprehensible," Haruyuki muttered, and checked both of their health gauges.

Immediately before the direct hit from the missiles, Haruyuki's had been lower, but apparently, his metal armor had cut the damage from the explosion; both gauges currently had a mere

10 percent or so remaining. If one of them got in two or three clean punches, the battle would be decided, but as they lay sprawled out on the ground, Haruyuki and Ash Roller glanced at each other before speaking at the same time:

"Should we call it a draw?"

"How about we leave this a draw?"

Each nodding at the other, they pulled themselves to their feet.

Wordlessly, Haruyuki looked around at the Gallery gazing down upon them, and then shouted in a tense voice, "Um, sorry! We're going to end this duel here as a draw!"

He thought a few people at least would grumble, but to his surprise:

"Good game!"

"Thanks for the great show!"

"Looking forward to next tiiiime!"

The spectators shouted their appreciation and burst out, leaving only their thundering applause. As he watched this, Haruyuki abruptly became aware of a certain kind of deep emotion filling his heart.

This was the duel. There might be thrills and excitement, but there was no resentment or anger. The duelers might be rivals competing against each other, but they were not enemies to hate.

Considering the cool rationality of the burst point system, perhaps the creator of this world had envisioned a more bloodthirsty survival game. But the players had of their own will rejected the expectations of the creator. That feeling was certainly included in the name "Burst Linker," something not set by the point system: the feeling that they were comrades.

The ISS kits and the Acceleration Research Society were trying to destroy this world. Bush Utan, whom Haruyuki had fought a few days earlier, and Takumu in the fight the day before, didn't seem like they were having fun. Even the members of the Society themselves, Dusk Taker and Rust Jigsaw, were at a complete disconnect from the pleasure of the duel.

That was wrong. That was definitely wrong.

As Haruyuki stood there stock-still, fists clenched, a hand wrapped in a leather glove came down with a slap on his left shoulder.

"Good fight, you crazy crow. Way to see through the weak point of my mighty V-Twin Punch."

"I'm sure the same thing won't work again next time, though, huh?" Haruyuki replied, and Ash Roller snorted with laughter.

"Absolutes! Check it. Next time, I'll be popping wheelies standing up, man," the skull face bragged before glancing upward. He was checking the timer. Six hundred seconds left. It wasn't a long time, but enough to talk for a bit.

Ash Roller sat down on one of the more reasonable-size rocks dotting the intersection and jerked his chin toward Haruyuki, as if to tell him to start talking.

Haruyuki nodded and took a seat on a rock opposite him. "Umm, I wanted to talk to you about Bush Utan."

In name at least, Ash was a member of an enemy Legion, so Haruyuki couldn't get into the details about Takumu, but even so, he expended every effort to tell Ash Roller as much information as he actually could.

That the ISS kits were essentially a colony, that they were linked to kits "genetically" close to them. That the wearers of the kits were guided by that link when they went to bed every night and connected with the main body. That Haruyuki and his Legion comrades had attacked that main body the night before on an information level and damaged it considerably.

"So right now, you might be able to destroy the ISS kit parasitizing Utan in a normal duel. But...there are two problems there," Haruyuki said, staring at Ash Roller, who had taken in the whole story without comment. "The first is, the ISS kits probably can't be damaged without using an Incarnate attack. And the second is, even if you destroy the kit, that doesn't resolve the essential problem. Now that he's experienced the Incarnate firsthand—he calls it 'IS mode'—after Rust Jigsaw launched that massive attack from the tenth shuttle in the Hermes' Cord race, Utan's really suspicious of the veteran Burst Linkers who kept the existence of the Incarnate System a secret. And I think that feeling is creating an urgency in him, like he doesn't care how legit or not the power is as long as it makes him stronger. Like there's no *point* if he doesn't get stronger. And as long as he feels like that, I'm pretty sure if you smash this ISS kit he has now, he'll just go looking for another one."

"Yeah, I know. I think so, too." Ash flipped up the skull-patterned shield of his helmet with his right hand. Beneath it, a face mask reminiscent somehow of a science nerd looked up at the sallow sky of the Wasteland. His quiet voice flowed out, voice effects weaker, surprisingly subtle.

"I already told you how that kid U, his parent ended up at total point loss, yeah? Only natural, I guess, but it was a huge shock for him. Ever since, he's had, like, this enormous terror…unhappiness or annoyance or something, just hanging out inside him. I'm supposedly his big bro, so I prob'ly shoulda done something for him. But y'know, I still hadn't…come to terms with this whole total-loss thing, either. I didn't know, y'know, what I should even say to U."

"Come to terms?" Haruyuki asked.

Ash nodded slowly and turned pale-green eye lenses on him. "When the number of burst points becomes zero, the Brain Burst program itself forcefully uninstalls, and you're done being a Burst Linker. Master Raker taught me right off the bat this was the biggest rule of the Accelerated World. You must've gotten it, too, Crow?"

"Y-yeah. Ku—Black Lotus told me that pretty clearly the day I became a Burst Linker."

"Right. But when I really think hard about it, I've actually never been backed up against that wall, where I'm seriously for real on the brink of total loss. I mean, if you really pushed, maybe the worst I've come up against is when I went up to level two and I had a pretty narrow margin, and then I lost to level one you. That got me a bit freaked."

Feeling the man's eyes on him, Haruyuki reflexively shrank into himself.

Thinking back, Ash Roller had been his first fight as a Burst Linker and the first opponent he had lost to. Later, his parent, Kuroyukihime, had lectured him about all sorts of things and come up with the perfect strategy for him to challenge Ash Roller to a rematch. But in the space of a single day, Ash had gotten to level two, and thanks to his newly won ability to ride up walls, Haru's carefully planned strategy had been useless.

Although he despaired of winning at that point, he had frantically racked his brain and realized that the weak point of the old-style motorcycle was that the drive power was in only the rear wheel, which allowed him to turn the tables and win the match. That duel had been the starting point for Haruyuki's tactics.

The "margin" that Ash Roller spoke of was a word originating from the unique ways players leveled up in Brain Burst.

In normal RPGs and other games, the player automatically leveled up when their experience points reached a certain fixed number. But in Brain Burst, to go up a level, a player had to spend experience points they had saved up—their burst points. Specifically, the number of points required to go from level one to level two was three hundred. In other words, when the player executed a level-up in the system menu, their points decreased by three hundred all at once. Thus, when moving up a level, a player needed to ensure they had sufficient wiggle room to lose several duels in a row without being forced to face total point loss—they needed a margin, in other words. It only made sense when he thought about it a little.

Hearing this from Ash Roller, Haruyuki composed a pathetic smile and confessed, "Th-the truth is, I wasn't thinking at all, and I went up a level as soon as I had saved up three hundred points. I was almost at total point loss."

"For real?! Back then, Suginami wasn't even Negabu territory, was it? Can't believe you made it back from that okay." Ash Roller sounded exasperated, and Haruyuki shrugged again.

"Y-yeah. My partner, Cyan Pile, helped me out, and I kinda..."

He started to tell the story, but he couldn't really remember exactly how he had gotten his points back up at the time. So Haruyuki turned the straying conversation back to its original route. "A-anyway, what did you mean before by 'come to terms' with total loss?"

"Ohh. Okay, so look. I can totally see how the whole system of forced uninstall when you lose all your points is a totally mean, for-real-awful rule. But I also kinda feel like if you're gonna be a Burst Linker and get this massive present, acceleration, then a risk that size is only natural. Honestly, I can't totally come down on either side. I mean, like, it's easy to say it's mean...But the flip side of me and you getting all the way to level five here is however many guys got those points stolen from them and ended up in total loss. It's like indirectly, the points I won and used totes casually were points taken from U's parent by someone else when *he* was pushed to total loss."

Haruyuki was speechless as he listened to this speech that was slightly—no, considerably different from the usual yee-haw century-end rider.

As if reading his mind, Ash snorted and turned away before continuing, as if embarrassed. "But then, I think a Burst Linker's gotta be ready right from the start for total loss at least. The one dishing it out and the one taking it, y'know? And in that sense, I really respect your parent, the Black King. Dunno if I should be saying this when I'm in Great Wall, but...she's amazing. She's undisputedly number one in the Accelerated World when it comes to being totally ready to leave this world. I wanna get that kind of mega cool, too. But y'know...like, if I was up against you in a duel, Crow, and say I found out you'd be at total loss if you were crushed one more time, would I be able to mercilessly slam that final blow into you, all cool-like...I honestly got no idea. At the very least, I can't say I wouldn't hesitate."

"Ash." This time, Haruyuki was genuinely surprised and turned serious eyes on the biker.

"Hey you!" he responded in a slightly threatening voice. "You look like you're gonna be all, *I'd have no problem putting you at total loss*. Come on, now!"

"N-no no no no way! I'd hesitate, too! I'd super hesitate!"

"Dude, for serious?! You sound all like, *I'd hesitate, but I'd still put you at total loss*. Come on!"

"B-but you just said it like you would hesitate! Right now!" Shaking both hands and head at top horizontal speed to dodge Ash Roller's follow-up jab, Haruyuki remarked, lips flapping, "But I mean, it's only natural to hesitate. My parent…Black Lotus, I mean, I know she hesitates. No matter how hated her opponent is. Because at the core, they're both Burst Linkers. And I owe you for this one, too, but that time the guy stole my flying ability this spring, he was an enemy, we were in total conflict, and I hated him from the bottom of my heart. And still, when I was defeating him in the Sudden Death Duel, I hesitated a little. I wondered if maybe we could have met a different way, had a different duel… and now I feel like that hesitation is maybe something we'll never be able to get rid of completely as long as we're Burst Linkers."

This time, it was Ash Roller who fell silent.

Eventually, he lowered his eyes to the brownish-red earth between his feet and muttered slowly, "Maybe so. But, like, because of that hesitation, I couldn't say anything to the U kid. I'm s'posed to be his big bro; I really should've said one or the other, clear as day. *I totes will never forgive the dude who pushed your parent to total loss. I'm def gonna get revenge.* Or else, *We all fight carrying around the risk of total loss. You can't mope about it forever.* One of those things. But I couldn't. Which is why U just filled up with anger and fear and went looking for something other than the power he had. This guy sitting right here made one of the reasons he went chasing off after the ISS kit."

Ash Roller slammed a foot on the ground with a *crunch*, and Haruyuki couldn't immediately figure out what he should say. But before he could open his mouth, something began flashing red in the top of his field of view. The timer had crossed into the last hundred seconds.

"That reminds me, Ash. Didn't you say you had a wish you wanted me to grant?"

"Oh. Y-yeah. Right, right." The biker lifted his face and yanked down the skull shield of his helmet before continuing in a suddenly wilder voice. "It's kinda connected with the whole U thing. Well, it's no big, actually. Sorry, Crow, but can you, like, mega quick and cool, teach me?"

"T-teach you? What?" Haruyuki cocked his head, and Ash Roller responded without hesitation and with a singular objective:

"The Incarnate System."

6

If someone were to ask Haruyuki what his favorite of the five weekdays was, he would have responded without a moment's hesitation that it was Friday. This was probably the same as the majority of students—and maybe grown-ups as well. The thrill of the two unbroken days off in a row was hard to beat.

However, when it came to his least-favorite day, he was a bit on the fence. Naturally, along with most people, he was not too happy with Monday, but the first day of the week held the joy of being able to see the object of his respect and affection, Her Excellency the student council vice president, after a two-day absence. And at least for this term, the lunch special on Monday was the feast of the gods that was minced meat cutlet curry.

Thus, if he proffered an amnesty for Monday in an act of extreme benevolence, next in line would have to be Thursday. After all, Thursday had gym class first period, a completely unforgivable timetable.

"Hey, Arita! Hey!"

Drenched in sweat, legs shaking, Haruyuki reflexively moved to throw the basketball he held in both hands in the direction his name came from.

But the figure of his teammate with hands up in the air was soon blocked by a player from the opposing team, and his own teammate disappeared from view. In the lower left of his vision, the digital numbers counting down the five- and twenty-four-second violations were steadily decreasing. Panicking, he held the ball high above his head with both hands to toss it toward the very front line in a blind long pass.

But just when he was on the verge of releasing the pass like a bolt of lightning, someone reached up and seized the ball from behind.

"Gotcha!"

Leaving behind an odious voice, the tall student—a basketball team regular named Ishio—magnificently dribbled the ball toward his own side of the court. While the girls standing around the court cheered, in the blink of an eye, Ishio made his way through the two players guarding and went in for a leisurely layup. The ball swooshed through the hoop, and the right side of the score of 22–36 displayed in the overlay in the lower right of Haruyuki's vision changed to 38.

"No big deal!" The teammate who had called out to Haruyuki clapped him on the shoulder. But Haruyuki could hear only the echoes that lamented the other boy's bad luck at ending up on the same team as Arita, instead of his own bad luck at ending up on the team opposite Ishio.

The dual basketball courts of the gym were divided up into girls' and boys', with the twenty boys being further split up into four teams, so each game was only twenty minutes. An upset victory in the remaining seven minutes and thirty seconds was clearly impossible, so Haruyuki prayed he would at least not make any more incredibly obvious mistakes as he started to return to his given position.

"Haru," a different voice murmured behind his back. "The important thing is the overall image. Just like in the Territories."

The one dropping this little bit of advice on him before moving away was Takumu Mayuzumi, who'd happened to end up on the same team. Although they were losing, they could be said to be putting up a rather good fight, given the fact that the other team had an actual basketball team player on it; there was only a sixteen-point difference. And the reason the gap wasn't greater was because Takumu was working hard as a forward, even though ball games were far outside his area of specialization.

The overall image? Just like in the Territories? Haruyuki puzzled the words as he ran noisily after Takumu, aiming to catch the ball after a throw-in or charge dribbling into enemy territory.

The Territories in Brain Burst took place every Saturday evening, group duels fought over territory between Legions. A normal duel could go up to only a tag team of two against two, but the Territories unfolded as large-scale battles of a minimum of three against three, with some instances of more than ten against ten.

Which meant the fight couldn't be won by simply relying on individual battle prowess. Players had to be aware of the overall situation in the large stage as they avoided the enemy's major attacks, while also looking for weaknesses at the same time. They needed to have a comprehensive image of the state of the war.

So was Takumu trying to say that a basketball game was the same as that?

But Haruyuki's team was already doing something like that. Since the enemy team's main firepower was clearly Ishio from the basketball team, their strategy was to have two people guarding him at all times to block his movement. Haruyuki and another boy were conservative centers, while Takumu was the lone forward. But unable to really stop Ishio even with two people—and with only Takumu as the core of their attack—it was clear they wouldn't be able to score as easily as that. Still, if they abandoned defense and shifted to an attack-style formation, the suddenly freed Ishio would simply run circles around them.

So then we can't just think of this in terms of battle strategy, Taku. It's like our opponent has a King on their side and we have a level one on ours, Haruyuki mentally replied to his friend. Of course, he was the level one. Given that he was slow, short, and bad at handling the ball, his presence alone in a basketball game was basically nothing more than an annoying obstacle.

And then at that moment, Takumu was knocked down onto the court with a heavy *thud*. An opposing player had panicked, seeing that Takumu was charging the enemy net for a three-point shot, and slammed into him. A sharp alert sounded and the word FOUL glittered blue in the center of his field of view. Blue was the enemy team's color.

"T-Taku!" Haruyuki raced to his side, but Takumu raised a hand to indicate he was okay, and then stood up again.

He calmly took his three free throws, and the points he gained changed the score to 25–38. As Takumu quickly ran back, Haruyuki started to call out to him, but then swallowed his breath.

The word *image* his friend had used before—what if it wasn't meant on the level of a weak point or a strategy? What if he had meant something bigger?

At the beginning of class, the in-school system had randomly divided them into teams. The moment Haruyuki saw that Ishio was on the opposing team, he had told himself it was all over; three of his four teammates had no doubt done the same thing. So before the game even began, they had been seized by a negative image.

Takumu was different, however. Because of his quiet manner and intellectual appearance, it didn't really show on the surface, but he was a natural-born fighter. Which was why, when they were in elementary school and he was horribly bullied at his kendo lessons, he didn't quit going. This was also why he couldn't stop himself from checking into the rumors about the ISS kit, which had the power to overwrite the weak point written into his avatar because of that bullying.

And even in this pointless twenty-minute mock game in their completely meaningless gym class, Takumu refused to have a negative image, even knowing the clear differences in fighting power. So, right, it was exactly like the Territories in Brain Burst.

In those battles, both sides expended every effort in tactics and strategies, and the first one who tossed out the words *It's impossible* was the one who lost.

"Sorry, Taku." His muttered apology probably didn't reach his friend, but Haruyuki looked at the broad back of his good friend and clenched his teeth.

Six minutes, twenty seconds remaining. He would at least shed his negative image in that time. He would do whatever he could without thinking it was impossible. So then what could he do? Beautiful baskets, sharp dribbling, these things were beyond Haruyuki. But there should have been something that one enormous obstacle could do. Obstacle…

Haruyuki's eyes flew open, and he immediately began fiddling with his virtual desktop at top speed.

There was a variety of functions in the gym ball-sports app carefully produced by the Ministry of Education, but ball games and AR displays were fundamentally incompatible—because obviously, the display got in the way of seeing the key bit of the whole operation, the ball—so AR was basically used only to display an overlay for the points and the time in the game at the edge of a player's field of view. They could have played just as well without their Neurolinkers, but they weren't allowed to because the school was legally obligated to monitor the heart rate, body temperature, and blood pressure of students exercising.

But when Haruyuki opened a tab for the court status in the app, it gave him a bird's-eye view just below the center of his vision. Five round red marks, five blue moved irregularly in a diagonal rectangle. These were obviously the current positions of the players. He narrowed them down to two with a filter function. The remaining red circle was himself. The blue was the enemy ace, Ishio.

The instant the game started again with the enemy throw-in, Haruyuki moved noisily and held out his arms right above the line connecting the ball he could see with his eyes and Ishio moving behind him. He tried to ruin any pass opportunities for Ishio simply by waving his arms frantically and making his already wide body larger. The members of the Gallery burst out laughing at his ridiculous movements, but the enemy player holding the ball clicked his tongue lightly and passed sideways to another player. Yet Haruyuki ran several meters to the left at the same time and began waving his arms up and down again.

This was the "something" he could do.

The opposing team's strategy was a "post" play to bulldoze through the game, using the ace posted around the basket. Since Haruyuki knew the ball was eventually going to be thrown toward the low post area, he first had to get an accurate understanding with the AR display of Ishio's position behind him, and then be an "obstacle" in the trajectory connecting Ishio and the ball.

Given the momentum Haruyuki generated, a perfect man-to-man defense clinging to the ace himself was simply not possible, but if he guessed at the pass route and optimized the distance he moved, Haruyuki might be able to keep filling this role until the end of the game.

The opposing player indicated he was going to throw the ball directly to one side once more, so Haruyuki also started to move in that direction.

However, on the verge of doing so, he put on the emergency brakes. Ishio, three meters or so behind him, was running in the opposite direction. It was a feint. With the right foot that slammed into the ground, Haruyuki managed to absorb the inertial mass and throw his body to the right. His earnestly outstretched right hand smacked hard into the ball the opposing player threw. As it was about to bounce off somewhere, he unconsciously killed his force with the way-of-the-flexible trick from Brain Burst and pulled the ball toward him, holding it tightly against his chest.

"No way!"

Haruyuki was thinking the same thing his opposition shouted, eyelids peeled back. But if he let himself be dumbfounded there, Ishio would come up from behind and snag the ball from him again.

"Hey!"

Haruyuki heard the voice from his left and reflexively threw the ball, this time without bringing it above his head. The player on his team who caught it—a member of the swim team called Nakagawa—dribbled the ball for a few meters into the enemy camp and passed to their team's ace, Takumu, running up on the right side.

Catching it firmly, Takumu headed toward the enemy basket in a fierce charge—Haruyuki would expect nothing less from a blue type—and finished up with a magnificent jump shot, making good use of his height. A light beep sound effect echoed in his ears, and the score display changed to 27–38.

"Nice, Arita!" Nakagawa called out to him, having promptly returned to their side of the court. Grinning, the typically buff swimmer raised his right hand, and Haruyuki, reflexively thinking, *He's going to hit me!* somehow managed nonetheless to lift his right hand and accept the high five.

Takumu ran up from behind and simply exchanged a quick smile with him, but that was still enough to communicate what needed to be said.

In the just under six minutes that were left, Haruyuki ran, ran, and ran. A waterfall of sweat poured down his face and drenched his body, he panted heavily, and his legs and arms trembled, but he didn't stop moving. His field of view—no, his mind—was filled with nothing but the ball in front of him and Ishio behind him. He imagined the course he should take in relation to those two and simply traced it out. Image and execution.

In one corner of his mind, becoming somewhat hazy at last, Haruyuki abruptly remembered that he had had a very similar experience only a few days earlier.

Exactly. When he was cleaning the animal hutch in the rear yard by himself. After thinking hard about exactly how he was going to clean up the mountain of old leaves piled up there, so many that it seemed it would be impossible to remove them by hand, he had imagined the result and then simply trusted in that, setting his hands to work. That had also been a difficult job, but in the end, the seemingly infinite number of dead leaves was gone.

Of course, a basketball game and cleaning a hutch were totally different. But maybe at the root, they were similar in what could be called the essence of action. He was pretty sure, though, that he had started to realize something more important at the time.

Words someone had spoken to him in that other world echoed faintly in the back of his mind.

…An image…strongly projected from the consciousness… overcomes restraints and becomes real.

Words to explain the other power hidden there. The ultimate power surpassing the normal system framework, close to a supernatural phenomenon. A miracle that shouldn't exist in the real world. And though that logic might be incredibly simple—

Even as he thought this through, Haruyuki continued to intently run back and forth. Naturally, he couldn't prevent every single pass to Ishio with his hastily prepared block. Sometimes, he was unable to get in the way of the ball being handed over, and in those instances, the enemy ace racked up points. Although they had closed the gap to a five-point difference with Takumu and Nakagawa's counterattack, from there, it was one step forward, one step back; only the remaining time steadily decreased.

However, at some point, Haruyuki had removed the timer and even the score display from his consciousness. From the Gallery came the occasional commotion, mixed with laughter, but none of it reached Haruyuki's ears.

Hah. Hah.

Listening only to his heavy breathing and the pounding of his heart echoing in his ears, he focused intently on tracing the expected image for the next second. He had nothing left over for attacking, but if he could simply counterbalance the weight of the opposing team and his own team one-for-one, the remaining four players should be more than even.

Once they were down to two minutes left, the two players on his team who had been guarding Ishio also went on the offensive, pushing through the gaps in the bewildered enemy defense to shove the ball through the hoop.

Three-point difference.

"Over here!"

Frustration building—and with good reason—Ishio returned to the far end of his team's side and raised a hand to accept the throw-in directly. His two former guards from the red team tried to obstruct his movement forward once more, but in a lightning-fast spin, Ishio pulled out and away from them. Apparently, the "real technique" of the basketball team regular had been locked away until then.

Vision blurred by sweat, Haruyuki stood, paralyzed, in the face of Ishio charging at him. One-on-one, dead-on, the Neurolinker AR display was of absolutely no help to him.

Physical Burst!!

Haruyuki desperately fought back the urge to call out the command.

If he used Physical Burst—which accelerated his perceptions by a factor of ten while his mind was still lodged in his physical body—it would be a simple feat to steal the ball from Ishio, no matter what dribbling technique he tried to use. But this so-called cowardly acceleration was strictly forbidden by his Legion. And besides, it was an insult to Ishio, who was taking on the challenge of a true fight.

"Ah…Aaaaaah!" What Haruyuki could do unaccelerated was simply shout as he spread out his arms as far as they would go.

The flesh-and-blood left hand of Ishio flashed before Haru's eyes, and the ball disappeared from view. The instant Haruyuki realized Ishio was dribbling behind his back, Ishio was already dashing past Haruyuki's left side.

Even though he knew he couldn't possibly catch up with the enemy ace as he charged ahead toward his team's basket, Haruyuki went after him.

After he had run a few steps, an unfamiliar red font flashed before his eyes. A warning that his heart rate or his blood pressure or something had gone outside the normal range. But he ignored it. He resolutely chased after the hazy figure in the center of his field of view, which was starting to flicker and white out around the edges.

And then he stared, dumbfounded, as a silhouette as tall as Ishio stood on the other side of the ace, blocking him. At some point, Takumu had returned to directly below the basket. With him going into a match-up defense, Ishio pulled out all the stops. Ball between the legs—crossover.

"Hngh...Hah!" Spitting out the last of the air remaining in his lungs, Haruyuki dove with everything he had toward the ball Ishio was attempting to dribble behind his back.

The tips of his painfully outstretched hand touched the bumpy rubber—or didn't. Haruyuki wasn't sure. Because his vision went completely black then, and his thinking abruptly decelerated. The front of his own body hit something big and hard, and just as he realized it was likely the floor of the gymnasium, he heard a high-pitched voice shout from somewhere in the distance.

"Haru!"

Definitely Chiyuri, who was herself in the middle of a game on the neighboring court.

Come on. Focus on your own game. With this final thought, listening to the footsteps racing over to him, Haruyuki lost consciousness.

Something thin was inserted into his mouth, so he tried sucking on it, and a sweet, cold liquid flowed in. He drank it in a daze, eyes still closed. After sending the liquid down to his stomach in gulps that made it almost hard to breathe, he inhaled deeply.

When he tentatively opened his eyes, he was confronted with a bright white light. He hurriedly closed his eyelids, blinked several times, and then opened his eyes once more.

The source of the light was panels embedded in the ceiling. That, and the white curtains enclosing his field of view in a square. It would seem that this was not the gym. And beneath his body was not the hard floor but rather smooth sheets—a bed.

Before he could wonder where he was, the curtain at the foot of the bed was pulled open with a light sound.

"Oh! Arita, you're awake?" Appearing there was a woman with midlength hair pulled back, wearing a crisp white doctor's coat over a patterned T-shirt—Umesato Junior High's health teacher. Last name: Hotta. Which meant this was the nurse's office, situated at the eastern end of the first floor of the school's second building.

"Oh…um…I…," Haruyuki muttered, and an exasperated smile appeared on Ms. Hotta's somewhat masculine face.

"It's important to try hard in games, but you have to watch your own condition, too, okay?" she said. "If your blood pressure had gotten any lower, you'd have been in an ambulance."

"O-okay. I'm sorry."

So that's it. I collapsed in the middle of the basketball game from anemia or dehydration or something, and they brought me to the nurse's office.

Now that he finally understood the situation, Haruyuki glanced over at the time display in the lower right of his field of view and saw that second period had started a long time ago. He had apparently been unconscious—or sleeping—for over half an hour.

The health teacher deftly flicked around her virtual desktop and checked that Haruyuki's vital signs were all back to normal before nodding lightly. "Rest here during second period. And get plenty of fluids, okay? I have a meeting in the teachers' room to go to, but don't hesitate to press the call button if anything happens. Okay, be good!"

Shhk! The curtain was closed once more, and the sound of footsteps softened by slippers receded. Finally, he heard the door opening and closing, and then the nurse's office returned to silence.

Ms. Hotta had probably stayed to watch over Haruyuki until

he woke up, even after the meeting started. *What a hassle for her. But, well, I guess it's her job and all.* Vague thoughts drifted through his mind, while a thin straw stretched out again from the left side of his face toward his mouth.

He took it unconsciously and sucked. A nicely chilled sports drink poured pleasantly down his throat. Here, Haruyuki finally wondered curiously just what the straw was attached to and turned his gaze to the left. Maybe some automatic water-supply device? It couldn't be a robotic nurse?

But the straw extended from a completely uninteresting thermos. And holding the bottle was a pale, slender hand that did not belong to Haruyuki.

As he gave commands to his still-decelerated thinking, his gaze now stopped on this hand. The slender arm extended from the sleeve of an open-collared black shirt. A dark-red ribbon on the chest of that shirt. Piano-black Neurolinker equipped on the graceful neck. Jet-black hair flowing over that.

"Bwhaaah!"

The instant he noticed the person sitting right next to the bed—the existence of whom he hadn't even been aware of until that point—sports drink jetted forcefully from his mouth and nose. He watched a drop of liquid fly onto that black shirt, and immediately, his temperature and heart rate shot up.

"I-I'm—" he shouted hoarsely, moving both hands in a panic. "I'm sorry! W-wi-wipe it off or it'll st-st-stain—"

"Mm. It will?" The person sitting on the simple folding chair set the thermos on the bed in a calm motion. "I'll wipe it off, then." She raised both hands and removed the hook-type ribbon before unbuttoning the open-collared shirt from the top.

He saw the skin of her chest, impossibly pale, and even caught a glimpse of the top of the gently rising curve.

"Hngoah!" Haruyuki uttered in a strange voice, throwing back his head, unable to close his eyes. But fortunately—or so he *should* say, at least—the two hands stopped their reckless movement.

"Kidding. Don't worry about it getting wet. The fabric's a washable shape-memory polymer." The person buttoning her shirt back up, her expression unmoved, was of course the only owner of a black uniform at Umesato Junior High, the student council vice president, Haruyuki's parent Linker and Legion Master, Kuroyukihime.

Seated with perfect posture on the chair, having returned her shirt to its original state, the beauty in black clothing opened her mouth once more, with a look on her face that allowed him to feel a faint tremor beyond its sternness. "Haruyuki. Ms. Hotta said this, too, and I won't say that it's bad to work as hard as you can in gym class. But given that you have the Neurolinker right there, you should heed the vitals warnings it sounds. This time, you managed to get away with a little light dehydration. But if things had taken a turn for the worse, this could have led to a serious incident."

"I—I know. I'm sorry. I accidentally got caught up in the game." He had meant to fight hard, but the only result was that his classmates had laughed at him, and in the end, he'd collapsed during the game. And then news of that foolishness had spread even to Kuroyukihime. Haruyuki hung his head, but her pale right hand reached out to cover his left.

"You don't have to apologize. I'm not reproaching you. It's simply...don't make me worry too much." Her voice dropped, and he raised his head. Kuroyukihime murmured, her expression more gentle, "When I heard from Chiyuri that you had collapsed, I thought I might pass out myself, you know. I just barely kept myself from using the forbidden physical acceleration command to race to the nurse's office."

The forbidden command was the Physical Full Burst permitted only to level-nine Burst Linkers. It was treated as a higher level of the "Physical Burst" command that Haruyuki had almost used facing off against Ishio, but Physical Burst couldn't begin to compare with Full Burst. That was because not only was consciousness accelerated, but movement of the physical body in the real world was also accelerated nearly a hundred times the normal speed.

Of course, the price paid for this was nothing to scoff at. The user lost 99 percent of their accumulated burst points and was, in an instant, pushed to the brink of total loss. Kuroyukihime was likely joking, but even so, Haruyuki reflexively shook his head quickly back and forth.

"I-I'm glad you didn't use it. I didn't really collapse, it was more like I was just too tired and got dizzy. So then Chiyu was the one who told you?"

"Mm. At about the same time you were carried here. She's quite fair in that way."

"F-fair?" When he cocked his head, not quite understanding what she meant, a faint, wry smile crossed Kuroyukihime's lips, and she indicated her left side with her eyes.

"Chiyuri and Takumu were sitting here with me for a while, until second period started. If they'd stayed, they would have been counted absent, so I sent them back to class. They were very worried. You should probably mail them."

"R-right."

Haruyuki nodded and launched the local net mailer from his virtual desktop. To his two childhood friends, he sent a report that he had regained consciousness and that there was nothing wrong with him, along with a brief thank-you for staying with him. And then he had an abrupt realization and looked at Kuroyukihime. "Um, is it okay for you not to go to class? Skipping without a note leaves a record on your permanent file, doesn't—"

"Now, just who do you think I am? I submitted confirmation that I'm a health aide, naturally. Ms. Hotta signed it for me easily enough." She grinned as she delivered this line, and he could only feel sorry for how completely thoughtless his question had been.

Kuroyukihime changed the nuance of her smile slightly before leaning forward. "To reward Chiyuri's sense of fair play, I did consider issuing an aide pass for her as well, but she understood my selfishness," she whispered mischievously. "After all, just yesterday, I used some tricks so we could be alone in the student council office, but we couldn't really have a real conversation. Well, given the situation, that was unavoidable."

"Oh. Uh. Yehuh." At the shining, unutterable beauty of those black eyes this close up, Haruyuki unconsciously turned away.

At lunch the previous day, Kuroyukihime had suddenly burst into eighth grade's class C and shouted that she was requesting the immediate presence of the president of the Animal Care Club. Having been appointed to that very position after announcing his candidacy through a misunderstanding, Haruyuki had followed her to the student council office, bracing himself to be yelled at for some reason or another, when it turned out it was all simply an excuse for the two of them to be alone together.

Of course, Haruyuki was also happy to talk with Kuroyukihime alone—it was, in fact, a dreamlike experience beyond happiness.

But she was too impressive and important to him. It wasn't just that she was his parent as a Burst Linker and his Legion Master. She had saved his life, pulled him free of the bog, and given him hope. The sword master he had sworn his absolute and eternal loyalty to. And that didn't even begin to describe what she was to him. Perhaps there was just one word that could sum her up: *miracle.*

Kuroyukihime lived charging single-mindedly toward the distant stars, and although she had her own issues to deal with, she had set her eyes on someone like Haruyuki, spoken to him, and reached out to him; this could well be called a miracle. Now she was at the center of his world, a massive jewel glittering dazzlingly. She was too beautiful, to the point where he felt she might disappear if he touched her, nothing but a fleeting memory.

He had only recently been able to relax around her enough to the point that he could speak normally, but when he realized they were alone together in a closed room, his heart started to pound, and his breathing became shallow. The current situation was much more critical than the day before in the student council office. After all, they were neatly surrounded by thick white curtains on all sides, and Haruyuki was lying in bed, with Kuroyukihime pushing a hand over the edge of it, leaning forward and staring at him.

His thoughts threatened to shoot off into some inexcusable territory if he stayed silent, so Haruyuki forced himself to pull back on the joystick and restart the conversation. "Uh, I'm sorry about yesterday. Now that I think about it, I didn't actually explain the situation to you."

"Mm. Well, I got the gist of it from your mail. And I did want you to tell me the details, but then you ended up here, and it all flew completely out of my head."

"I-I'm sorry." He apologized for the second time in a row, rubbing the fingertips of both hands together.

The reason Haruyuki had raced out of the school and run home the day before was because of his fear for Takumu, of course. And instead of that fear being absolutely unfounded, Haruyuki had discovered his best friend was on the verge of falling completely under the control of the ISS kit. But through a duel with Haruyuki, Takumu had gotten himself back, and the kit itself had been completely destroyed in the fight in the BB central server the night before.

Although he had given Kuroyukihime, Fuko Kurasaki, and Utai Shinomiya a rough overview of all this in a mail after his duel with Ash Roller that morning, he hadn't been able to include all the little details in its short message. Haruyuki himself didn't fully understand the events in the central server, and another, more important matter had been added to his list of things to do before the mission to escape the Castle commenced.

To wit, Ash Roller's entirely unexpected "wish."

Even though he should have had a million things to say to Kuroyukihime, Haruyuki closed his mouth once more, unable to figure out exactly where to start.

"Even still, that you would try so hard in gym class that you'd collapse...," Kuroyukihime said gently, as if she understood

Haruyuki's confusion and was trying to ease it to some degree. "Perhaps this might sound rude, but it's a little unexpected."

"Y-yeah. I was super surprised, too."

"Did something change for you?"

At this question, he cocked his head, puzzled. Now that she was asking, he did feel like there was something, but at the same time, he felt like nothing at all had changed.

"Umm. It's not that anything particular happened. But I was messing up all over the place in the game, and Taku came and said to me that the important thing was the image. So I decided to at least stop playing the game with a negative image in my head. And then I guess I just got into it before I knew it. That reminds me, I wonder how the game ended."

"Takumu said you lost by one point."

"We…did?"

According to his hazy memory, Haruyuki's team had been down three points with a minute or two left on the clock and opposing ace Ishio going on a serious offensive against them. If they had narrowed that down to a one-point difference, then they had blocked that swift offensive attack and managed to score on the rebound, which is where the game ended. He figured Takumu managed to pull that off with some shocking counterattack.

And then Kuroyukihime made a surprising statement, smile on her lips. "The truth is, it was Takumu and one other boy, the basketball player in your class, who carried you to the nurse's office."

"Huh? Ishio? Carried me?"

"Mm. He left a message for you. He said, 'You crushed me this time, but that trick won't work on me again next time.'"

"Ah! Cr-crushed?! But I mean, his team won the game."

"Apparently, his own personal definition of winning is that it's a loss unless he wins with a twenty-point difference."

"H-huh, really?" He couldn't tell if this message from Ishio was humility or arrogance, and unconsciously, he smiled wryly.

The reason he had been able to stay in Ishio's way during the game was because the opposing team stubbornly refused to change their strategy. If they played basketball in gym class and he ended up against Ishio again, the simple method of using the AR display to block him would no longer work. It was the same as in Brain Burst duels or the Territories. In that world, too, succeeding a second time with a strategy that worked once was very rare. Because it wasn't an AI he was fighting, it was a human being with his own image power.

His thoughts drifting along that thread, Haruyuki was abruptly aware of the important "something" he had felt during the game starting to flicker back to life in his mind. "Oh!"

"Mm? What is it?"

"Oh no. It's no big deal. I mean, I might be way off, but..." Pushed by Kuroyukihime's gaze wordlessly encouraging him, Haruyuki moved his mouth again before it came to a complete halt. "...'An image strongly projected from the consciousness... overcomes restraints and becomes real.'"

Kuroyukihime's eyes opened wide for an instant, and then she smiled gently. "It had to have been Fuko who said that to you."

"Th-that's right. How did you know?"

"I told you before. She is the most genuine user of the positive will I know. And those words are very Fuko, and her belief in the light side of the Incarnate System above all else."

Haruyuki didn't think he completely understood the meaning behind Kuroyukihime's soft words. But not daring to ask her about it, he continued speaking himself. "That's obviously a description of the Incarnate System in the Accelerated World. But when Takumu said that to me about one's 'image' being important during the game, I just somehow thought, like, maybe when we really try hard in this real world...we're doing the same thing? Of course, it's not like we can use superpowers like Incarnate attacks on this side. But, like, my going up against *the* Ishio in a basketball game or managing to clean the animal hutch by myself, it's a miracle greater than superpowers for me. Umm, basically, I guess I'm trying to say...um..."

Here, Haruyuki reached the limit of his power of speech, and all he could do was flap his mouth open and shut like always.

Fortunately, however, it looked like he had communicated what he needed to say to Kuroyukihime. Her obsidian eyes opened wide once more, and a long breath slipped past her glossy lips. "Haruyuki. When exactly will you stop surprising me? I certainly never dreamed you would reach this mental state so quickly, and under your own power at that."

"Huh? M-mental state?" Haruyuki parroted back, dumbfounded.

"Yes." Kuroyukihime peered into his eyes and nodded deeply. "The words you've just given voice to are precisely the entrance to the second stage of the Incarnate System. To move past the basic expansions of range, power, defense, and movement and learn the so-called practical techniques, you must understand exactly what the imagination is not through reason, but rather through intuition. Just how big, how deep this power given to us is, this power to imagine."

"Im...agine..."

"Mm. Up to now, you thought the overwriting through the image that is the basis of the Incarnate System was a game system logic that existed only in the virtual world, yes? But that's incorrect. Imagination holds unlimited power in this real world as well. Of course, you can't do anything that would defy the laws of physics. But drawing on the aid of the power of the image, it is possible to overwrite a wall that appears to be an absolute limit. Just as you yourself proved during the basketball game."

Kuroyukihime's words shook Haruyuki somewhere deep in his heart, but at the same time, they also generated a serious confusion in him. He unconsciously leaned forward and, staring at Kuroyukihime—who similarly leaned forward—he asked in a hoarse voice, "The power of imaging takes you beyond your limits. That fundamental is the same in the Accelerated World and the real world. I feel like I basically get that. But how are that and this 'second stage of the Incarnate System' connected?"

Kuroyukihime didn't respond to his question right away. She lowered her eyes, as if seized by uncertainty after having come this far, and bit her lip lightly.

Haruyuki had the vague sense that he could guess at why. Kuroyukihime carried a kind of fear about the Incarnate power she had learned. She feared that her power—unlike the positive power Fuko/Sky Raker used—was negative, calling up destruction and despair.

But Haruyuki fervently believed that couldn't be true. Because Kuroyukihime's Incarnate attacks (though he had seen only her long-range attack, Vorpal Strike) were so beautiful as to render him speechless. Even if it was awesomely powerful, a technique that beautiful couldn't be the result of negative imaging.

"Kuroyukihime." Haruyuki leaned a few centimeters closer and gently touched her right hand with his left. "First, Raker, and Niko after her, taught me very important things about the Incarnate System. But…you're my 'parent.' I want to know everything about you. I want you to teach me everything. Please. Please tell me about your Incarnate."

Her reply wasn't quick in coming.

The sun at half past ten on that June morning had already risen to very close to the center of the sky, and the light coming in through the windows didn't reach the corner on the other side of the nurse's office. In the space cut out by the snowy white curtains on all four sides of his bed, dimly illuminated by the lowered light of the ceiling panel, only the sound of the two of them breathing echoed faintly.

Finally, Kuroyukihime's fingers moved gently to tangle themselves among Haruyuki's. A subdued murmur followed. "In that case, we'll first need a direct cable." As she lifted her face, the only thing he saw there was the same enigmatic, mysterious smile as always.

Haruyuki let out his breath and then said, panicking slightly, "Ah! I-I'm sorry! My cable's in my bag in the classroom."

"Mine, too. But they have cables here." As she spoke, Kuroyukihime manipulated her virtual desktop with a light touch, likely searching the equipment list. She nodded soon enough, removed her fingers from Haruyuki's hand, stood up, and disappeared quietly beyond the curtain.

He could hear the sound of a drawer opening and closing, and when she returned seconds later, her hand held a white XSB cable. But…

"I-isn't that a little short?" Haruyuki blurted the instant he saw the cable, which looked to be just barely fifty centimeters long.

But Kuroyukihime shrugged lightly. "Then we just have to make it reach. Fortunately, we're out of view of the social cameras here."

"Huh? B-but how—?" he started to say, and then swallowed his words hard.

Because Kuroyukihime hopped up onto the bed, entirely nonchalantly.

"Huh?! Um! That's…" Belatedly, he realized he was still wearing his white gym clothes and pulled back. Thanks to the quick-drying fabric, his sweat had already dried, but he must have still stunk.

But Kuroyukihime reached out her left hand, seeming to pay all this no mind, and pushed gently on Haruyuki's chest to make him lie back down before lying down herself immediately to his right. From extremely close up, she turned a somewhat mischievous smile on him.

As usual, the engine of his mind raced emptily while his heart rate shot up into the red zone.

Her sigh contained a smile as it gently touched his ear. "Ha-ha! After everything, it's a bit late to get this nervous now. We did sleep together in the same bed the night of the Hermes' Cord race, didn't we?"

"Y—! Yee—! W-w-w-w-we did, but!"

The aforementioned race event had happened a mere two weeks earlier in the Accelerated World, but because so many things had happened since then, it seemed like something out of the distant past. But the memory of that night was deeply etched into the back of Haruyuki's mind.

Then, too, they had direct-dueled from the same bed. Although Haruyuki had challenged Kuroyukihime over and over again with his recently acquired Aerial Combo, she had fended off his attacks effortlessly with her ever-more-powerful "way of the flexible," and in the end, he had taken a hit from her level-eight technique Death By Embracing and been killed instantly.

I have a feeling it's gonna turn into something like that this time, too, Haruyuki thought as the girl brought the end of the fifty-centimeter-short XSB cable toward his Neurolinker. Reflexively, he started to move his head away, but the plug was inserted whether he liked it or not.

"Ah!"

Not heeding Haruyuki's strangled cry, Kuroyukihime next connected the plug on the opposite end to the piano-black communication device equipped around her slender neck. A wired connection warning blinked red in his view.

"Yesterday, I made you use a point for my own selfishness. So today, how about I treat you?" Those whispered words meant that rather than both of them accelerating simultaneously to dive into the initial blue world, Kuroyukihime alone would accelerate and then challenge Haruyuki.

"O-okay. Thanks," Haruyuki replied.

He watched her light-peach-colored lips move slightly to call out, "Burst Link."

And then the dry thunder of acceleration filled his hearing.

7

That day, the setting for their second duel was a Steel stage, every inch of the landscape formed with riveted steel panels. As for the characteristics of the stage, to begin with, it was hard. It conducted electricity well. And footsteps were abnormally loud. Even more so when the duel avatar was a metal color, metallic down to the soles of their feet.

Clang! came the high-pitched metallic impact as Haruyuki dropped down onto the stage and waited for the sound of two more feet, head lowered. However, he heard nothing even after a few seconds had passed, so he lifted his face and surveyed his surroundings.

What was originally the Umesato Junior High nurse's office had changed into an empty cube, no beds, no desk. The floor, walls, and ceiling were all thick panels of steel shining a sharp rusted color. In line with Brain Burst's starting-distance rule—which stated that opponents who were basically on top of each other in the real world should appear separated by a minimum of ten meters in the Accelerated World—she stood quietly at the room's eastern wall.

Sleek, semitransparent jet-black armor, reminiscent of obsidian. Armor skirt patterned after water lilies, incredibly slender body, mask that tapered into a V. And the long, sharp swords of all four limbs that sent a chill up the spine...

Haruyuki took in the beautiful yet ferocious figure of the Black King, Black Lotus, a sight he would never grow accustomed to no matter how many times he saw it, and finally understood why he hadn't heard any footfalls. The sharply tapered points of her feet floated above the floor, albeit by only a centimeter or so. She was one of the few hovering avatars in the Accelerated World.

Kuroyukihime stayed like that a few more seconds, staring at Haruyuki's avatar, Silver Crow, but eventually, she moved forward as if gliding. She paused before him, and the violet-blue eyes on the other side of her black mirrored goggles shone vibrantly.

"I can tell by just looking at you, Haruyuki. You made it through yet another fierce battle."

He quickly guessed that the words and their gentle echo were referring to the intense fight between him and Takumu the evening before. He still hadn't explained to Kuroyukihime all the details of the previous night through to that morning, but she had apparently already seen through to the fact that he and Takumu had spoken fist to fist as Burst Linkers.

And she was right; it had been a painful, difficult fight. To bring his friend back from the dark wrappings of the ISS kit, Haruyuki had lost his left arm and wing; he had kept standing even as his entire body had split and cracked into pieces. Encouraged by the mysterious golden-yellow girl, he had summoned the Destiny—albeit just one arm of it—the original form of the Armor of Catastrophe, and mustered every ounce of his Incarnate.

The end result was that Takumu had released his special attack upon himself in order to save Haruyuki from the clone of the ISS kit that had been about to parasitize him, and Haruyuki could see even now how that battle lingered on inside himself. If he had to put it into words, it might have been the feeling of confidence in himself. It was precisely because this confidence existed that, in the battle that took place within Brain Burst's mysterious central server, he had been able to release his new Incarnate attack with a range that surpassed his Laser Sword.

However, shrinking back at being praised was second nature to

Haruyuki, and he hung his head, rubbing at both arms. "N-no, that's—I mean, someone's always coming to my rescue and stuff..."

"Ha-ha! That you're able to think like that is already proof of your growth." Kuroyukihime laughed briefly and lightly patted Haruyuki's back with the flat of her sword hand. "Now show me, Haruyuki. Everything about this new Incarnate attack you've learned."

Here he truly and desperately wanted to squirm and fidget again, but they were in the Normal Duel Field rather than the Unlimited; they could stay here for only a mere 1,800 seconds. Given that Incarnate training generally took several weeks at least to learn a single technique, thirty minutes was too short. He couldn't waste a single second.

Haruyuki took a deep breath, stored it in his abdomen, and nodded. "Okay. Here I go."

Taking a few steps forward, he stopped about three meters away from the windows on the south side of the empty room.

Originally, snow-white wallpaper had covered the walls, but now they were panels of rust-colored steel. Each and every rivet in the grid punched into those panels communicated an overwhelming hardness. But that hardness was, in the end, nothing more than a parameter registered in the server. It should be possible to overwrite it with his will to pierce it.

Haruyuki slowly lowered into a fighting stance and readied his left hand at his waist, lining up his fingers as if for a palm strike. When he imagined a piercing light concentrating into his fingertips, the silver light of his overlay began to illuminate the dim room. As he focused on his image, a faint resonance echoed, and the light moved up his left arm to the elbow. Although the activation speed of his Incarnate was faster than it used to be, Haruyuki was unaware of the fact as he slowly pulled back his left hand.

"Laser Sword!!" At the same time as he shouted the name, he twisted his hips sharply and thrust his left arm forward.

Skrrriiiink! With a crisp sound, silver light in the shape of a sword stretched more than two meters from his left hand and gouged deeply into the thick steel wall.

However, not stopping there, Haruyuki pulled his right leg far back and readied his right arm above his shoulder, rather than at his waist. He brought back his left arm and positioned it horizontally, level in front of his body. This time, the fiercely glittering silver light was born in his right arm.

"Yaaaaah!" The battle cry gushed naturally from his mouth. The sharp tip of the light extending a dozen or so centimeters from his right hand met the back of his left hand—and shot forward.

"Laser Lance!!"

He had launched the technique only once before, that very morning in a dream—and drawing on the help of Chiyuri to boot—but Haruyuki was confident he could do it again. The gleam of the Incarnate discharged in the shape of a lance hit the precise spot where the wall had been damaged three seconds earlier by the light sword digging into it, savagely piercing the area once more.

The lance of light, momentarily stopped, broke apart into several ribbons and disappeared. Immediately after that, the steel plate of the wall itself shattered into pieces and scattered, apparently unable to fully absorb the power it had been hit with. On the other side of the large hole that appeared, one of the steel pillars that stood in the space corresponding to the front yard of Umesato Junior High in the real world was sliced in half and toppled to the ground with a heavy *thud*.

It was easily ten meters between Haruyuki and the pillar. The sword of light he had released actually reached more than three times his normal swing range.

"Phew." Haruyuki let out a sigh and lowered both hands, while behind him, he could hear a crisp *clang*, like a bell ringing. When he turned around, Kuroyukihime was bringing together the swords of both arms to create something like applause.

"Wonderful. Wonderful imagination, Haruyuki."

"Uh…Th-thank you." As always, unaccustomed to being complimented, the boy bowed his head, even as he pulled in his neck.

But he yanked his head back up again at what came next from his Legion commander.

"This Incarnate of yours is already essentially in the domain of completion as a basic range-expansion technique. Both the Laser Sword—the sword you can extend from either hand at high speeds for hand-to-hand combat—and the Laser Lance, which releases the power built up in your right hand for midrange combat—are good techniques with clear, conscious targets. However, because of that, although you can of course refine the techniques and polish the accuracy of your sights or the speed of activation, you can't expect any great leaps and bounds forward."

"Huh?"

So does that mean my Incarnate...ends here? Haruyuki's shoulders started to drop at the thought, but stopped abruptly as Kuroyukihime continued:

"It's a little soon to be disappointed. I just told you, the Incarnate System has a second stage." Hovering soundlessly toward him, she lowered her voice and murmured as if admonishing a small child. "You...Your will contains infinite possibilities. Everything starts with you believing that. The techniques you showed me now belong to one of the four basic types of Incarnate: range expansion. Although the various basic techniques might look different, if they are of the same type, then the essential performance is very similar. Do you understand so far?"

"Y-yes." Nodding, Haruyuki remembered the unique range-expansion technique that Niko—the Red King, Scarlet Rain—had shown him.

Niko's technique launched a high-speed ball of fire living in her hand to burn up the distant object she targeted. The long-range technique clearly surpassed Haruyuki's, given that it launched so quickly that she had no need to even shout the name of the attack and it easily traveled fifty meters. But even so, all these techniques shared the essential nature of being a single long-distance attack.

As if waiting for Haruyuki to come to this understanding,

Kuroyukihime nodded and raised her right sword slowly as she spoke. "In contrast, the second stage of the Incarnate is, to wit, the practical technique. Here, you combine two or more of the four basic types of images, or you materialize an entirely new image to bring about an even larger overwrite. Rust Jigsaw's Rust Order, which destroyed the race before, and Fuko's Wind Veil, which protected us *from* that attack, are indeed this kind of second-stage techniques."

"And your Vorpal Strike's also like that, right? That technique combines range and power expansions, doesn't it?"

"Mm." Kuroyukihime nodded, a tint of embarrassment showing on the other side of her half–mirrored face mask—or maybe it was just his imagination. "Well...I guess that's how it is. Although it might be more accurate to say that's how it ended up. At any rate, Haruyuki, the time has finally come for you to proceed to this second stage."

The first part of her statement was curious indeed, but he didn't have time to think about what she meant. He stood up tall and shouted, "O-okay! I'll do my best!" However, here, another doubt floated up in the back of his mind. "Um, but before, in the nurse's office, you said something about how...to learn the second stage of Incarnate, I had to understand the meaning of the power of imagination or whatever in the real world, too, right? What specifically does that mean?"

"Mm-hmm. Well, that is—" Kuroyukihime cut herself off and stared at the tip of her right hand, the sharp sword still held up before her. For some reason, a faint hint of tension drifted across her purple-blue eyes, and she continued in a murmur, "It's hard to convey the meaning in words, so how about we shift to a show? The truth is, Haruyuki, recently, I've also been tackling a new practical technique."

"What..." Swallowing hard, he stared at the black avatar's mask. A new practical technique—a super attack power surpassing Vorpal Strike? And she was going to show it off in this tiny room?

"Oh! Th-then, we should go out...," Haruyuki started to say, and Kuroyukihime stopped him by shaking her head lightly.

"No, it's not that grand. There's more than enough space here."

Then the Black King turned the tip of her right sword precisely on Haruyuki and stood perfectly still.

Wait. What? I'm the test platform for the new technique?

Actually, that's totally possible. I mean, she's the master and shield sister of Sky Raker, and Raker didn't hesitate to shove me off the top of the old Tokyo Tower. Which means it wouldn't be the slightest bit weird if Kuroyukihime's way of teaching the Incarnate was even more spartan than Sky Raker's. Don't be scared. You're lucky. I mean, to be the first person to experience the as-yet-undisclosed technique of undoubtedly the strongest person in the Accelerated World...There's no better training than this. Stand tall and take the hit.

His thoughts bounding ahead in a mere millisecond, Haruyuki gritted his teeth and held his breath.

Right hand still extended before her, Kuroyukihime narrowed her eyes beneath her goggles, the same air of concentration drifting up around her. At the tip of the sharp sword, a yellow light—an overlay—popped up. Pulsing faintly, the light thinly enveloped an area about twenty centimeters from the tip of the sword.

Watching this with wide eyes, Haruyuki felt a slight pinch of confusion.

Because...it was warm. The light enveloping the sword was so gentle, so fleeting, and so warm that he couldn't actually believe it could generate massive devastation.

But at the same time, in contrast with the tranquility of the light, Haruyuki knew that Kuroyukihime was mustering up every ounce of imagination in her entire body. Her slender avatar trembled; her legs shook intermittently.

"Haruyuki...Your hand."

Before he stopped to think about—and get confused by—her words, Haruyuki stretched out his own right hand as though compelled. His finger approached the tip of the sword the girl extended and gently touched it. If Kuroyukihime's Incarnate was an attack type, then at this point, she would generate an overlay, and Haruyuki's fingers would drop off, regardless of how hard his metallic armor might be.

But that didn't happen. Instead, something he hadn't even thought to anticipate was made incarnate.

The sharp black sword melted away.

The tip split into four. And then one more a little below that. Separated into a total of five pieces, the slender, delicate organs caught the light coming in through the large hole in the wall and glittered brightly.

This—

Fingers. A hand.

A modest transformation generating absolutely no sound or light other than the hazy overlay.

Haruyuki reflexively wondered why she would deliberately lower her attack power before finally realizing something: that a practical Incarnate technique could be an incredible miracle, surpassing even the most massive range attack.

No Burst Linker could learn an Incarnate that was not in alignment with their own attributes. The Red King, Niko, had once told him that this was the basic principle of the Incarnate System.

Judging from her form, her limbs clearly swords, the attribute of the Black King was obviously "severance." She cut through everything she touched. Rejected it. An aloof black lotus flower unable to approach anyone. There was still so much that even her sole "child," Haruyuki, didn't know about Kuroyukihime. No matter how close they were, looking at each other, no matter how they talked alone together, the depths of her heart were shrouded in a deep darkness, invisible to him.

But he felt like this was okay. That it was even a part of the beauty of this person Kuroyukihime.

And yet at that moment, she was showing him that she rejected her own attribute. She was showing him that she had negated the words she had once spoken to him—"I don't even have a hand to hold"—with her imagination.

This Incarnate certainly contained a kind of declaration. That as the leader of Nega Nebulus, she would face the members in a different form than in the past. That she would reach out a hand, open her heart, and form real bonds in not just the Accelerated World but in the real world, too.

"Kuro...yukihime..." Murmuring her name, Haruyuki realized with a sharp pain that he really did know nothing about the person before him. That he had used the superficial words *aloof beauty* without knowing anything at all.

His vision blurred and twisted. Tears welled up beneath Haruyuki's mirrored mask as he gently intertwined the fingers of his right hand with those five wire-thin digits. Jet-black and white silver touched, and he was aware of a fleeting warmth. And then—

A hard, ephemeral sound, like millions of tiny bells ringing, accompanied Kuroyukihime's right hand shattering into tiny shards of crystal.

"Ah!" The cry slipped out of Haruyuki at the same time the girl collapsed, as if she had used the last of her strength. Automatically, he stretched out his right arm to support her slender waist.

Black Lotus held up to her chest the arm she had lost almost to the elbow and took shallow breaths for a while as if—no, most *certainly*—enduring pain. But finally, she lifted her head and said calmly, "Seventeen seconds. Breaks the old record by a considerable margin. I suppose...it's because you're here."

The declaration implied that Kuroyukihime had attempted this "practical Incarnate" technique and smashed her own hand countless times before that moment.

"Kuroyukihime." Haruyuki replied with this one word in a trembling voice, unable to hold back the emotion swelling up inside him. Spurred by impulse, he squeezed the avatar in his arms and said earnestly, "Kuroyukihime. Thank you so much. I feel like I understand—to learn the second-level Incarnate, you have to confront not your duel avatar but your own real-world self, right? You have to constantly think about what you're afraid of, what you hope for, what image you'll create, not just in the Accelerated World but in the real world, too. That's it, isn't it?"

"That's it exactly." The voice in his ear was so quiet, it was practically soundless, but it echoed crisp and clear in the duel stage they shared. "For those who use a purely negative will, this process is unnecessary. Because rage and hatred and despair are indivisible from one's real-world self right from the start. However, to generate a positive will—the power of hope—the process of inverting mental scars is absolutely essential. You face head-on your own trauma, shaped into the form of a duel avatar. You accept it, and you sublimate it into an image of hope. This is no easy feat. It's simple to fall into the holes in your heart, but the climb out is a steep one. I've spent vast amounts of time as a Burst Linker, and even I can barely manage to change my sword into fingers. However..."

She paused and looked up into Haruyuki's eyes, so close their masks were practically touching. "But you should be able to do it. You realized all on your own what the image is, after all."

This was perhaps a situation where normally, he'd reflexively cry out, *I can't*, or *Me?!* But right now at least, Haruyuki brushed aside that timid insect and nodded deeply. Their masks bumped against each other, but he maintained that contact and said, "Okay. I...I'll try. Although I probably won't make it in time for the mission tonight. Still I'll fight, I'll find it. My image of hope."

"Mm. I'll fight, too. So that next time I can hold it at least thirty seconds, and hold your hand properly." This time, her murmur contained the force to fluster Haruyuki as usual.

"Uh! Um! Uh." Blinking rapidly beneath his silver mask, Haruyuki managed to reply somehow. "R-r-right. And using the Instruct menu and stuff's probably more fun with hands."

Instantly, the violet-blue eyes before him glittered dangerously, and the chill in her voice increased slightly. "I suppose. I was planning to make this duel a draw for you, but the operation is a bit of a hassle without hands, so I'll just have to win like I always do."

Fortunately, Kuroyukihime used the sword of her left hand to accept the draw request Haruyuki submitted.

The direct duel over and now back in the real world, Haruyuki stared vacantly at the ceiling for a few seconds before finally becoming conscious of the situation all over again. He was lying in a bed in the nurse's office with Kuroyukihime right beside him, their bodies pressed up together like a romantic comedy manga from the last century—

"Haruyuki."

The soft breath touched his left ear, and after a jerk of surprise, Haruyuki timidly looked in that direction. Instantly, he forgot his nervousness and his surprise and opened his eyes wide.

Still lying on her side on the sheet, Kuroyukihime was staring intently at her own pale right hand. Her small, shiny, pearlescent nails glittered, reflecting the illumination from the light panels above them. She blinked her dark eyes once and then shifted them to focus on him.

"Haruyuki, I wonder if you remember. The day I gave you your first lecture about Brain Burst...I reached out a hand to you in the initial acceleration space and asked you, 'Do these two virtual meters feel that far to you?'"

How could he forget? At that time, Haruyuki had averted his eyes from the outstretched hand and answered in his heart that they did indeed.

Kuroyukihime nodded sharply, her smile blurred with a plaintiveness as she continued. "The truth is...those two meters were far for me as well. Because for a long time—a really long time—I didn't offer my hand to anyone. I had been afraid for so long to hold someone else's hand. Even my Legion members, people I should have been emotionally connected with—Fuko, Utai, Current, Graph—I rejected their hands in perhaps the truest sense of the word. But, well, ever since the day I met you in the virtual squash corner—No, before that, ever since I noticed the little form of a pink pig running as hard as he could, head hanging, avoiding people's eyes, in a corner of the local net..."

Here, Kuroyukihime closed her mouth. But Haruyuki felt certain that he had caught the words she couldn't speak, even through the direct cable that still connected them.

Another smile and a faint murmur. "So, Haruyuki? Have we crossed those two meters?"

He couldn't say anything in reply. The feelings welling up in him were simply too great and filled his heart. Instead, he mustered up every bit of courage he had and raised both hands to wrap them around the pale right hand she still held in the air.

It was warm. The same warmth as the hand of Black Lotus that he had touched for a brief instant in the Steel stage. It seeped into the palms of his hands, to be transmitted to his nervous system and shine golden in the center of his consciousness.

Kuroyukihime raised her left hand as well and placed it over Haruyuki's right. The only things that existed in the world filled with warm light were their four hands intertwined and her calm, beautiful, smiling face.

The girl slowly lowered her long lashes, changing the angle of her face. As if sucked in, Haruyuki leaned his torso forward slightly. Kuroyukihime also brought her body closer in the same way, eyes still closed. Now there were only a mere fifteen centimeters between him and her pale face—and its peach lips. They drew a little closer. Down to ten centimeters.

The clatter of the door sliding open put a stop to things.

Kuroyukihime pulled herself away from him so fast, she practically teleported. In one swoop, she yanked out the direct cable, leapt off the bed, and returned to the chair beside it. A mere two seconds later, the edge of a white curtain was lifted, and the face of Ms. Hotta appeared.

"How're you feeling, Arita?"

Haruyuki was frozen in place, eyes and mouth all gaping, and the teacher furrowed her brow.

"Your face is pretty red. Maybe your temperature's gone up again?"

"No. I'm fine." This was as much of an answer as he could manage.

Meanwhile, Kuroyukihime sat neatly on the chair, face perfectly calm, not even a drop of sweat on her forehead. Her powers of mental control were formidable, truly. At some point, her hands had even picked up the thermos once more.

As she proffered the straw of that very thermos in a gesture perfectly befitting a health aide, Haruyuki had no choice but to accept it and suck.

8

During the ten-minute break at the end of second period, Haruyuki changed out of his gym clothes, back into his uniform, and returned to eighth grade's class C.

Immediately after he pulled the door open and set foot inside, he was showered in no small amount of applause, and he froze in place. When he thought about it, though, he didn't know what it'd be like when a frail girl collapsed from anemia or something, but if a boy collapsed from trying too hard in a regular gym class, that was basically comedy gold. Pulling in his head and bobbing it in small bows, Haruyuki dashed to his seat, sat down just as the bell sounded for third period, and heaved a sigh of relief.

When he lifted his face, his eyes met those of Chiyuri, who was looking back with an expression of concern from her desk, which sat kitty-corner to the front and right of his. He gave her a nod to say that he was fine and glanced back at Takumu, behind him, searching for brief eye contact.

Takumu's expression was actually apologetic; he apparently thought it was because of his advice about the image being important that Haruyuki had tried so hard that he collapsed.

It's not your fault. In fact, thanks to you, I realized something important. Thank you. Putting this thought into his gaze, he started to grin, and Takumu also finally turned the corners of his mouth up slightly.

During third and fourth periods, lunch, and then his afternoon classes, Haruyuki studied with half his brain while the other half thought furiously about what second-level Incarnate he could find and nurture.

He understood that he had a far more pressing duty to focus on at that moment: Castle Escape Mission Part II, scheduled for seven o'clock that evening and closing in fast. He had to dive into the Unlimited Neutral Field with Ardor Maiden aka Utai Shinomiya, meet the mysterious young azure samurai Trilead Tetroxide again, and, with his help, return alive from the Castle and the territory of the Four Gods. Considering the fact that they would be plunged into the terrifying state of Unlimited Enemy Kill if they were defeated by even one of the samurai avatars patrolling the interior of the Castle, much less the God Suzaku, no matter how much he focused on the mission, it would never be too much.

But Haruyuki simply couldn't stop himself from thinking about his own Incarnate. Because at the moment, he had one other situation he couldn't put off for later: the fact that he was going to initiate his eternal rival—or that's how it had turned out at any rate—the fin de siècle motorcycle-riding Burst Linker, Ash Roller.

When Ash had abruptly asked him to teach him the Incarnate System in their last duel before school, Haruyuki had been stunned into silence for almost a full five seconds. Once he somehow managed to get his brain moving again, the very first thing he asked was, to him, the most natural question in the world.

"Wh-why me?"

And the century-end rider had said, "It's just, you're, you know. You're, like, Master Raker's apprentice, right? So then, like, you're my junior or my bro or something?"

It took him another second to understand that *bro* meant younger apprentice, and he stopped himself from retorting that *bro* didn't exactly make clear what their relationship was at all. He instead replied with a more practical question. "Th-then shouldn't you get Raker to teach you properly? You're her child, Ash. I'm sure she'd teach you very nicely, regardless of the fact that you're in different Legions. She'd make sure to take the time and do it right."

"That's just it. That 'do it right' is the whole problem."

Haruyuki caught an echo of something like fear in the voice slipping out from beneath the skull mask and instantly understood what the issue was for Ash. It was like he was scared—no, he actually *was* scared. Of the terrifying spartan teaching style in which Sky Raker aka Fuko Kurasaki "did it right" and pushed Haruyuki off the top of the old Tokyo Tower to initiate him into the Incarnate System two months earlier.

"Um," Haruyuki said, after staring at Ash Roller out of the corner of his eye for a while. "This might sound a bit grandiose, but...the Incarnate System isn't so easy as that. I mean, just getting it without working hard like some dodgy Neurolinker study kit or something—"

"Don't be a Chatty Cathy about every tiny deet! I get it! Mighty me's totally *comprendés*!" Ash shouted, and the palm of a gloved hand was thrust before Haruyuki's eyes. "But let me just say this. The lesson you got from Master was the mild version, special for guests!"

"Huh? Th-that was?"

"One hundred percent! And, like, basically, my masterful self's, like...Dunno if I should say it like this, but I'm not planning to learn the Incarnate System and then go running around the Unlimited Neutral Field ripping danger dudes to shreds or something. Only gonna use the Incarnate tech in one fight—maybe just one time. All I gotta do is slam tough-guy action on Kid U, who's swallowed up by the ISS kit, and get him to wake up already. That's all."

At that unexpected pronouncement, Haruyuki considered the skull face's profile.

Face turned up to the sky of the stage, Ash Roller muttered in a quiet voice tinged with an usual gravity, "For my mighty self, Brain Burst's basically nothing but a fighter."

And when Ash said this, Haruyuki couldn't bring himself to reject his rival's request. Because Haruyuki himself was the one who told Ash Roller that now was the time to strike a blow against Bush Utan and destroy his ISS kit.

The duel time ended there, so Haruyuki didn't get the chance to say yes or no to Ash's wish, but he was sure his intention—that he had resolved to grant this wish—had been conveyed to his longtime rival.

As half his brain spun and whirled in thought, the bell sounding the end of sixth period rang, and the air in the classroom suddenly perked up.

The sixth-period teacher left, to be replaced by their homeroom teacher, Sugeno, and the short homeroom session began. At the end of the various announcements, when the matter of Arita passing out in first period was brought up, Haruyuki gratefully accepted the wise words "Giving it your all's fine, but the golden rule of the athlete is to properly self-monitor," and then the bell for the end of the day rang.

He first talked briefly with Chiyuri and Takumu about the plans for that evening before his friends ran off to track and kendo practice, respectively. They confirmed the general gist of things—once they were done with practice and club work, they would change and meet at Haruyuki's, have a meeting with the whole Legion, and start the Castle escape mission—and then parted for the time being.

Haruyuki changed into his sneakers at the outside doors, and while he headed toward the rear school yard by himself to take care of his club duties, he kept intently asking himself the same question.

Perhaps it was because these doubts still existed in the bottom of his heart that he had felt a slight impatience with Kuroyukihime in the nurse's office, as he sought instruction in Incarnate.

If it was just about technical knowledge of the Incarnate System—a conscious use of imagination circuits, which were a subtextual control system in Brain Burst—he could brag that he had learned it to some extent. But Incarnate was not simply a technique. It held an overwhelming power outside the game rules, but it also carried the terrifying risk of the player's own mind being pulled down into dark places. This was no mere metaphor. For Burst Linkers who unlocked a negative will, even their personalities in the real world were twisted. Like the marauder Dusk Taker. And Takumu the previous day.

If he was going to initiate someone into the Incarnate, he had to make sure to carefully warn them not to be pulled to that dark side. It probably wouldn't be enough to explain the danger in words. First, he would need to show actual examples of the miracles that the Incarnate could bring about. Like Sky Raker making her wheelchair dance without using her limbs or Black Lotus turning her sword into a hand.

From this point of view, Haruyuki's Laser Sword and Laser Lance were fairly weak. As a phenomenon, they were nothing more than one-off attack techniques. There was any number of other Burst Linkers who had special attacks with the same range and power.

If he really intended to lecture Ash Roller on the Incarnate System, then rather than the four basic technique types, Haruyuki would have to show him what Kuroyukihime called a second-stage power. If he couldn't, then he probably wasn't qualified to teach anyone about Incarnate.

"Still, that said...," Haruyuki muttered with a sigh as he rounded the second school building from the east side and walked along the mossy backyard.

In the nurse's office, Kuroyukihime had said that to learn the second stage of Incarnate, he needed to face his own flesh-and-blood self head-on and invert the mental scars that were the template for his avatar, in order to give birth to an image of hope. But to be honest, Haruyuki didn't really understand himself why he was born as Silver Crow—a metal color with slender limbs, a smooth head, and ten metal fins.

He'd wanted a thin body because he was fat. He'd dreamed of flying because he lived his life crawling along on the ground. It was easy to say that. But for some reason, he felt like that wasn't the whole of it. After all, this theory had nothing to say about the reason for the metal color.

Then he suddenly heard a faint voice: *And it's basically for sure that peeps with a mental-scar-shell strength that goes beyond a certain level turn into metal colors…*

He froze on the spot and looked around.

It was the slightly husky voice of a girl. But there was no one in the dim yard. He listened hard once more, but the only sounds he heard were the shouts of the sports teams practicing on distant grounds and the members of the band tuning their instruments in the music room.

But he wasn't just hearing things. Because even if Haruyuki had known the phrase "mental scar shell," he didn't know any girls around here who used the Kansai dialect the voice spoke in.

Throb.

Suddenly, a point in the center of his back, between his shoulder blades, ached fiercely. Unthinkingly, he staggered and put a hand out against the wall of the school building beside him. *Throb. Throb.* The pain just wouldn't go away.

It wasn't muscle pain from gym first period. Haruyuki already knew this pain wasn't coming from some abnormality within his body.

"*Ngh*…Why, now…*that*," he muttered hoarsely, clenching his fists and enduring the agony.

Exactly. *That*: the Armor of Catastrophe parasitizing Silver Crow, the Enhanced Armament "the Disaster," born from the mutation of the Destiny Arc—it was excited.

Smash. In his ears, a fierce bestial voice roared, entirely different from the previous voice. *Kill. All of them…Rip them apart… Chew them up…Eat them!*

Haruyuki, still leaning against the wall, groaned at the heat of the rage and hatred that enveloped this voice; it instilled a terrible fear in him.

Two weeks before, in the final stage of the Hermes' Cord race, Haruyuki had been carried away by his rage toward Rust Jigsaw and summoned the armor. Although it had basically controlled him for a time, Chiyuri's special attack Citron Call Mode II had rewound time for his avatar, and the armor had returned to a parasitic state—a fragment of a hook wire left behind by the fifth Chrome Disaster, Cherry Rook.

He hadn't heard the armor's voice since, but the previous evening, when he was fighting Takumu, who was on the verge of being swallowed up by the ISS kit, Haruyuki had tried to summon the original form of the armor, the Destiny, to bring him back. And although it hadn't been the Armor of Catastrophe itself, the parasitic element might have awoken in the summoning process.

But. As he endured the pulses of lightning-like pain, Haruyuki felt something was out of place somehow. This was...different from the voice of the armor before, he felt. The brutal destructive urge was the same, but behind that lay some massive emotion, beyond the anger and hatred. An emotion that howled and raged and...wailed.

If he simply closed his eyes and ears to it, the voice would pass at some point, but Haruyuki unconsciously tried to tune his consciousness to it.

Instantly, an intense pain, the most powerful yet, enough to make him dizzy, raced up his spine to the center of his head, and he fell to his knees on the ground. His hearing was filled with a ferocious howling.

Smash. Smash. Smash smash eat eat eat eat eat eat!!

...This is...sadness...? Are you crying...?

The response to Haruyuki's questioning was a third merciless burst of pain. Unable to even groan now, he squeezed his eyes shut and pitched forward, about to fall onto the moss-covered ground.

Before he could, someone supported his shoulders with small

hands from the front. A soft, gentle sensation enveloped his upper body. Before he could comprehend that someone was holding him up, Haruyuki wrapped his arms around that someone, clinging to them for dear life.

The someone was cool, a temperature to soothe and calm and absorb blazing crimson flames. Each time the small hands patted his back, the pulses of pain receded.

He let out a long breath and released the tension from his stiffened body.

Brain still half-frozen, he absently opened his eyes to see thin concentric lines of deep crimson against a black background, like the sparks from incense on a summer evening. It took a little time for him to realize they were pupils—eyes.

He pulled his head back just a little, and his field of view grew. Fifteen centimeters in front of him was the face of a young girl, large eyes open wide and looking worried.

Neatly trimmed front fringe. The rest of her hair was tied back with a slender ribbon. A surprisingly thin neck, and a white dress-type uniform below that. A brown school backpack on the shoulders—

"Shi...nomi...ya...?" Haruyuki asked hoarsely, and the girl nodded sharply.

Utai Shinomiya, the nonschool member of the Umesato Junior High Animal Care Club, of which Haruyuki was president. Fourth grader in the elementary division of Matsunogi Academy, a member of the same business group as Umesato. And in the Accelerated World, Ardor Maiden, a level-seven Burst Linker who had once occupied one corner of the Four Elements, the upper echelon of the first Nega Nebulus.

Haruyuki let out a thin sigh of relief at the appearance of someone he could trust unconditionally and tried to pull his face—still far too close to hers—back a little more.

But he couldn't. Because both his arms were wrapped tightly around Utai's body, which was small even for her age.

After looking down for about two seconds at Utai's dress and his own round stomach pressed together, Haruyuki finally realized his position—as though he was unafraid of divine wrath raining down on him—and shouted out, "Noheeeah!"

His arms swung out to the sides, spring-loaded, and he jumped back half a meter, still on his knees. "I—! I-I'm sorry! I-it's not like that. That's not what…" He waved both hands wildly.

A red system message popped up in the middle of his virtual desktop. Without checking that it was a request for an ad hoc connection, he hit the Yes button. A chat window had no sooner appeared in the bottom part of his field of view than Utai's adorable fingers were typing furiously in the air.

UI> There's no need to feel awkward, Arita. This is most likely out of view of the social cameras.

I-is it? So then isn't that actually way worse?

Rather than giving voice to this fleeting thought, Haruyuki tried a more rational approach. "Uh, umm, I was walking along and I got a little dizzy, probably just from pushing too hard in gym class, but I'm okay now, sorry to worry—"

But as if seeing right through him, Utai cut off his speech with a gentle, sad smile. She stood up from where she was kneeling on the ground with him before moving her fingers once more at a slightly lower speed.

UI> You don't need to panic like that. I understand. What you experienced now is most likely something called "overflow."

"O-over…flow?" He cocked his head at this word he was hearing, or rather seeing, for the first time. But the string of text that followed made Haruyuki open his eyes wide.

UI> The higher-level version of zero fill. If zero fill is an empty will—resignation and helplessness filling your heart, rendering you unable to move—then overflow is a negative will: overflowing with rage, hatred, and despair, and losing control. Of course, this is essentially a phenomenon that happens to the avatar in the Accelerated World, but I've heard it also happens in

THE REAL WORLD, ALBEIT RARELY, TO BURST LINKERS WHO USE NEGATIVE INCARNATE.

"Negative...will," he whispered, and gasped as he looked up at Utai. Shaking his head fiercely, he squeezed out, "Uh, um, I-I totally haven't been practicing a negative Incarnate by myself..."

Once again, Utai smiled gently before stepping over to his side and placing her left hand on his plump cheek. At the same time, she typed with just her right, UI> I TOLD YOU, I UNDERSTAND. THAT WAS INTERFERENCE FROM THE ARAMOR, WASN'T IT?

He inhaled sharply, but if she had seen through him to that extent, he couldn't exactly deny the statement. "Yes, it was. Something...Um, I remembered something someone said and it suddenly started raging."

UI> SOMETHING SOMEONE SAID? WHAT EXACTLY WAS IT?

"Umm, I can't remember who it was. Actually, I'm pretty sure it was the voice of someone I don't know. But it was something like 'the mental scar shell' does whatever and then you 'become a metal color.' Or something."

Twitch. Not Haruyuki, but Utai's hand on his cheek.

The eyes with the crimson threads running through them opened as wide as possible. Lips trembled slightly but naturally, and instead of a voice crying out, her right hand tapped falteringly at her holokeyboard. UI> WHO WAS IT? ARITA, WHO SAID THAT TO YOU?

"Sorry, I'm trying as hard as I can to remember, but...I can't. I don't know. All I remember is that it was a girl's voice."

UI> IS THAT SO? I'M SORRY, PLEASE FORGET IT. ARE YOU FEELING ALL RIGHT NOW? She changed the subject rather suddenly, but Haruyuki quickly forgot the strangeness of it and nodded. When Utai pulled away her hand, he heaved himself to his feet and brushed off the knees of his uniform.

"Yeah, I'm okay now. Thanks. It's almost like you can use Incarnate even in the real world, Shinomiya," he said casually, in the way of a thank-you, and Utai seemed bashful in response, a rare display of age-appropriate behavior. Her cheeks colored slightly and she looked down as she filled the chat log all at once, typing at her fastest speed yet.

UI> I'M GLAD IT DIDN'T TURN INTO ANYTHING MORE SERIOUS. I DON'T THINK YOU NEED TO WORRY TOO MUCH ABOUT INTER-FERENCE FROM THE ARMOR. IT WOULD ACTUALLY BE STRANGE FOR AN ENHANCED ARMAMENT WITH THAT SORT OF HISTORY NOT TO CAUSE ANY OVERFLOW. WHATEVER INTERFERENCE IT CAUSES, AS LONG AS YOU DON'T CALL OUT THE COMMAND TO EQUIP IT IN THE ACCELERATED WORLD, IT WON'T EXERT ANY CONTINUOUS INFLUENCE OVER YOU. EITHER WAY, IF WE SUCCEED IN THE ESCAPE MISSION, I'LL BE ABLE TO PURIFY THE PARASIT-IZING ELEMENT RIGHT THEN AND THERE.

"...Yeah, I guess so." The slight delay in Haruyuki's response was the momentary hesitation he felt about the mission to purify the armor, the most important matter before him at that moment—rescuing Ardor Maiden, escaping the Castle, all of it was nothing more than groundwork to that end.

But was there anything for him to hesitate about? If the Armor of Catastrophe wasn't completely removed, then at the meeting of the Seven Kings in three days, a bounty would be placed on the head of Silver Crow by joint effort of the six major Legions. He absolutely couldn't let that happen.

Fortunately, head still turned to the ground, Utai didn't seem to notice the change in Haruyuki's tone; her fingers continued to flash. UI> WELL THEN, SHALL WE TAKE CARE OF OUR CLUB DUTIES? I'M CERTAIN HOO IS QUITE HUNGRY.

She waved away her keyboard with one hand and picked up her bag from where it sat on the ground a little ways off. With-out looking at Haruyuki, she began walking briskly toward the animal hutch in the northwestern corner of the school yard, and Haruyuki chased after her.

Hoo, the northern white-faced owl, had moved from Matsunogi Academy to Umesato Junior High only a mere three days earlier.

But the small bird of prey drowsing on the wooden perch inside the hutch already seemed entirely at ease in his new environment. He didn't even crack his eyes open when Haruyuki approached the hutch, but the instant he became aware of the sound of Utai's feet after she set down her bag and backpack beside the sink, his round eyes flew open and his wings moved restlessly.

"He's such a mercenary," Haruyuki said with a wry smile, and unlocked the door's electronic lock. He stepped quickly inside and collected the water-resistant paper that was spread out around the perch, along with the tub for bathing. In their place, Utai set out the paper they had washed and left to dry the previous day, before checking that Hoo's weight and temperature were normal.

Haruyuki stepped outside once again, and as he splashed the paper with water from the tap sticking out from the side of the hutch, he caught sight of the white cooler peeking out of the bag off to one side.

Inside was Hoo's food. From what he'd seen the previous day, it was some kind of meat, but according to Utai, it was not chicken or pork or beef. Which reminded him, at today's feeding, she was supposed to show him how she dressed the meat, but she had noted that "a certain amount of mental damage can be expected, so please prepare yourself." Cocking his head anew at just what exactly that was supposed to mean, Haruyuki quietly reached out his hand.

UI> YOU COULD EAT IT, ARITA, BUT YOU PROBABLY WOULDN'T LIKE IT.

The words scrolled across the chat window, and his hand froze. He turned around to find Utai grinning at him, having come out of the hutch at some point without his noticing.

"O-oh, uh, I wasn't going to eat it as a snack or anything. I'm in eighth grade now, after all." Haruyuki shook his head back and forth, forcibly forgetting the time he had come across fried eggplant and chicken meant for a curry and it had turned into a whole thing with Chiyuri, while he hung the freshly washed paper on small hangers. He dried his hands with a handkerchief and looked at Utai.

The elementary school girl, four grades lower than him, gave him a look as though she was carefully considering the situation, but soon she nodded crisply. UI> ALL RIGHT. I'M GOING TO PRE-PARE HOO'S DINNER.

She moved over to the sink, reached a hand into the bag there, and pulled out the cooler. She undid the clasps on all four sides and pulled off the lid. Spurred on by curiosity, Haruyuki poked his head forward to peer inside and, two seconds later, inhaled sharply.

Alongside the cooling packs were small light-pink creatures about five centimeters long, probably mice before they had grown any hair. Naturally, they weren't alive, but they still looked like mice.

Plucking up one of the four creatures, Utai placed it on top of the cooler lid in the sink as she typed with her free hand, UI> HIS FOOD IS FROZEN PINKIE MICE. PET OWLS ARE BASICALLY FED MICE, CHICKS, OR INSECTS LIKE CRICKETS OR MEALWORMS. BUT THE MICE ARE TOO BIG LIKE THIS, SO YOU HAVE TO DRESS THEM.

Then she put her hand back into the bag and pulled out something that gave Haruyuki another start. It was very small, but it was indeed a knife. She slid it out of the smooth natural-wood sheath, and a blade about six centimeters long appeared, glittering with a bluish sheen.

UI> NATURALLY, I HAVE A PERMIT TO CARRY AND USE THIS SMALL KNIFE. ALTHOUGH IF I PULLED IT OUT ON A PUBLIC ROAD OR ANYTHING, I'D STILL BE TAKEN INTO CUSTODY IMMEDIATELY.

Utai's comment was definitely not an exaggeration. Presently, in 2047, carrying any kind of blade, regardless of size, was basically illegal. If you had a professional reason, you could obtain a permit from the public safety commission, but he remembered seeing on the news that the review you had to go through was pretty severe.

"I—I can't believe you got a permit," Haruyuki murmured unconsciously, and Utai simply smiled faintly.

She held the pinkie on the lid with her left hand and brought the tip of the knife down onto it deftly with her right. She guided the blade, and its target was neatly split in two. And it didn't look like she had even scratched the plastic of the lid. The knife moved two more times, and the mouse was instantly transformed into four thin pieces of meat. The color was indeed the same as that of the meat Hoo had happily downed the day before. Apparently, the internal organs had already been disposed of, but a little blood did flow out and wet the knife.

As she worked, Utai radiated a tension that seemed to change even the air pressure around her, and Haruyuki couldn't bring himself to speak to her. Although right from the start, he hadn't had the courage to ask her to let him do it. The remaining mice were dressed one after the other until, in not even a full two minutes, the contents of the cooler were transformed into the state he had seen the previous day.

Having finished her work, Utai washed the small knife and dried it carefully with what appeared to be a piece of cotton before slipping it into its sheath. She wrapped the fabric around the knife and the sheath, put the whole thing in her bag, and stood back up. Without looking at Haruyuki, she typed on her holokeyboard, UI> NORMALLY, YOU USE SCISSORS TO DO THIS. IT'S EASIER THAT WAY.

"So then why the knife?" he asked softly.

Utai cast her eyes downward as if in thought before replying. UI> I THOUGHT IT MIGHT AT LEAST BE A WAY OF PAYING RESPECT, BUT THAT MIGHT IN THE END BE MEANINGLESS CONCEIT. NOW THEN, LET'S GO FEED HOO.

Haruyuki followed Utai as she picked up the cooler and the leather glove, and returned to the hutch with her, contemplating the sentence still displayed in the chat window. But no matter how he explained it to himself, he felt like he was a little off somehow.

The pair entered the enclosure and the owl on the perch flapped his wings as if to express his impatience. The instant Utai raised her gloved left hand, he flew over, almost circling the interior space.

Just like the day before, Haruyuki held the cooler with both hands while Utai picked up the pieces of meat and fed them to

Hoo. In the end, the answer to his homework question had been "mouse," but now that he was thinking about it, he was pretty sure all the owls that showed up in fiction caught mice. There was no reason Hoo would be eating pigs or cows.

Staring at the owl intently swallowing one piece of meat after another, Haruyuki wondered absently at the very obvious fact that Hoo was also alive.

Although Hoo was of a species not native to Japan, sold only as a pet, he still wasn't an artificial protein synthesized in a factory, much less a polygonal object. Inside this four-square-meter cage, every day, he ate, slept, and felt things. Things Haruyuki couldn't even imagine...

Perhaps sensing him biting his lip, Utai looked back and cocked her head. Haruyuki hurriedly shook his head and said quietly, "Oh! S-sorry. It's nothing big. It's just, I was thinking maybe I was kinda rude yesterday when I said he looked happy when I was watching him with the water."

Here he realized he was maybe being rude to Utai now rather than Hoo, and he panicked further. "Oh! Um, I—I don't mean that he's, like, unhappy or anything with you taking care of him. I'm sure he's pretty happy about that. I mean, I'd want you to take care of me—Aah, that's not what I mean. Umm."

At this point, Haruyuki's "run-away meter" had climbed fairly high, but he couldn't do that while holding the cooler in both hands, so he earnestly focused on putting words together.

"Umm, Hoo was probably born through artificial breeding, so I guess he's never known anything outside of a birdcage. But he is still a bird. And birds want to fly high...I guess. Oh! Of course, I'm not saying let him go or anything. I don't mean he's, like, unhappy here. But at the very least, it's not great for me to just decide how he's probably feeling or whatever."

The more he talked, the more incoherent he became, so here, Haruyuki reluctantly closed his mouth.

However, whatever he was trying to say seemed to have reached Utai, to some degree at least. She nodded once and started feeding Hoo again with a thoughtful look on her face. Four pinkie mice worth of meat slices disappeared one after another into the beak, and finally, after some gentle petting on his head, the screech owl, looking deeply satisfied, spread its wings and lifted off from Utai's left hand. It carved out a counterclockwise arc in the hutch, flying leisurely through the air.

No matter how many times Haruyuki saw the owl in flight, the sight was still so beautiful as to take his breath away. As he watched, fascinated and somehow at peace, text scrolled across the chat window with a modest sound effect.

UI> I think what you were trying to say is "respect," Arita.

The instant he saw the word in quotation marks, Haruyuki bobbed his head up and down several times. Yes, that was exactly what he had been feeling earlier.

Hoo—or rather, all pets, including Hoo—was not simply a thing for people to keep. Pets lived alongside their humans. And it didn't make sense to decide whether they were happy or not by human measures. All you could do was treat them with respect.

And it wasn't just pets. Rather than taking the easy way with scissors, Utai had used a properly sharpened knife and dressed the pinkie mice with the utmost seriousness. She didn't forget to respect even mice who were destined to be a meal.

Looking up at Hoo back on his perch, Haruyuki was struck deeply by the text that began to scroll a little slower across the chat window.

UI> I believe it's very important to have respect for all things. "Respect" here meaning not ignoring or slighting anything. The subject of that respect also must include even your own self.

"Huh? Respect for yourself?" Haruyuki took his eyes off Hoo and stared at the girl standing at his side. "Isn't it...different for yourself? Like, isn't that being conceited...or narcissistic?"

This was all Haruyuki could say, given that, far from respecting his own self, he honestly preferred to avoid even looking at his own reflection in the mirror. But Utai paused for a moment before moving her fingers again, gentle smile still on her face.

UI> PERHAPS IT MIGHT END UP LIKE THAT IF YOU TAKE IT TOO FAR, BUT I THINK THAT BY DISRESPECTING YOURSELF, YOU ALSO DISRESPECT THE PATH YOU'VE WALKED UNTIL NOW, THE HOURS YOU'VE SPENT, THE PEOPLE YOU'VE KNOWN. I'M SURE YOU ALSO HAVE INSIDE YOU, ARITA, A FLAME THAT CANNOT BE PUT OUT NO MATTER HOW MUCH WATER IS POURED ON IT, NO MATTER HOW THE WIND BLOWS IT.

The girl gently reached out with her right hand and placed it neatly in the center of Haruyuki's chest, directly above his heart.

UI> THAT FLAME USES YOUR PAST EXPERIENCES AND MEMORIES AS FUEL—AND EVEN YOUR SINS AND MISTAKES. IF YOU PROBE INTO A PERSON'S MIND, THE FIRING OF A NEURON—THAT FLAME, BOTH INSTANTANEOUS AND ETERNAL, IS THE ESSENCE OF LIFE. I BELIEVE THAT CAREFULLY CONTINUING TO BURN THIS FLAME WHILE REMEMBERING TO RESPECT YOURSELF AND OTHERS WILL ILLUMI-NATE THE PATH YOU ARE TO TAKE.

Utai Shinomiya didn't even look at the long, difficult text or her holokeyboard as she typed with her left hand. The whole time, the crimson sparks of her eyes were focused on Haruyuki. From her small palm still pressed against his chest, Haruyuki felt like some kind of energy—perhaps even a real flame—was being generated and poured into his heart.

"My flame…The path I should walk down…" The heat in his veins raced around his body and finally collected in his back, between his shoulder blades.

The real-world Haruyuki, of course, did not have wings. On the contrary. He was round and short, and he was so lacking in any real physical abilities that he collapsed if he tried even the slightest bit in gym class.

But he could move forward. He could keep a modest flame burning in his heart to light his way, and he could put one foot in front of the other. Instead of running hard and looking backward—look forward. Move forward. It was all a matter of imagination. If he had the image of moving his feet forward in the real world, those steps would be doubled and increase tenfold in the Accelerated World.

"My image...my will," he murmured before he took a deep breath and changed tones completely. In a clear voice he offered, "Thanks, Shinomiya. I feel like I can find the answer to something I've been wrestling with for a while now."

Utai took her hand off his chest, and a rare, clear smile spread across her lips, allowing teeth like pearls to peek out.

Leaving the animal hutch, they washed their hands at the tap and then signed the club log file to indicate that the work was complete. After that, they submitted it to the in-school net.

It was four fifteen PM. The meeting at Nega Nebulus's temporary headquarters aka Haruyuki's house was at six PM, so even taking into consideration the time it would take for them to get there, they had a little time to spare.

Maybe I'll go to the student council office with Shinomiya today and chat with Kuroyukihime and wait for Taku and Chiyu to finish practice. This thought rolling through his head, Haruyuki went to pick up his school bag sitting beside the sink.

Suddenly, Utai's entire body stiffened and froze in the middle of drying her hands with a handkerchief next to him. And then Haruyuki felt the presence of something creeping up behind him.

Bloodlust...!

He started to whirl around, but before he could, two arms stretched out around the shoulders of Utai and caught her firmly. At the same time, a cheerful voice sang, "I got you, Uiuiiiiiiii!"

UI> PLAS SSDTOP PLS

Utai frantically slapped her hands at her holokeyboard as she was hoisted up into the air, but the letters scrolling out into the chat window didn't come together into words. All Haruyuki could do was catch in midair the white handkerchief she dropped.

The assailant executing this masterful backstab had no sooner flipped around Utai's small body than she was clutching it to her chest and crying out with delight, "Aaah! Uiui, you're as cute as always! I just want to tuck you away in my pocket and bring you home with me! Or make a little mascot doll out of you and put you on my dashboard!"

Uttering this questionable declaration of love was a girl in the uniform of a school that was not in this area. She was quite a bit taller than Haruyuki, her too-perfect proportions wrapped in a light-blue blouse and checkered skirt, thin knee-high socks reaching up quite a ways past her knees. Her long, soft hair flowed down over her shoulders.

Utai's right hand scrabbled even more frantically in the air before dropping down, as if it had expended all its energy.

Here, the predator, having confirmed total control over her target, finally looked at Haruyuki and smiled gently. "Hello, Corvus. I see you're working hard at the Animal Care Club."

"Oh. Th-thanks. Hello, Master." Face stiffening, Haruyuki exchanged greetings with the deputy of Nega Nebulus, level-eight Burst Linker Sky Raker, aka Fuko Kurasaki. Then he asked, ever so timidly, "Uh, um, wh-why are you here at Umesato?"

"The one thing everyone should have is a friend in a position of power. Sacchi was kind enough to issue me a visitor's pass."

In that era, the tightening of security at elementary, junior high, and high schools had been pursued wholeheartedly, so that people outside the school, even children of the same age group, could not freely come and go. Authentication occurred at the gates of the school via Neurolinker, and unless a pass had been issued, security guards would come running the instant a stranger stepped over the threshold.

"Oh, nice." Haruyuki nodded his head before suddenly shaking it.

"W-wait, I'm not talking system-wise. We're supposed to meet at my place at six, right?"

"Goodness! Am I not allowed to simply want to see you sooner

rather than later? I have to have some urgent business?" She grinned and, given that he was a healthy junior high school boy, there was no avoiding the way his head exploded a little.

But on the brink of disaster, Haruyuki remembered that before him was the actually scary Master Raker. His slackening cheeks tightened abruptly, and he shook his head in tiny increments.

"N-n-n-n-no, that's, it's not that you're not allowed, I'm really h-h-h-h-happy." This was no time for him to get carried away—because, at present, Haruyuki was keeping something important from Fuko. And that was the fact that he had to secretly initiate her "child," Ash Roller, into the Incarnate.

He stood frozen in place, stiff smile plastered onto his face, and Fuko gently stretched out her hand to pinch his cheek lightly.

"H-huut?"

"Corvus. Perhaps it's just my imagination? Somehow, I feel like you are keeping something from me."

He desperately suppressed the urge to spring up into the air and shook his head from side to side again. "N-no, there'sh no reashon I would hide shomshing from you!"

"I wonder? My instincts on this sort of thing are almost never off." As Fuko gently tugged on Haruyuki's cheek between her pinched fingers, a charming smile, sweeter than the finest-quality fresh cream, spread across her lips to fill her face. Still, he mustn't forget that she still held her first victim tightly to her chest.

He placed his hands on his legs and stood taller as he continued to shake his head, and Fuko's fingers moved from his cheek to his ear. As her fingertips toyed with his earlobes, she brought her face in close and murmured, "So then I suppose I simply got the wrong idea?"

"Wrong idea? About what?"

"Nothing serious. It's just I had a little time after I left school today, so I thought I might go sit in a duel Gallery. And when I did, I just happened to come across Ash in the Gallery of the same duel, so we started to chat."

"…"

"And somehow, he seemed a little off, a little strange, you know? So I caught up with him in the real and gently questioned him."

"……"

"And wouldn't you know, he told me he had completely disregarded me, his parent, and gotten you to promise to teach him something very important? Verrrrry top secret, verrrrry critical, a name I hesitate to say in a public space…" Here, soundlessly, Fuko's lips moved: *In. Car. Nate.* "…system and its use?"

Ash Rolleeeeerrrrrrr!! Way to crack under pressure! I mean, if you're going to spill it right away, then just get Raker to teach you to begin with! What exactly was the point of me worrying and working on this all day?! Anyway, you seriously owe me for this mess now! he screamed in his mind, but he couldn't turn back time.

He stopped the ongoing side-to-side motion of his head and moved it sharply up and down in resignation. "Um," he said. "Uhh, I-I'm sorry. I was. Hiding something. From you."

"Oh, you were?" Terrifyingly, her perfectly kind smile still on her face, Raker nodded once more. "I'm so glad you told me. If you had tried to feign ignorance any further, I would have given you the full course of special training with Ash, Corvus, but now I'll let you do just half."

"…H-half…?"

"Yes. Once we succeed in today's Castle escape, your special training will begin in the Unlimited Neutral Field. I think it's getting to be time for you to proceed to the next level as well, Corvus."

"…T-today…?" he said, dumbfounded, and, although he was reassured by Fuko referring so easily to the mission's success, proceeded to cast around wildly. But of course, there was no sign of anyone in the dim school yard besides Haruyuki, Fuko, and Utai (clutched firmly to Fuko's chest).

"B-but how are we going to meet up with Ash? If we don't pick a fairly definite time, it's difficult to meet in the Unlimited Neutral Field, isn't—"

"That's not a problem." Fuko answered Haruyuki's question with the utmost ease. "I already have Ash locked up—or rather, standing by in my car parked nearby. I'll be bringing him along to your condo, Corvus, and having him dive with us. Naturally, not from your house, but rather the parking lot close to you."

"Huh? Ash came all the way here? In the real?"

Haruyuki opened his eyes wide, forgetting momentarily his own punishment status. So then that meant if he wanted to, he could meet Ash in the real world? The century-end rider who in his mind had a mohawk and a riveted leather jacket in real life, too?

Unfortunately—he wasn't sure whether to call it that or not—Fuko shook her head slightly. "He's here, but it's better if you don't meet in the real yet. He is, after all, still a member of one of the six Legions, Great Wall."

"R-right, he is." Slowly letting out the breath he had been holding, Haruyuki nodded. They might have been pupils together, but Ash was still a subordinate of the Green King, who stood in opposition to Kuroyukihime. There was a line where he had to pull back.

"I understand." He lifted his face, finally looked directly at Fuko, and nodded deeply. At some point, Haruyuki teaching Ash the Incarnate had turned into both of them being taught together by Fuko, but his exhilaration was greater than his regret. "I feel like I just came across a new clue. Having you teach me again, Master, is exactly what I want!"

"Well said. Good attitude."

He watched Fuko smile, pleased, and wondered if it wasn't a little too soon, when the still-captive Utai weakly moved both hands and tapped at her keyboard.

UI> I'LL ALSO COME ALONG FOR THE TRAINING.

After finally releasing Utai, Fuko said hello to Hoo in the animal hutch—it was their first meeting, but they apparently got along quite well as fellow "flying types"—before the three of them headed toward the student council office.

Although there weren't very many students left on campus after school, walking alongside an elementary school girl and a high school girl was a bit of a trial for Haruyuki. Slipping past the amazed eyes that lasered in on them, they moved from the entrance to the depths of the first floor of the first school building, and the instant he pushed through the door, Haruyuki heaved a sigh of relief.

But once they were in the closed room of the student council office, he was forced to deal with a different kind of nervous tension. Because with the addition of Kuroyukihime, who welcomed the party with a smile, he had definitely arrived in the situation where he was the lone, dull boy in a troupe of sleek, refined girls. Not to mention that these three girls had been the head and senior members of the former Nega Nebulus, which had once occupied the top spot of the Accelerated World's seven major Legions; there was no reason Haruyuki would be able to relax among them.

You know, now that I'm thinking about it, the current Negabu has Chiyuri and Takumu now, so it's four girls and two boys. If we don't get more boys in here, it's gonna be all lopsided. But it'd be better to get someone who's not too scary, if we can. Oh, right! Maybe that guy'd join. Maybe I'll try inviting him when we see him.

These and many other random thoughts wandering through his head, Haruyuki sat in one corner of the sofa set and sipped the tea Kuroyukihime had made. At some point, the clock on the wall had gotten all the way around to five PM.

"Goodness! Is it already so late?" Fuko stood up as if in a panic and clapped her hands together. "I simply can't leave Ash locked up—waiting forever in the car, so I'll go on ahead, all right? I'll park the car near Corvus's house and come by myself at six."

"I feel like you've already left him alone plenty long," Kuroyukihime remarked wryly.

"I told him to earn ten points in free duels before diving into the Unlimited Neutral Field, so I'm sure he's not bored,"

Fuko responded with a composed expression. "All right, then, everyone—I'll see you later."

Fuko waved a hand and left the student council office, and almost as if to replace her, Chiyuri and Takumu appeared, practice over. Their hair was still damp from the quick showers they had taken, and the party, now five, walked together to the mixed-use condo in north Koenji.

Since Chiyuri's mother should have already prepared a light supper for all of them again that day, hot on the heels of the previous two days—a fact for which Haruyuki was both deeply grateful and deeply apologetic—they simply stocked up on drinks at the shopping mall in the condo building and got into the elevator. Chiyuri and Takumu got off at the twenty-first floor to transport the foodstuffs, while Haruyuki, Kuroyukihime, and Utai went up to the twenty-third floor ahead of them.

As they were making these preparations, Haruyuki felt his nervousness increase with each second they drew closer to seven PM.

His other self, the duel avatar Silver Crow, had been left deep in the Castle enshrined at the center of the Unlimited Neutral Field. If he couldn't escape from there, the purification of the Armor of Catastrophe couldn't happen, and thus, his future as a Burst Linker would become very uncertain. Takumu and the others had declared that even if a bounty was placed on his head in the name of the Seven Kings and he ended up not being able to duel, they would supply him with the points he needed. That sentiment filled his heart with joy, but he couldn't simply sit back and count on that. He didn't want to cling to acceleration to the point where he became a burden on the Legion.

"Don't get caught up in a negative image, now," a voice murmured in his ear the instant he walked into the living room of his house and set down his bag.

At some point, Haruyuki had started to droop forward, and he lifted his head with a gasp.

The voice belonged to Kuroyukihime, and she was standing immediately behind him. Placing her right hand on his chest, she pulled him around to face her. "It's important to have an image of every situation. But there are times when you need to focus hard on what's in front of you and charge ahead. Now is one of those times."

UI> It's exactly as Sacchi says. Right now, let's simply believe and move forward.

If even Utai, his fellow prisoner of the Castle, was typing these words as she poked her head out from behind Kuroyukihime, then he couldn't very well hang his head.

Haruyuki thrust out his chest and replied with a single word: "Right!" At this, the cold sweat oozing from both hands seemed to mysteriously suck back in.

Once the sushi and various other rolls prepared so lovingly by Chiyuri's mother were laid out on the six-person dining table and the tea had been brewed, Fuko joined them, with perfect timing.

Haruyuki looked around at the lineup of Legion members, the same as it had been two days earlier, and asked timidly, "Um, are you sure it's really okay? Leaving Ash in the car, I mean?"

Chiyuri and Takumu—already filled in on the situation—smiled wryly along with Kuroyukihime, and Fuko composed her face in the same cool expression as before.

"He's pouting a little, but I can't exactly bring him up here."

"So then at least bring him some of the sushi later," Chiyuri suggested, smiling as she brought a plastic container out from the kitchen and began to quickly divide up the rolls. Haruyuki pictured the century-end rider eating cucumber rolls, and the corners of his mouth unconsciously turned up.

"How about it, Fuko? Time to recruit him for our team?" Kuroyukihime uttered unexpectedly, with a serious face.

"Ye—H-huh?!" Naturally, it was Haruyuki who shouted.

But the other members didn't seem so surprised. Takumu even nodded calmly with a quick "That's one way, isn't it?"

Haruyuki stared, dumbfounded, with wide-open eyes, and Fuko cocked her head slightly, looking perfectly composed.

"It's not that I haven't thought about it, but…he's, well, he has a surprisingly strong sense of duty. I can't say whether or not he'd approve of lowering the Wall flag after raising it already. And, of course, there's also the concern that the Green King, Green Grandé, would use the Judgment Blow instead of approving Ash's withdrawal."

"Hmm. To be honest, I never really know what Grandé is thinking." Kuroyukihime crossed her arms, frowning. "I feel like I've grasped the personalities of the other Kings to a certain extent, but that shield of a man alone, well…"

At the meeting of the Seven Kings the previous week, Haruyuki had also seen the Green King close up, but the only thing he got from it was that the Green King seemed super hard. Grandé hadn't said a single thing from start to finish but had simply nodded once when it was concluded that they would give Silver Crow a week.

It's kind of incredible that he rules over a major Legion of more than a hundred people like that.

Haruyuki hurriedly brought his straying thoughts back to the subject at hand: Ash Roller in Nega Nebulus. He had never even considered it, but he didn't actually hate the idea. Ash was his eternal rival, someone he had fought countless times since that first day when he'd become a Burst Linker, but when Haruyuki lost his purpose after his wings were stolen, that man had passionately rebuked him and brought him to his own parent, Sky Raker. Haruyuki owed him. It was hard to picture from the swaggering way he carried himself, but Ash Roller was a real stand-up guy, honestly compassionate.

And then Haruyuki realized something and lifted his face with a gasp. "Uh, um, Kuroyukihime, Master? I think that, for the time being at least, Ash can't transfer to our Legion."

"Why do you say that with such certainty?"

"Ash's little brother, Bush Utan—" Haruyuki cut himself off here and suggested that they talk while they ate, since it was a long story.

Once Fuko had returned from delivering the package of sushi Chiyuri had put together to her car—although it was apparently not her vehicle, but rather in her mother's name—in the large parking garage in the basement of the condo, they all sat down together once more to eat.

Chiyuri's mother's specialty was Italian food like pasta and lasagna, but she also demonstrated ample skill when it came to Japanese food, and Haruyuki, who didn't get to eat sushi all that often, stuffed it all in his mouth in a trance. Everyone else also rose to the challenge, maneuvering their chopsticks until the large plate was half-empty, and then finally, the conversation resumed.

"Haight, haight. Ahout Ahoo Hohaa." Haruyuki started to speak with a mouth full of sushi, and Takumu stopped him with a slight smile.

"I'll explain about that. I'm a big part of it, so…"

Haruyuki opened his eyes with a gasp and hurried to chew up the vinegar-seasoned rice in his mouth, but while he was furiously masticating, Takumu had already started to explain, so he had no choice but to accept the role of listener. The briefing by the biggest brain in the Legion was indeed easy to understand, but Haruyuki couldn't help but get nervous. Because, just as Takumu had said he would, he explained everything that had happened to him, without leaving out a single detail.

How two days earlier, after hearing about the ISS kits from Haruyuki, he had gone to investigate on his own. How he had come into contact with a Burst Linker called Magenta Scissor in the Setagaya area and been given the kit in a sealed state. And then how the previous day, he had been attacked by the PK group Supernova Remnant in the Shinjuku area and had counterattacked and destroyed them with the power of the ISS kit in the Unlimited Neutral Field. The direct duel with Haruyuki after that. And the mysterious "dream" the three of them shared that morning.

Haruyuki had simply informed Kuroyukihime, Fuko, and Utai

of the general overview of this chain of events in a mail, because it had seemed impossible to properly put into text why Takumu had sought power and how he'd overcome that. Of course, given that they would have to explain that at some point, it was probably preferable that Takumu was telling the story now himself, but Haruyuki couldn't help but feel uneasy. Like maybe Kuroyukihime would reprimand Takumu for getting the ISS kit at his own discretion like that.

However...

"I see. Well done, Takumu," the head of the Legion put forth immediately with a gentle smile after hearing the whole story. Fuko and Utai also nodded calmly.

"What? I thought you'd be super mad and break the table slamming your hand onto it, so I got sushi ready as an emergency measure," Chiyuri said, actually bringing both hands out onto the table.

"I am indeed the Legion Master." Kuroyukihime smiled a broad, wry smile as she responded. "But I don't believe that I can—or would like to—control my members completely. All of us Burst Linkers have our own daily ongoing battles, in the Accelerated World and in the real world. Whether you're a parent or a master, all you can do is simply have faith and offer encouragement. And it's basically still adorable when you three act on your own. More so than the Four Elements of the first Nega Nebulus."

At this last bit, Fuko and Utai both stuffed sushi rolls into their mouths and feigned ignorance.

In the midst of this harmonious scene, Takumu blinked quickly behind his glasses and then finally bowed his head deeply. When he lifted it again, his pale face had completely regained its usual intellectual expression. "Thanks to Haru and Chii, I was able to break free of the control of the ISS kit. At the same time, I managed to inflict some degree of damage to the main body in the Brain Burst central server. But, although that weakened the kits parasitizing Bush Utan and Olive Grab, they're still not completely gone."

"Th-that's right." Here, Haruyuki remembered what he had

wanted to say and connected that to words. "And Ash feels super responsible for Bush Utan getting sucked into the ISS kit. I think that, even if we did invite him to join, he wouldn't say yes until he had freed Utan from the control of the kit. The reason he wanted me to teach him the Incarnate System to begin with wasn't so he could get stronger, but because he wants to destroy Utan's ISS kit himself. That's all he wants."

"Corvus. You really do understand him very well, don't you?" Fuko said suddenly, just as he had taken a breath and was about to down some of his tea, and he unconsciously choked a little.

"Unh. What? You think so? To be honest, I still can't picture what he's like in the real at all, though."

"Hmm? Isn't he the same, though? Riding an electric scooter every morning, doing his hya-ha-ha thing?" Chiyuri opined, and Takumu nodded with a serious face.

Fuko, however, simply laughed gracefully, and then, without answering the question, clapped her hands. "Setting aside the Legion switch, if he wants to learn the Incarnate System because of his friend, then I can't stop him. I believe he's reached a level of actual power as a Burst Linker that will allow it. That's the reason I got Sacchi's permission to have him accompany us today."

After the escape from the Castle, we move straight into special training. Remembering Fuko's words, Haruyuki felt a shiver run up his spine.

Utai, to his right, finished eating a *kanpyo* roll before setting her fingers racing over the tabletop. UI> WELL THEN, OUR SCHEDULE TODAY'S GETTING PRETTY FULL. (1) CASTLE ESCAPE. (2) ARMOR PURIFICATION. (3) INCARNATE TRAINING. IT DOES COST TEN POINTS TO DIVE INTO THE UNLIMITED NEUTRAL FIELD, SO IT'S ACTUALLY A BARGAIN TO TAKE CARE OF EVERYTHING ALL AT ONCE.

"Hee-hee, it truly is. Once we've finished all that, how about we do a little Enemy hunting while we're at it?"

"Ah, in that case, I wanna go check out one of the four great dungeons!" Chiyuri proposed innocently, and the three veteran

Burst Linkers fell silent all at once before shaking their heads back and forth, looking serious.

Utai typed out in an excessively stiff motion, UI> IF WE TRIED TO GO IN ALL THE WAY WITH THIS MANY PEOPLE, IT WOULD TAKE AT LEAST SIX MONTHS.

At the same time as the three junior members dropped their jaws in amazement, the clock on the wall hit six forty-five.

They worked together to clear the table, took turns using the restroom, and then moved to the sofa set on the west side of the living room just as the clock hit five minutes till seven.

Looking around at the assembled, Kuroyukihime carried out the final briefing. That said, unlike the previous outing, they didn't have a particularly detailed plan.

After diving into the Unlimited Neutral Field, Kuroyukihime, Fuko, Chiyuri, and Takumu would move from Suginami to the Chiyoda area and stand by in front of the Castle's south gate. When Haruyuki and Utai dove, they would appear in the coordinates of the automatic disconnect from the last time—the shrine in the basement of the Castle's main building—so with the cooperation of the mysterious young samurai avatar Trilead Tetroxide, they would return to the south gate, break the seal, and escape. Working together with Kuroyukihime and the others waiting outside, they would evade the fierce attacks of the God Suzaku and flee to the other side of the large bridge that stretched out from the gate.

Since they couldn't predict what Suzaku would do, all they could do was play it by ear in the actual moment. However, unlike the last time, when he'd had to collect Ardor Maiden from the ground, this time he just had to flee as fast as he could. The bridge was only five hundred meters long. If things went well, they might be able to charge through before Suzaku finished materializing after detecting the intruders in its territory. No, they'd *definitely* be able to.

Clenching his fists as he whispered this to himself, Haruyuki suddenly remembered something and looked at Fuko, seated across from him. "That reminds me. What's Ash going to do? If you're going to meet up in front of the condo, he'll have to match the timing here pretty closely."

"It's fine. I gave him very strict orders to dive a second before seven," Fuko responded briskly. And indeed, in that case, it would be impossible to leave Ash waiting for her and the others in vain. Just the opposite, actually. One second in the real world was a thousand seconds in the Accelerated World; in other words, Ash Roller would be waiting in front of the condo for sixteen minutes and forty seconds.

Just like our master—tera nil mercy, he thought secretly, while Chiyuri asked in a slightly concerned tone:

"Isn't that dangerous? I know it's only sixteen minutes, but he'll be all by himself in the Unlimited Neutral Field."

Fuko smiled gently at Chiyuri's kindness toward Ash, ostensibly an enemy, as she crisply uttered even more merciless words. "I don't believe that our dive time has been leaked to the outside, and if, hypothetically, Ash *did* have the misfortune of being attacked by a large Enemy or a hostile Burst Linker, we'll have appeared during the hour of regeneration time. We will at the very least avenge him."

"I guess that makes sense. Okay, if it comes to that, I'll kick ass, too!" Chiyuri readily agreed with the elder girl, and the two boys felt shivers run up their spines.

And then it was finally one minute before seven.

Their six Neurolinkers were already daisy-chained together with five XSB cables, and they were connected to the Arita home server through the second cable extending from Haruyuki's neck. All he had to do was press the button displayed in his field of view, and they would all be connected to the global net.

Sitting to his immediate left, Kuroyukihime stared into his eyes and murmured in a gentle, ringing voice, "No matter how many hours, how many days it takes, I'll be waiting, Haruyuki. For the moment when you and Utai open the Castle gate once more and come flying out."

"O-okay!" Haruyuki nodded once and then hurriedly shook his head. "N-no! We won't make you wait that long! At most, five hours—No, we'll escape in three hours!"

UI> THEN LET'S AIM FOR TWO HOURS. WE HAVE OTHER PLANS AFTERWARD, AFTER ALL, Utai typed in a very Utai-like way. Everyone laughed.

Nodding deeply, Kuroyukihime straightened up resolutely in her seat and shouted, "Well then, I'll begin the countdown! Ten seconds to acceleration! Eight, seven, six..."

Everyone joined in the countdown with her.

"Five, four, three, two, one!"

"Unlimited Burst!!"

9

With his eyes closed, Haruyuki passed through the acceleration process: his Neurolinker amplifying his thought clock while simultaneously freeing him from his real-world senses. His body floated for an instant, and he waited for the sensation of coming down on a hard surface before lifting his eyelids.

Before him, the familiar Arita living room was already gone. In its place, a floor with a complicated pattern of blue-black tiles that held a sharp metallic luster. Walls that looked lined with thin blades. The ceiling a network of slender joists. The only illumination came from the several curious purple candles placed along the walls, so the room was dim overall, and he both felt and knew that this place was deep underground.

It was the small room connecting the great hall with the deepest depths of the inner sanctuary of the Castle, which itself stood in the center of the Unlimited Neutral Field—what a certain person had called the Shrine of the Eight Divines. The fact that the design differed from what he remembered meant that the Change peculiar to the Unlimited Neutral Field had happened, and the attributes of the place did not match the Heian stage of their last visit.

"This is the Demon City stage." A clear, youthful voice came from immediately beside him, and Haruyuki turned his eyes in that direction.

Standing there, both hands neatly arranged before her, was a small duel avatar with white-and-crimson armor, reminiscent of the garb of a shrine maiden. One of the Four Elements of the first Nega Nebulus, the blazing shrine maiden Ardor Maiden. Naturally, this avatar was controlled by Utai Shinomiya.

"I'm glad it's not some stage with a lot of terrain traps or wild creatures," he quickly responded to that voice, something he had never heard in the real world. "The terrain's probably harder than the Heian stage, but the Castle building can't be destroyed anyway." As he spoke, he glanced up to check the status in the top left of his field of view. Although his health gauge was completely recovered since he had left and dived back in, his special-attack gauge was at zero.

He then looked at their surroundings, but of course, none of the other Legion members were there. In the last dive, unlike Haruyuki and Utai, Kuroyukihime and the others had left properly through a leave-point portal, so they would have appeared ten kilometers away to the west in Suginami. They had probably just joined up with Ash Roller and started to move. Which meant the only people there were Utai and Haruyuki—

Or, no, that wasn't true. There should have been one more person appearing there with them.

"R-right. He's…"

"He's already here," Utai replied to Haruyuki's muttering, and he jerked up his head to look around again.

"I've been expecting you, Crow, Maiden." The clear voice of a boy, reminiscent of an early summer breeze, came from the gloom near the wall.

Turning his eyes in that direction, Haruyuki saw a single silhouette pop out of the darkness in the modest light of the candles.

The overall look closely resembled that of Ardor Maiden. Head armor shaped like pulled-back hair, a sharply defined face mask. Swollen arms like traditional Japanese clothing. The *hakama*-like armor of the legs spread out horizontally because the avatar was sitting properly on his knees. His color was a deeply serene azure.

Before the smallish avatar lay a silver stick-shaped object—a straight sword in its scabbard. It wasn't especially large, either, but perhaps reflecting the overwhelming potential it contained, the space around the sword looked just the tiniest bit distorted. It was the fifth star of the Seven Arcs, the most powerful Enhanced Armaments in the Accelerated World, the Infinity.

The azure avatar, perfectly described by the words *young samurai*, looked directly at Haruyuki and Utai with sky-blue eye lenses before bowing deeply, still in the formal kneeling position. Bringing his body back up, he plucked the straight sword from the floor and stood easily.

The young samurai took a few steps away from the wall, and Utai returned his bow, bending at the waist with wonderful grace. Haruyuki hurriedly dipped his head as well. After he lifted his chin, he struggled with the words for a minute before opening his mouth.

"Uh, um, uhh, it's been a whil—Actually, it hasn't been that long. Good evening, Lead. Were you waiting long?"

The young samurai avatar smiled gently at Haruyuki's awkward greeting and shook his head. "No. Although I did wait, it was a mere two seconds of real time. Please don't concern yourself with it."

That said, those two seconds were two thousand seconds on this side—more than thirty minutes. If it had been Haruyuki sitting in the formal kneeling position for that long, his legs would probably have fallen asleep, even in duel avatar form.

And before that, in the current age when Neurolinkers had spread far and wide, no one simply "waited" anymore. For instance, if you were meeting someone somewhere, your Neurolinker would tell you how many minutes before you needed to leave the house and what train at what time to get on so that you could move to your destination in the most optimal fashion, and it would even display in detail where the person you were meeting was at that moment and what time they were expected to arrive. If you went out to eat, you could see how busy the restaurants in the area were in real time, so you could go without

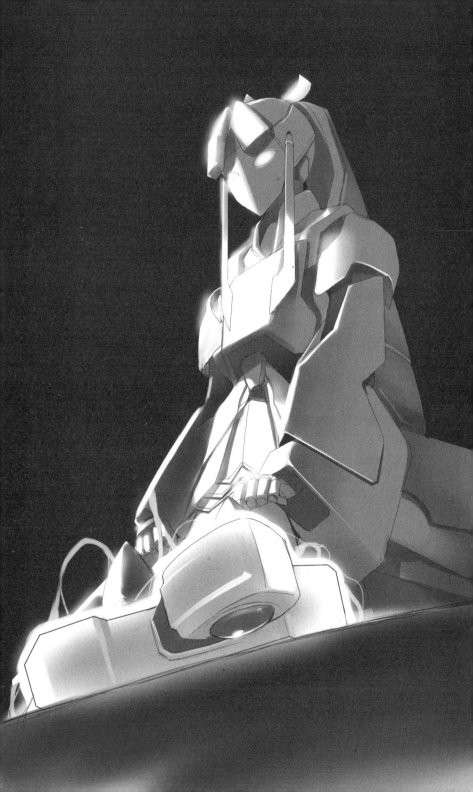

having to wait in line, and if you were taking a taxi, the push of a button would send your request to the car closest to you. Of course, there were occasions when, due to unforeseen circumstances, time was spent waiting, but Neurolinkers were equipped with all kinds of meaningful ways to use time.

Thus, Haruyuki felt sorry from the bottom of his heart for having made the other Burst Linker simply wait for a whole thirty minutes in this place where there was absolutely nothing to do, and he started to lower his head in a bow once again.

But the young samurai put a stop to Haruyuki's apology, as if accustomed to sitting for long periods with no AR or full dives, and said calmly, "Please don't worry about it. Really. Waiting for the two of you to arrive was also a very thrilling experience. So much so that I might almost think it would have been better to have spent the whole day waiting."

"I-it was? Um, me, too. I know the situation I'm in is really bad, but I was super excited to get to see you again, Lead." Haruyuki didn't usually say this sort of thing, but the words fell from his mouth, and the azure avatar pulled in his shoulders and offered a bashful smile in response.

"Lead" was a nickname. The other avatar was formally Trilead Tetroxide. Haruyuki hadn't checked the name—which, according to a search by Takumu, was a molecular formula meaning three lead and four oxygen—in the Brain Burst system. That was simply how the other avatar had introduced himself.

Since you couldn't see the health gauges of other Burst Linkers in the Unlimited Neutral Field, if he were going to attempt confirmation of another Burst Linker's name, the only way Haruyuki could think of was to submit a request to join the Legion from the Instruct menu. But he couldn't do something like that out of the blue, and to be honest, he, strangely, didn't care whether or not Trilead was the other avatar's real name. Haruyuki simply thought that if he was hiding his actual avatar name, then he must have some reason for doing so.

At any rate, having any doubts about Lead now would mean

that the mission to escape the Castle itself would not happen. Because without his cooperation, Haruyuki and Utai probably didn't have a hope of getting out of the inner sanctuary. Thus, he had already decided to trust Lead completely, and Utai seemed to have done the same.

The shrine maiden, even smaller than the young samurai, dipped her head again and said much more smoothly than Haruyuki had, "I'm also very happy to see you again, Lead. There are so many things I wish to discuss with you. However, our Legion comrades are waiting for us outside the Castle, so I apologize for our selfishness, but I hope you might be able to offer your opinion on the fastest route of escape."

Haruyuki also had a ton of things he wanted to ask Lead about—how had he gotten into the Castle, why hadn't he used the one-off portal in the great hall upstairs to escape himself, what did he mean when he said he'd never fought a normal duel—but it's true that this was not the time to have a lazy chat. Kuroyuki-hime and the others were probably still on their way there, but he wanted to keep the time they spent waiting outside the south gate to a minimum. He also thought they would certainly have the chance to talk while they moved, and so he nodded wordlessly.

"It's not selfish at all," Lead responded firmly, standing up taller. "The first time we met, you were both kind enough to trust me unconditionally. In which case, it is only natural that I live up to that faith. I would gladly aid you in your escape." The young samurai stopped and set the scabbard of his long sword, still in his left hand, on his waist. He raised his now-free hand into the air leisurely and continued, "Currently, there are two ways to exit this Castle normally. But one of them is impossible in practical terms." He moved his left hand farther and indicated the far end of the not-large room.

A fence—actually, a barricade—stood there, with a design like countless short swords intersecting diagonally. On the other side of the fence was a vast space filled with a blue darkness. Beyond this expanse, ten times, a hundred times larger than the gymnasium at Umesato Junior High, he could see two tiny lights.

The one pulsing blue like the surface of a body of water was a path to the real world, the light of a portal. In front of that was a golden light, flickering faintly. According to Trilead, that was the last of the Seven Arcs in the Accelerated World, the seventh star crowned with the name Youkou, known as the Fluctuating Light.

Just like he had two days earlier, Haruyuki took a few steps forward as if sucked in and stared at the golden glow. Because it was so far away, he couldn't make out the actual source of the light or the pedestal it should have been sitting on. But even still, he felt something.

The desire to own a rare item? No.

The instinct to enhance his fighting power? No.

The light, which should have been nothing more than a single Enhanced Armament, even if it was an Arc, didn't seem like just a simple item to Haruyuki. As proof, the Fluctuating Light he saw as save data in the "dream" he'd shared with Chiyuri and Takumu that morning, inside the Brain Burst central server—which was, in a certain sense, a region more impenetrable than the Castle—had glittered and shone more brightly than any of the other stars in the center of the galaxy. Almost as if it were the absolute core of the Accelerated World itself.

"The final Arc, Youkou." Lead's voice came abruptly from his immediate left, and Haruyuki pulled himself back from his own thoughts with a gasp. "If you could obtain that item and activate the portal behind it, it would be possible to exit the Castle normally. However, that is simply too difficult. Because that fence—it was a sacred rope the other day, but the moment you go beyond it, extremely powerful Enemies begin to appear in the space on the other side."

"Begin to appear? Does that mean it's not just one?" Utai asked from Haruyuki's right, and Lead nodded slightly.

"Yes. Two appear at first. And then they continue to appear in pairs as the intruders move forward or stand in place. I've confirmed there are at least six, but that probably isn't all of them.

Based on a guess that there will be at least two more, I call them the Eight Divinities."

"E-Eight Divinities," Haruyuki murmured tensely. They hadn't even been able to do anything against just one of the super-high-level Enemies guarding the gates outside the Castle, the Four Gods. "What if that portal actually leads to the next boss room, and sixteen Divinities popped up there?"

Lead seemed to give serious consideration to this casual thought passing Haruyuki's lips, so Haruyuki hurriedly shook both his head and his hands from side to side.

"N-no, sorry. Forget that. Uh, umm, anyway, so it seems like you totes can't get to the portal without defeating the Eight Divinities. You can't just avoid their attacks, huh?"

"Yes, that's exactly right, Crow. I think it's most likely that it is totes not possible to obtain Youkou unless you defeat all the Enemies."

"Forget that 'totes' bit, too," Haruyuki added quickly, afraid he had accidentally taught the completely straightforward Lead and the dictionary in his head a weird word. "Uh, um, it definitely doesn't look like leaving through that portal is realistic. So then, the second way? We were kinda thinking it might end up being this. We have to go back to the south gate and leave through that…right?"

Lead turned back to Haruyuki and smiled as he nodded. "That is correct. Although if you insist on it, Crow, I have no issue with using the north or the west gate."

"N-no, the south gate's good! Our friends are waiting there and all," Haruyuki replied before cocking his head. "The east's no good?"

"I would hesitate slightly to recommend the east gate. The particular attack of the guardian beast Seiryu is a bit trouble-some."

"Huh? What does it do?"

"It is called Level Drain."

"So we'll forget about the east," he answered immediately.

"N-no, forget about the north and west, too. Please, let's go to the south gate."

"Totes understood, Crow." Lead nodded with a serious look on his face, and unusually, Utai, standing off to the right, let a small giggle slip out.

"Both of you are in such perfect sync, I can't get a word in."

"Huh? A-are we?"

"You perform a splendid *shite-kata* and *waki-kata*," Utai commented, using words Haruyuki didn't know, before growing serious once more and bowing toward Lead again. "Lead, do forgive me for asking, but I would deeply appreciate your help in this endeavor."

"I will expend every effort. Now then, let us first go upstairs." Lead moved away from the sword barricade and began walking toward the stairs at the back of the small room, leading upward. Utai followed.

Haruyuki took a few steps after the two Burst Linkers before looking back one last time at the Shrine of the Eight Divinities. He stared at the golden light flickering on the other side of the ultramarine darkness and murmured in his heart, *I will come here again someday. I'll travel the proper path to come see you again once I have power befitting you...so please wait for me.*

It sounded more like he was talking to a person rather than any Enhanced Armament, but Haruyuki clearly saw the seventh Arc flash brightly, as if it had its own will and was responding to him. Or he felt like he did, anyway.

The stairs that had been thick planks two days earlier had transformed into a spiral staircase that was a combination of polished stone and steel.

Right around the time he had lost track of how many times they had gone around, they finally arrived aboveground. They emerged from the staircase into the great hall, which was now both threatening and imposing, exactly what he would expect from a Demon City stage. Decorating the walls were countless protruding spears. Tapered chandelier on the ceiling, like a kind of drop trap. The only things that remained unchanged were the two objects lined up in the center of the great hall, the black granite pedestals where the fifth and sixth stars of the Seven Arcs were once enshrined.

"Right. So then, actually," he started to say casually, and then clamped his mouth shut. Lead, ahead of him, looked back, perplexed, and Haruyuki apologized with a quick "Sorry, it's nothing."

What he had been about to say was, *Actually, the one who has the other Arc from those pedestals is me.*

The fifth of the Seven Arcs glittered beautifully on the waist of the young samurai avatar before him. And the sixth Arc, the Destiny, was sleeping lightly, deep inside Haruyuki himself—inside Silver Crow. However, it was no longer the mirrorlike silver it had once been. Now a dark chrome, Destiny had transformed into Disaster, the Armor of Catastrophe, a cursed power and the greatest in the Accelerated World.

Haruyuki couldn't remember all of that strange dream, but way, way back, at the dawn of the Accelerated World, a lone Burst Linker had succeeded in infiltrating the Castle and obtaining the Destiny. Rather than use it himself, he had given it to his partner. To the girl with golden-yellow armor who appeared in Haruyuki's dream. However, after that, something—a very sad and scary something—had happened. But no matter how hard he tried, Haruyuki couldn't remember the details. He earnestly dug through his hazy memories, but all that came back to him were several fragmented images.

An Enemy with an enormous, terrifying form.

A group of Burst Linkers lined up around the edge of a large hole, looking down.

And several people in one corner whispering to one another things he didn't really understand. "Main Visualizer," "override," "mental scar shell." The words hazily wafted through his ears, but when he tried to catch them, they disappeared without warning, like soap bubbles. If he tried to chase after them, it would almost certainly happen once more: the overflow, calling up extremely negative feelings alongside intense pain. Right now, he had to at least avoid collapsing and being unable to move.

At any rate, because of some incident that included these images, the Destiny had changed shape—or perhaps even its essential nature—to become the Disaster. Thus, the Enhanced Armament Haruyuki currently possessed could no longer be called one of the Seven Arcs. When he thought about explaining this history to Lead, who knew nothing of it, no matter how much time he had, it wouldn't be enough, and he didn't have enough information to begin with to even explain things properly.

Sorry, Lead. Haruyuki apologized in his heart to the blue back of the young samurai, whom he felt strangely close to. *Someday, I'll definitely tell you everything. Not just about the armor, but why I became a Burst Linker, what I fight for, what I'm aiming for, everything; I won't leave anything out. And when that time comes, you, too…*

Here, he forced his thoughts to a halt, quickened his pace, and came up alongside the pair walking before him. They passed between the two pedestals, so close their shoulders were almost touching, and headed toward the south of the Great Hall.

The exit and its imposing ornamentation came into view, and Haruyuki spoke up once more in a quiet voice. "Huh? The terrain's different?"

When they had entered the great hall two days earlier, he was sure they had gone down a hallway running east–west. But now, the path he could see beyond the doorway was stretching out to the south—and he could see stairs leading up beyond that.

Responding to Haruyuki's confusion was not Lead but Utai. "The Change happened, and the stage transformed from Heian to Demon City, so the structure of the maze changed with it, not just the design."

"Hngh! So then my 'memories' are no good anymore."

The reason Haruyuki and Utai had been able to make it to

the great hall without getting caught by patrolling Enemies two days earlier was because he hazily remembered the path taken by an unknown avatar in a mysterious "dream." But if the terrain had been transformed along with the Change, then naturally, he couldn't make use of those memories now.

Fortunately, however, Lead nodded as if to reassure them. "It's all right," he said smoothly. "I know the way."

"Huh? So does that maybe mean that you've memorized the map of this Castle for the hundred or more different stages?" he asked, stunned.

The young samurai nodded, somewhat bashfully. "That said, I actually only remember the way from this great hall to the exit of the inner sanctuary."

"Th-that's plenty. Great! For a second there, I thought we'd have to play the dungeon right from scratch to get out. I mean, I definitely wouldn't hate that, but, you know…I actually like that sort of thing."

Lead flashed a quiet smile at Haruyuki's strange relief, but his face took on its serious look again soon enough. "But speaking from my own experience, the level of difficulty of Demon City is a fair bit higher than Heian. The strength of individual sentinel Enemies is not as great, but because there are more of them, it's difficult to move without being seen."

In his mind, Haruyuki cocked his head curiously at Lead's unbalanced knowledge; he didn't know the name Nega Nebulus, but he knew the stage names. Still, he set aside his questions for the time being and murmured, "I get it. Mobs are more likely to aggro, so sneaking's harder."

This time, it was not only Lead who gave him a puzzled look but also Utai. It seemed neither was familiar with the general terminology of net games. The thought struck him that it would be fun to make them talk with Pard, but he quickly tucked it away and continued without the jargon.

"Um, basically, moving takes more focus than in the Heian

stage. But still, let's make it happen somehow. I'm pretty good at sneaking around."

"That's very reassuring." Haruyuki was half joking, but Lead took in his utterance with a serious face. "But there is just one place where we will not be able to slip by in the Enemy's blind spot, no matter what we do. Thus, we will be forced to fight once. I'd appreciate it if you could prepare yourselves mentally for that."

"W-we will? Okay, got it. It's fine. W-w-we'll fight. If they're weaker than the Heian stage, I feel like we'll be able to manage it. I'm sure it'll be okay, probably." The mere thought of fighting one of those Enemies was enough to make a fountain of sweat gush up inside, but Haruyuki tried to cover it with a display of bravado. He clapped his hand to his chest and jumped forward about three meters. Whirling around, he asked Lead, "So then, maybe you could tell us, just so we know, about when the fight'll happen?"

Lead's reaction was unusually slow; after two seconds or so, he apologized for some reason. "I'm sorry, Crow. My explanation was insufficient."

"Huh? H-how was it not enough?"

"The unavoidable fight is when we leave this great hall. A single sentinel Enemy is patrolling there."

"…Huh." At the same time as Haruyuki let a stunned noise slip out, he heard a heavy metallic sound behind him. Nervously turning around, he saw through the large exit an even larger silhouette peeking into the great hall.

In the Heian stage two days earlier, the Enemies guarding the inner sanctuary of the Castle had all taken the form of Japanese-style warriors, but in the current Demon City stage, they resembled something like knights. The large frame closing in on them was three meters tall and covered in thick metal armor. In its left hand, a kite shield the size of a door. In its right, a rough greatsword that looked as though it had been hewn from a piece of steel.

The area beneath the open helmet and the long horns growing

out of it was swallowed up by darkness, making it invisible to Haruyuki, but from within that darkness, two sharply glittering purple eyes stared down at him. That gaze indicated he had entered the reaction range of the knight Enemy.

"...Huh," he inadvertently murmured again, hoarsely, and slowly moved to step back. But before he could, the knight stepped into the great hall with a weighty, thunderous sound.

"*Voraaaaaa!*"

If forced to transcribe the battle cry that slammed into his avatar with a physical force, Haruyuki would string the letters together something like that. He staggered backward, while an impossibly massive sword was brandished high above his head.

"Hey. Wait," he said, stunned, but the Enemy was obviously not going to listen to him, a tiny avatar that didn't even reach up to its waist. The purple eyes blazed, and the knight moved to slice him neatly in two.

The sharp noise of the sword cutting through the air kickstarted Haruyuki's halted thoughts.

An arc of blue light came flying from behind him and drove into the sword of the Enemy knight, pushing it back the slightest bit. Not letting this opening slip away, Haruyuki dashed backward with everything he had.

Moving forward past him was the young samurai with the azure armor, Trilead. The previous attack had definitely been his, but the straight sword on his left hip was still in its scabbard, and both hands were wrapped in blue light.

Haruyuki opened his eyes wide as Lead brought his weaponless right hand straight up into the air.

"Ha!!"

A battle cry like a scream. His sword hand flashed up and down, and a sword of light in the shape of a crescent moon—the same as the one Haruyuki had seen before—emerged and raced through the air. The metallic clash again. The blue arc struck the knight's neck and carved out a definite mark on the thick armor.

"*Voruuuuu,*" the knight groaned, moving its gaze from Haruyuki to Lead, shifting its target. In other words, the knight's AI was, as Haruyuki suspected the last time, based on a simple hate principle, unlike the AI of the Four Gods.

"*Vora!!*" the knight roared, and whipped the massive sword sideways through the air.

This single slice would no doubt have mown down even the enormous trees of the Primeval Forest stage, but Lead dodged it with a sliding step. For the third time, an arc of light shot out from his sword hand to dig into the surface of the shield in the knight's left hand.

Haruyuki pushed Ardor Maiden farther back behind him in an unconscious gesture as he continued to watch the duel with wide eyes.

It was the first time he had seen the mysterious Burst Linker Trilead Tetroxide fighting. Haruyuki had expected it to a certain extent from the way the young samurai carried himself, but he was indeed extremely skilled. The way he stepped smoothly, like water flowing; the speed with which he moved from evasion to counterattack; and above all else, the blades of blue light launched from both hands in rapid succession were no mere special attack. Given that he wasn't calling out the name of the attack and the fact that it had the power to dig into the incredibly hard armor of the knight Enemy, it was clearly a power generated outside the system by his imagination—an Incarnate attack.

At the same time as his Burst Linker's instincts had him collect all this information instantaneously, Haruyuki felt a single question rise up in him.

Why didn't Trilead take out his sword? The weapon equipped at his left hip was the Arc Infinity, which held an attack power that it was likely no exaggeration to say was the greatest in the Accelerated World. If he could generate that kind of power with no weapon, it wasn't inconceivable that he could do several times, maybe a hundred times more damage if he used the Arc.

"My apologies, Crow! There is a reason why I can't use the sword right now!" Lead shouted out, almost as if he had read Haruyuki's mind, as he jumped aside to dodge the knight's sword. "This Enemy must be defeated without the Arc!"

"G-got it!" Haruyuki shouted back immediately, and hurriedly added, "It's okay to use I-Incarnate?!"

He asked because the conversation with Kuroyukihime and the others from two days earlier still lingered in his ears. The higher the level of Enemy, the more ineffective Incarnate attacks became, and at the same time, Enemies were more likely to be drawn to the Incarnate waves. Just the one knight before him was so terrifying he was practically passing out; he wasn't sure he'd be able to stay in place and not run like the wind if another one or two came along.

Fortunately, however, Lead nodded quickly. "In this room, it's all right as long as we don't use it for more than ten minutes in succession!"

"Got it!" Haruyuki shouted again, and then belatedly readied his own hands in front of him. His brain, stunned at the sudden appearance of the Enemy, was finally switching into battle mode.

Happily, the knight Enemy wasn't using long-distance attacks. Of course, their opponent was a Castle guard Enemy, likely on par with Legend-class Enemies, so if he took a real hit from that sword, Haruyuki would be killed instantly. If it kept picking out new targets, they clearly couldn't focus their might, but he was sure they had a chance of winning if they worked together with Lead and attacked from a distance.

He took a deep breath and brought the image of light speed into both hands, taking aim through the scope in his mind at the back of the knight chasing Lead. The Enemy brandished its sword and pieces of its thick armor slid over each other. The instant Haruyuki saw the less-protective chain mail at the back of the neck...

"Laser Lance!!"

Shouting out with his entire body and soul, Haruyuki launched the Incarnate technique he had only just developed. From his extended right hand, a lance of silver light gushed forward and hit his target at the base of the knight's neck, dead-on. The massive creature staggered, albeit slightly, and the sword attack aimed at Lead slid off course and slammed violently into the floor.

At the same time, the health gauge of the knight Enemy was displayed in Haruyuki's view. The right edge of the first of the three bars stacked up there decreased about 2 percent.

"Whoa," he cried out unconsciously.

Including the clean hit Lead had gotten on the knight's body before, the amount of the gauge they had taken still wasn't even a tenth of the first bar. At this rate, how many minutes—how many hours—would it take to carve away the swollen gauge?

"Both of you, please hold out against it for three minutes." A firm voice echoed from behind him. "I will take over after that." The owner of the voice, silent until that point, was, of course, Utai Shinomiya—Ardor Maiden.

They'd probably only barely be able to cut away another couple percent from the knight's gauge in three minutes. She said she would take over from there, but could the completely long-range Maiden actually draw the Enemy's focus?

"R-roger!" Haruyuki shouted, and knocked the fleeting question out of his brain.

"I understand!" Lead's voice came from a little farther off at the same time.

Nodding at their replies, Maiden held a long Japanese *yumi* bow that had appeared in her left hand at some point. It was immediately enveloped in crimson flames and began changing shape, as though melting. The item, now transformed into a short, flat stick, opened out thinly into a hand fan with a satisfying *snap*. From both sides of the shrine maiden's innocent face mask, additional snow-white armor slid out, meeting in the center to produce a curious screen. Then her entire body was wrapped in a thick crimson aura.

After watching this much out of the corner of his eye, Haruyuki moved to Lead's side. They communicated their strategy through eye contact alone. That said, it wasn't anything complicated. They would both increase the knight Enemy's hate to about the same amount and split its focus as much as possible while attacking.

"*Vorrraaaaaaa!!*" the knight roared, as if irritated that it hadn't yet gotten a direct hit. Until that point, it had been bringing the massive sword down in one strike at a time, but now it began swinging from side to side as it advanced on the two Burst Linkers.

Haruyuki and Lead drew the Enemy as close as they dared before leaping off to the sides, and then with perfect timing, together…

"Haah!!"

"Laser Lance!!"

Blue and silver light shot out. Two light-effect colors bounced off the knight's side. Damage: 4 percent.

The following three minutes were excruciatingly long, hard, and just the teensiest bit exciting. However much they were splitting the Enemy's focus, they couldn't quite manage to flee a safe distance. Although they dodged the sword closing in on them while the knight roared fiercely, sometimes they took splash damage from the blade hitting the floor.

If Haruyuki had been alone, he would no doubt have been eating a direct hit in less than a minute; he could keep slipping by the lethal blade thanks to Lead's precise instructions. Somehow, not only did the young samurai have maps for all the various structures of the inner sanctuary, he also apparently possessed complete knowledge of the attack patterns of the transforming guardian Enemies. He perfectly read in advance the trajectory of the sword the knight brandished from side to side, and even more than that, the placement of the log-like legs and the wind-pressure attack using the shield, and told Haruyuki how to avoid all of these.

Faithfully following these instructions to evade the attacks, Haruyuki aimed for any and every little opening to get a blow in whenever the knight targeted Lead. In a certain sense, moving in perfect sync like this to walk a tightrope where making a single mistake meant certain death was the real thrill of network games.

Once two minutes or so had passed, Haruyuki and Lead had basically stopped talking. Lead communicated instructions via a slight movement of his hand, and Haruyuki responded without a moment's delay.

If I had done it like this…If I had done it like this in the basketball game today, imaging not just the opposing players but even my teammates' movements and thoughts, and moving in line with that, then maybe…

In the middle of the intense battle, the thought flitted through Haruyuki's head, but he quickly stamped it out.

There's no way I could. Real-world me is totally different from Silver Crow. Not this light. Not this fast.

But…maybe I can aim for that at least. No matter how impossible it seems. If I hope I change, and I take one step, just one step toward that, maybe I can, too.

"Come here!" A sharp voice sounded abruptly from his rear, and Haruyuki opened his eyes wide with a gasp.

At some point, the three minutes Utai asked for had passed. He exchanged a quick look with Lead, off to his right, and then they both jumped way back at the same time. As the knight Enemy charged after them, raging even more fiercely, they led it in the direction of Utai's voice.

However, even though they had endured for the three minutes as instructed, the first bar of the Enemy's three-level health gauge was still nearly 90 percent full. What exactly was Utai planning to do?

Feeling slightly anxious, Haruyuki continued to dash backward alongside Lead until they reached the two pedestals in the center of the great hall.

Instantly, the right side of his field of view was dyed red, and he reflexively pulled his eyes away from the Enemy to look in that direction.

What he saw there was a scene that made even Haruyuki—who had come up against all kinds of supernatural phenomena within the Castle and hardened his nerves to pretty much anything—swallow his breath in dumbfounded amazement.

Flames. The source: the small body of the shrine-maiden avatar. From the tips of her *tabi*-covered toes to the ends of the long hair coils, she was enveloped in a conflagration burning red.

Since Ardor Maiden didn't seem to be taking any damage herself, they probably weren't real flames. It was likely overlay, the irregular light effect that accompanied the activation of the Incarnate System. But even compared with the overlay of another red-type avatar, the Red King—Scarlet Rain—the flickering hue was much closer to the look of real flames.

This aura, which took a full three minutes to muster, was several times more intense and more beautiful than when she had burned Bush Utan to ashes in the tag-team duel three days earlier. Cloaked in flame, the shrine maiden held her fan over her head and danced unhurriedly. The knight Enemy charged in with enough force to smash her to pieces.

"Grief-stricken flames of Dvesha." All of a sudden, a sonorous "song" rang out from the mouth of the shrine maiden. She waved her fan neatly, and a spray of small flames flowed off into space. Seeming to be nothing more than meager sparks, they fell at the feet of the knight Enemy.

Krrrr! Instantly, a deafening roar filled his ears and shook the air, and the supposedly incredibly strong floor of the Demon City stage burst into flames—and melted.

The knight Enemy sank helplessly up to its chest in the liquid—the magma—glittering with a dazzling orange light. The cold dark-gray shine of the metal armor immediately grew incandescent, like a lump of burning coal.

"*Vorooooaaaaaa!!*"

A roar—or a scream. The knight waved both arms frantically and tried to free itself of the magma, but the "lake" of molten floor was easily larger than five meters in diameter. All the knight did was vainly scatter droplets of fire; the large frame didn't seem to move up in the slightest.

"Become dust in the ground and be gone." Once again, a verse with a mysterious rhythm echoed in the hall.

The crimson aura enveloping the shrine maiden grew more and more intense, and the temperature of the magma lake increased further. Although Haru was plenty far away, a hot wind blew toward them and threatened to cook his own body. If he got any closer, he wouldn't be surprised if he did actually start taking damage.

After standing slack-jawed for over ten seconds, Haruyuki finally looked at the health gauge of the knight Enemy displayed above his head. The first bar was just on the verge of being similarly burned up.

Lead had said that even in the great hall, if they used Incarnate techniques for more than ten minutes, there was the possibility that it would call other Enemies over. Taking that into consideration, it was a little iffy as to whether or not the remaining two bars would be carved away during this grace period. This was perhaps the time for Haruyuki to join in with a long-distance technique, but for some reason, he felt like he shouldn't. This "flame dance" was a stage for Utai alone, and other people shouldn't force their way in. Lead, maybe feeling the same thing, simply stood quietly near Haruyuki.

The shrine maiden danced for another five minutes, the flames eddied and coiled, and the knight writhed. Eventually, the third health gauge bar was also burned up, and the Enemy disappeared in the center of the magma pool together with a magnificently large scattering effect.

Even after Ardor Maiden slowly lowered her fan and stopped moving, Haruyuki was unable to say anything. He was overwhelmed. By the power of Utai's Incarnate technique, its beauty, its ferocity. He couldn't help but tremble at this terrifying, destructive power.

As far as the logic of the technique, it wasn't that complicated. Melt the floor of the stage, turn it into a high-temperature liquid, and drop opponents into it. What was terrifying was what came after that. There was basically no escaping from it. If you couldn't fly like Haruyuki or you didn't have some kind of special movement ability like the fifth Disaster's wire hook, you'd never be able to get out of the lake of magma. The liquid was viscous, hindering movement, and even if you did manage to somehow make it to the shore, the inside wall of the hole was also melted. It would be like trying to climb a wall of glass covered in oil.

It was a fundamentally different power than the flame of purification that had burned up Bush Utan three days before. The category of Incarnate technique was—he didn't want to think about it, but it was probably the fourth quadrant, i.e., negative power targeting range. But why exactly had adorable, youthful Utai Shinomiya managed such a tortuous technique of destruction...

Part of Haruyuki's half-numbed brain was wandering along this track when Ardor Maiden, standing a few meters ahead of him, shook violently.

"Ah!" Reflexively, Haru dashed forward to catch Utai's back as she was about to collapse to the floor. Before his eyes, the white face mask covering the shrine maiden's face split apart and retreated beneath her hair parts.

Her crimson eye lenses blinked irregularly and looked up at Haruyuki. A weak voice flowed out. "It seems that...it was a bit too soon. To use in actual battle."

"Huh? What?"

"That. Technique. I've been practicing it for a year now. An experimental...technique for heavyweight, ground-based Enemies. More precisely...for the God Genbu."

"For Genbu?"

Naturally, Haruyuki had never actually seen Genbu, the super-high-level Enemy guarding the north gate of the Castle. He had no idea what it looked like or what kind of attacks it used. But he did know one thing: Another of the Four Elements that Fuko and Utai had been a part of in the old Nega Nebulus was currently sealed at Genbu's feet.

In Haruyuki's arms, Utai closed her eyes and continued speaking in bits and pieces. "My power...it was as if it didn't reach the God Suzaku. At the time of the mission to attack the Castle, I personally wished to lead the team against Suzaku. I foolishly thought...if it was fire, then I would be able to control it, no matter what kind of power it had...Perhaps if it had been Aqua Current and the water she controls, then opposite attribute... Or maybe Sky Raker, faster than the wind...Maybe they would have broken through Suzaku's guard. In which case...the annihilation of the Legion two years ago...it was my disdain for the enemy, my forgetting to respect it...my...fault..."

Haruyuki saw a single small droplet of water shining on the edge of her closed eyes and instinctively shouted, "That—That's not true! Absolutely no one thinks it was your fault, Mei!"

"No...that is a mistake for which I should be rebuked. Because...at that time, in my heart...I foolishly thought I might be the one to quell Suzaku's flames and make it through the gates alive...and I said nothing...What would you call that..." The murmured voice, colored with sorrow, finally halted there.

Unable to find any words to say to her, Haruyuki felt like he finally understood why Utai had stayed hidden in a corner of the Accelerated World for two years, without trying to contact Kuroyukihime and the others.

Before, Utai had said that it was because she didn't want to be the cause of secondary damage in a mission to rescue her avatar sealed away in front of the Castle. And of course, that wasn't a lie. But at the same time, she had been severely blaming herself. She was convinced that she was the cause of the Legion's destruction, and because of this sin, she had decided that no matter how much she wanted to see Kuroyukihime and Fuko, she couldn't be allowed that. For a period of two years.

But...

But these feelings of guilt were shared by Kuroyukihime and Fuko.

Kuroyukihime had decided that her taking the head of the first

Red King, Red Rider, on impulse and bringing about a war on all fronts with the remaining five Kings' Legions was the direct cause for the destruction of Nega Nebulus. She had hidden herself in the Umesato Junior High local net for two years.

Fuko worried that she had created all the underlying causes for the dissolution of the Legion when she resolved to cut off her legs to strengthen her own will and forced Kuroyukihime to perform the act for her. She had lived in seclusion in the old Tokyo Tower for two years as well, in the Unlimited Neutral Field.

It was all the same. The three of them were all the same. Because they all cared so deeply about their companions, felt tied to them by profound bonds, they punished themselves. Haruyuki was sure, absolutely certain that the other two Elements, and the other Legion members whose names he didn't even know yet, all went into hiding thinking the same thing. Eternally sacrificing themselves for the destruction of the old Nega Nebulus, never to stand center stage in the Accelerated World again.

"But...but..." Staring down at the face of Ardor Maiden in his arms, her eyes still closed fast, Haruyuki worked to push out his voice. "But Brain Burst doesn't exist for us to—to struggle or worry or hate or fight. It shouldn't, at least. Lots of sad and hard things happen in this world, but someday, we'll get past all that, and the day will come when we can again take the hands of the people we love and share everything with one another. The day is definitely going to come when you can share with your friends this pain you've been shouldering by yourself all this time. It's been two years already since the destruction of the old Nega Nebulus. So this day could be that day!"

As he moved his mouth frantically, Haruyuki vaguely understood the source of the destructive Incarnate that Utai had displayed earlier.

It was sin. It wasn't colored with the same level of darkness as despair or hatred, but it was definitely not a positive force. If those flames were to roast a criminal, then Utai must have tasted the same anguish as her target the whole time the technique was activated.

And at the same time, the sin Utai carried with her was probably not just tied up with the destruction of the Legion. There had to be a deeper, stronger emotion directly connected with the real-world her. After all, Kuroyukihime had said it herself. You definitely couldn't generate a second-level Incarnate technique without facing head-on the scars of your own self in the real world.

Naturally, there was no way Haruyuki would be allowed to enter into the depths of Utai's heart, given that it had been mere days since they met. Right now, he couldn't even imagine the things she had been through, what she had suffered, and why she had lost her real voice. But...but...

"If you have to be tormented forever, to hate people forever even here in the Accelerated World for all your mistakes and disagreements, then why did we even become Burst Linkers?" Haruyuki squeezed the feelings in his heart out into words, and Utai's limp body twitched in his arms.

The crimson eye lenses opened slowly. But their light still flickered weakly. Although Haruyuki wanted to say something more, another few words of some kind, his heart was shaking too fiercely and no words would come out.

At that moment, a voice cool and gentle as a breeze blowing over a grassy plain came to them softly.

"'For sport and play, I think that we are born; for jesting and laughter, I doubt not we are born.'"

It was Trilead, who had been silent the whole time. The young samurai had moved soundlessly out from behind Haruyuki to now face him, Utai between them, before he sank down on his knees without even bending his back.

After a brief period of silence, Utai replied in a hoarse voice, blinking slowly as she did, "'For when I hear the voice of children at their play, my limbs, even my stiff limbs, are stirred.'"

It was probably some old poem or something, but Haruyuki didn't know it. Still, he felt like he could get the meaning of it, albeit only on an intuitive level.

Lead shifted his gaze from Utai to Haruyuki and began to

speak quietly. "I am embarrassed to say this, but I have never before considered the kinds of fates Burst Linkers other than myself have borne or for what objectives they fight. However... however, I had the...vague idea...that the majority had fun playing this game. And that someday, I would be able to...join them."

He hung his head momentarily, the long hair tied behind him swinging. When he lifted his face again, the mysterious youth continued softly:

"However, before I met the both of you, I was the sole Burst Linker I knew. The person who is my parent and teacher told me that even if I was all alone, even if I could not exit this palace and step outside, I should throw myself into playing and having fun. That it was the only path leading to my future. I have long swung my sword alone, imagining the voices of children happily at their play on the other side of the high palace walls. After many, many long days, you appeared before me suddenly, Crow, Maiden. We spoke, we promised to meet again, and then today, we fought alongside one another. I find it impossible to put into words what I am feeling now."

Trilead broke off once more, and Haruyuki and Utai stared wordlessly at the droplet sliding down his graceful face mask. Rather than wiping his face, Lead gave voice to a few last words in a trembling voice.

"The only—the only thing I can say is that I'm glad I became a Burst Linker. I'm happy to have been able to know this Accelerated World. And it is you both, Crow and Maiden...who have given me this joy." Here, the young samurai closed his mouth and bowed once more, deeply.

For a time, silence ruled the great hall curtained in blue gloom. At some point, the lake of magma Utai's Incarnate technique created had cooled, leaving nothing but a slight, shallow indentation.

Finally, Utai sat up in Haruyuki's arms and looked at the other two Burst Linkers in turn. "I, too—that at least," she said in a clear voice. "I am without a doubt happy that I was able to become a Burst Linker at least. No—serving the Black King, fighting as a member of Nega Nebulus. And at the end of that road, meeting you both, C, Lead. I'm happy for all this as well. Which means… the path I have walked until now…was not a mistake."

She moved feet patterned after the split-toed *tabi* socks and brought them down onto the floor. Following Utai's movement, Haruyuki also slowly stood up.

Utai waited for Lead to also get to his feet before taking a step forward and looking back. "I'm sorry to have worried you. Now then, shall we go? I'm sure at the end of this road we walk down one step at a time, our future—our destiny stretches out to infinity."

Lead's claim that he had memorized the internal structure of the Castle inner sanctuary in all the various stages was most certainly not empty boasting. Without hesitating even once, the young samurai led them assuredly through the complicated map of the Demon City stage, which was completely different from the Heian stage of two days earlier.

They ascended stairs, crossed walkways over air, pressed trap switches, opened hidden doors, and descended using pulleys. Without guidance, who knew how many days or even weeks it would have taken them to make it through the medieval castle–style dungeon, replete with gimmicks? And on top of that, the place was crawling with Enemies of the same knight type they had fought in the beginning, along with some in heavier armor, some that looked quick and nimble, and even some wizard types.

Haruyuki was prepared for the fact that they probably wouldn't be able to avoid two or three random encounters, but Lead's instructions were perfection itself. Even when they were stuck with Enemy groups walking along on both sides, he calmly stopped them in the shadow of some object before they all ran as fast as they could once they were in the blind spot of receding opponents. Once, he even managed the stunt of deliberately setting an empty elevator in motion, and when the Enemies gathered there, they went down a ladder in the opposite direction. It was no exaggeration to say that he knew the place like his own backyard.

For a dyed-in-the-wool gamer like Haruyuki, the only titles he could "move" in this freely were online FPS games that he'd played for years or single-player action-adventure games he'd logged more than a hundred hours on. And the entire structure of the Castle was transformed during the Change, too. Exactly how many years had Trilead spent fighting—no, playing—in this place?

This question in mind as he followed instructions and ran, climbed, descended, and passed through the nth doorway, a scene suddenly appeared before Haruyuki's eyes.

A single small window on a wall. A vast expanse spreading out on the other side, columns of pillars, and a sky swirling with black clouds. Outside.

"Very nice work. The Castle inner sanctuary ends here," Lead said, completely nonchalant, and approached the window to open it casually. A cold wind blew in and coolly caressed Silver Crow's armor.

Moving to the window as if compelled, Haruyuki looked outside. Two columns of massive blue-black pillars stretched out in long lines a fair bit to the right of the window. He had seen this before. In the Heian stage, the coloring had been different, but similar pillars had stood at the main entrance of the inner sanctuary then, too. So that meant that ahead of them was...

"Th-the gate!" On the verge of unconsciously shouting in his excitement, he hurriedly got himself in check.

He could even catch a tiny glimpse of the enormous gates at the end of the columns of pillars, beyond the fog lingering above the surface of the ground. From the angle of the shadows the pillars cast, he could tell the gate was directly to the south—in other words, it was the very same Suzaku gate Haruyuki and Utai had crashed through two days earlier.

Finally. Finally, they had made it to a place where they could see the gate. All they had to do now was open it, go outside, shake free of the flames of the God Suzaku, and fly to the other side of the bridge.

Thinking about this, Haruyuki clenched his right hand into a tight fist before realizing something and taking a sharp breath. "R-right. How are we going to open it?"

The gates he could see on the other side of the heavy fog were without a doubt shut tight. There was no possible way the stone doors, very nearly twenty meters in either direction, would simply open if they reached out and pushed them. The reason the gates had automatically opened, albeit just a crack, when Haruyuki and Utai flew in was that someone—or rather the young samurai before him—had broken from the inside the seal plate that served as a lock.

The moment his thoughts reached that point, Lead nodded as if he had been watching Haruyuki's mind at work. "The seal of the Suzaku gate has regenerated, but I will break it once more now. The gate should open then."

"I-is that an easy thing for you to do?" Haruyuki asked timidly, and Lead cocked his head, as if searching for the words, before nodding slightly.

"I don't know whether or not it's *easy*, but it is something I've done once before. And the reason I didn't—no, couldn't unsheathe this sword in the battle earlier was because I needed to break the seal on the gate."

"What do you mean exactly?" Utai asked. Haruyuki also didn't understand the causal relationship between not drawing the sword and being able to break the seal.

Lead nodded again and gently touched the straight sword on his hip with his left hand. "Although it is beyond my position, this Infinity I have been allowed to possess now has several special effects. One of these is that as long as it is sheathed in the scabbard, the power of a single blow increases infinitely until it is unsheathed."

Haruyuki opened his eyes wide in amazement, but at the same time, this made a very deep kind of sense to him. If the sword did indeed have that kind of effect, then it wasn't something to be used against random sentinel Enemies. In fact, frugal

Haruyuki could see himself dragging it out forever and never actually using the thing.

However, Lead was apparently generous enough to use the power stored up in the blade for what was certainly many long hours on their behalf. Despite the fact that there weren't enough words of thanks simply for his guidance up to that point, he was going to go even further for them, and Haruyuki did feel a little guilty. But the fact of the matter was that there were no other proposals for them to achieve their number one priority of escaping the Castle. Thus, Haruyuki lowered his head deeply and said simply, "Thank you, Lead."

Utai, beside him, also arranged her hands on top of her *hakama* armor and bent deeply at the waist.

The young samurai shook his head, almost blushing. "It's much too soon for you to be thanking me," he responded in a light tone. "We still have to fight our way a little farther to the gate."

But contrary to Lead's words, after the road they had taken up to that point, it was no great effort to go out the small window of the inner sanctuary and head south in the cover of the pillars.

Naturally, just like the last time they had passed this way, terrifying groups of sentinel Enemies incessantly patrolled the wide road between the two columns of pillars, and they could hear suspicious footsteps and groaning voices from the deep woods to the left that made their blood run cold. However, once they knew they wouldn't be targeted as long as they hid behind the pillars, it wasn't a difficult thing to relax and clear one pillar at a time. Fortunately, all three avatars were small and lightweight; their footfalls were quiet, and their bodies didn't stick out from the sides of the pillars.

After about forty minutes, they had reached the shadow of the southernmost pillar, and all three heaved a sigh of relief together as they leaned back against the cool, curved surface. They looked at one another and exchanged small grins.

They had managed to make it this far. Within the Castle, there was only one sequence left. When he quietly opened the Instruct menu and checked the time elapsed since they'd dived, the digital readout showed 135 minutes. A little over the two hours Utai had set as a target, but they had basically done an amazing job.

That said, on the outside of the south gate at that time, Kuroyukihime, Fuko, Takumu, Chiyuri, and the spur-of-the-moment inclusion, Ash Roller, were impatiently waiting for the gate to open. All he wanted was to break through the guard of Suzaku ahead of them and share in the joy of the mission's success with all of them.

"Well then, it's about time for us to finish this, yes?" Lead murmured, nodding briefly, as if sensing Haruyuki's impatience. "The procedure is simple. Once the Enemies patrolling the main road on either side are at their farthest point away from us, I will fly out and destroy the seal. At the same time, you escape through the gate. If you are prepared, we will go on our next opportunity."

A nervous tension quite naturally rose up in him, and all Haruyuki could do was nod. In contrast, Utai had the air of wanting to say something, but she quickly pulled back and also assented with a nod. Lead glanced out at the front from the shadow of the pillar and raised his right hand.

The southern gate rising up like a stone monolith was about twenty meters to the southwest of the pillar they were hiding behind. In the center of the two gate doors was a steel plate with a relief of a phoenix on it; this alone was the same as it had been in the Heian stage. The seal of Suzaku.

The wide road that stretched from the gate straight out toward the north was patrolled by a total of eight groups of guardian Enemies. Additionally, a curving hallway ran in the east–west direction in front of the gates, with groups of Enemies coming and going on both sides.

The movement of all the groups was slightly out of sync, meaning that the space in front of the gates never seemed to clear out. But as they waited with bated breath, the timing of the groups' movement gradually started to match up. Finally, Lead splayed the five fingers of his right hand. Then he folded down one finger after the other. Four, three, two, one…

Now!!

Their soundless shouts overlapped, and the three Burst Linkers raced out from the shadow of the pillar.

They dashed across ground made up of blue-black tiles, running as hard as they could, cutting through the thick fog. In a mere three seconds, they had arrived at the plaza in front of the gates.

Lead quickly raised his left hand to stop Haruyuki and Utai, while at the same time placing his right hand on the scabbard of the straight sword—the Infinity, one of the Seven Arcs. An intense blue light jetted from the small body of the young samurai, the light of a young, fixed star.

Overlay. The brilliance of the Incarnate. When they fought the knight Enemy, Haruyuki had thought Lead was a fairly skilled user, given that he used the technique without calling out a technique name, but the speed at which he activated the system and the scope of his overlay far exceeded Haruyuki's expectations. Despite the fact that Lead still hadn't activated the technique itself, the hard tiles at his feet cracked in concentric circles, and the air burst with blue plasma.

The young samurai crouched down abruptly and grabbed the scabbard of the straight sword with his left hand and the hilt with his right.

"Ah…Aaaaaaaaah…!!"

Lead's severe battle cry, the first time Haruyuki had heard it. Unable to breathe, Haruyuki unconsciously pulled Utai in toward him.

Lead's normally cool eye lenses burned a hot white, and he called out the name of the technique with a deep echo.

"Heavenly Stratus!!"

His right hand moved so fast, it blurred as it shot out in a horizontal line. The blue blade raced through space, combining the superior attack power of the Arc itself, which increased every second it sat sheathed in the scabbard, and Trilead's Incarnate, which threatened to split the heavens. To Haruyuki's eyes, the arc the combined power cut in the air looked as though it would split the world itself in half.

From left to right, a single blow, a sword drawn and swung. The blade returned without a moment's delay and slashed downward from directly above.

The light slashed out to form an enormous cross and slammed into the thick steel plate joining the two doors. A sharp cross ran along the face of the phoenix that was carved in bas-relief. The vertical line stretched out top to bottom and pierced the door itself. The southern gate standing in their way like a cliff shuddered heavily.

It's opening!

Haruyuki held Utai even more tightly and pulled his clenched right hand to his side. With the movement, the ten metal fins folded up neatly on his back until now unfurled all at once.

"So that is your true form, then, Crow."

Hearing the murmur, Haruyuki looked to his side.

Silver sword still drawn and lowered, the young samurai narrowed his eye lenses as if dazzled. "It's beautiful," he said. "I truly am happy to have met you."

"Th-that's…I mean, me, too, meeting you, Lead…" He had gotten this far when suddenly the body of Utai, pressed up against him, stiffened. At the same time, Haruyuki noticed it, too.

The wide road stretching out at length behind Lead. The hall connecting it to the east and west. From all directions, groups of patrolling Enemies were thundering toward them. But why on earth—they were definitely out of visual range. After a stunned moment of thought, Haruyuki finally realized it.

The high-level Enemies were drawn by the Incarnate waves.

The Incarnate technique Trilead had activated to break the seal on the gate, Heavenly Stratus, was the highest-level attack Haruyuki had seen up to that point. Using it in an open space

where they were in plain sight, it was no wonder a wide range of Enemies would get aggro.

"L-Lead!" Haruyuki shouted, and quickly stretched out his right hand. "Hurry and grab on! You, too!!"

However...

The azure samurai simply smiled, a tinge of sadness in the calmness of it, and shook his head slightly. "No, I cannot go. Please, the two of you leave on your own."

"Wh-why?! If you stay here, the Enemies'll destroy you!!"

There were more than ten of the massive-framed knights and wizards, all seething with palpable animosity as they surged toward them. Even a master like Lead, armed with the Infinity, couldn't take on that many alone.

But before that, even, Haruyuki had unquestioningly assumed the whole time that Trilead would naturally be escaping with them. Which was why he had put off all the many things he wanted to ask the other Burst Linker, all the things he wanted to talk about. And yet, being separated for life here on opposite sides of unopening gates, he had no idea when they'd be able to meet again.

"Y-you can't! Lead!!" Haruyuki shouted with all the voice he could muster and stretched out his hand even farther.

But Trilead took a large step back and pointed at the south gate with the sword in his hand. "You must go!! As long as I'm here, I won't end up in a state of unlimited EK! And...I cannot leave this palace yet!! But I promise you, I will meet you and Maiden once again one day. And then I will tell you everything. The reason why this palace exists in the Accelerated World, the reason why it is so fiercely guarded—everything I know about it!!"

Faced with the firm spirit of the young samurai and his resolute declaration, Haruyuki could say nothing more.

"Shall we go, C?" Utai said sharply from his side. "Our staying here now will only make Lead's sacrifice be in vain!"

"Hngh!" Haruyuki closed his eyes tightly for a second, and when he opened them again, he was resolved; the wings on his back vibrated lightly. The thrust they generated pulled the two avatars soundlessly upward.

From an altitude of about two meters, Haruyuki shouted briefly, in a voice filled with a flood of emotion, "Lead. See you!"

The young samurai grinned. "Yes. See you!"

The two words were the promise young children exchanged in the evening to meet again the next day. Suppressing tears as he looked back, Haruyuki heard, mixed in with the footfalls of the herd of Enemies closing in, Lead's final words.

"Trilead Tetroxide is the name my parent gave me. My real name is…"

Checking the impulse to look at Lead once more, Haruyuki flapped both wings vigorously. As the two avatars charged toward the southern gate of the Castle, narrowly opened with just a seam, a voice like the deep blue of a cool breeze pushed at their backs.

"…Azure Air!"

10

Crimson.

That was the first thing Haruyuki saw after they slipped through the tiny crack in the gate and finally escaped to the outside world.

Swirling, raging, deep-crimson flames. But this was no ordinary heat energy. It was the form of a massive bird with two enormous wings, a long neck, and eyes glittering like rubies.

The super-level Enemy, the God Suzaku.

"Wh-why is it already materializing?!" Utai shouted hoarsely, clinging tightly to his neck.

Haruyuki was equally stunned. Suzaku, the guardian of the south gate, started to pop into existence above its altar, which sat on the near side of the bridge, at the moment someone intruded on its territory. That territory was the large bridge five hundred meters in length and thirty meters in width. Judging from what they had witnessed the last time, it took the God about five seconds to materialize and start to move. Haruyuki had calculated that they could pass through the gate and fly a fair distance in the time it took for Suzaku to appear.

And yet, for some unknown reason, the instant they flew through the gate, Suzaku had already finished materializing—only thirty meters away from them. Haruyuki frantically spread the wings on his back and braked desperately to avoid slamming into the phoenix.

The south gates at their back were already tightly closed. Even if they turned around, the gates wouldn't likely open again. The gates had let them in the last time because Trilead—real name: Azure Air—had broken the seal plate for them in advance, but the seal apparently regenerated whenever the gate opened and closed again.

Since it was probably safe to assume Lead had been attacked and killed by the dozen guardian Enemies, they obviously couldn't hope for him to slice into the plate for them again. And if they went back inside now, they wouldn't be able to endure seeing Lead anyway, not after he had faced his own death to send them off.

Our only choice is to slip through Suzaku's flames and fly to the other side of the bridge, Haruyuki resolved, banishing the fleeting hesitation.

The Enemy with the name of a god had stopped right in front of them and was staring at the two avatars with red eyes.

Little ones. This time, you will indeed pay for the crime of disturbing my sacred place and slipping through so cunningly.

You will burn.

Anticipating the breath attack that was coming, Haruyuki focused every nerve in his body on seeing through to its trajectory.

But rather than opening its beak, the bird of flames spread its enormous wings out wide and flapped them firmly once.

"It cannot!" Utai cried out.

At the same time, Haruyuki saw a pure red, super-hot wave generated by Suzaku's wings push toward them in a semicircle. It wasn't a line—it was a surface. No matter which way he flew, there was no escaping it.

No way. We're going to die here? Just like that? We worked so hard to get out of the Castle inner sanctuary, Lead gave his life to open the gates for us—all that, and we get locked up in the cage of unlimited EK here?

"I...will not allow it!!" the childish shrine maiden in his arms shouted with determination when Haruyuki started to descend, brain frozen. She reached out her small left hand as far as it would go. The incredibly slender palm released a crimson fluctuation that looked very much like Suzaku's wave attack.

The instant the two energy waves touched each other, a dazzling white light colored the world.

Suzaku's heat wave became a ring with a circle in the center and passed around Haruyuki and Utai with a roar. At the same time, perhaps in some kind of damage feedback, Ardor Maiden's left arm disappeared instantly at the shoulder.

"Unn, ah!" The shrine maiden convulsed with a thin cry. Unable to withstand the intense, and very real, pain the Unlimited Neutral Field generated, her head drooped.

Holding the unconscious Utai tightly with both hands, Haruyuki mustered every last bit of energy he had to reactivate his will to fight.

Fly. Fly! If you don't fly right now, there's no meaning in the fact that you were born a flying avatar!

"Unhaaaaaaah!!" Haruyuki howled, and vibrating both wings as hard and as fast as he could, he plunged forward.

Beyond him, Suzaku spread its wings once more. The same attack again. He had to make it through the damage zone before the God could launch it.

I have to make it in time!!

But. The air ahead of Haruyuki shimmered like a heat haze and started to glitter red. The surface of his avatar crackled as it burned. A dizzying heat assaulted them, and his HP gauge—nearly 90 percent full—started to drop...

Then...

Something else he hadn't expected blocked Suzaku's attack.

Two lances of light, one red, one blue, shot in from behind the enormous bird and pierced the left and right wings at the same time.

He recognized those colors. The blue was Lightning Cyan Spike, the special attack of Cyan Pile—his best friend, Takumu.

And the red was Vorpal Strike, the Incarnate attack of Haruyuki's parent, his teacher, the person he respected more than anyone in this world—Kuroyukihime.

On the verge of disintegrating Haruyuki and Utai, Suzaku's super-heated wave was ripped to pieces and dispersed.

And then, almost brushing up against the massive, flame-shrouded wings, Haruyuki finally made it past to the rear of the God. But the Enemy naturally whirled around and, catching Haruyuki with eyes burning with rage, opened its large beak. The breath attack.

As Haruyuki charged forward with all his might toward the south side of the large bridge, he crossed paths with a silhouette racing in from that direction at a terrifyingly high speed. Accelerated to the limit, Haruyuki's perceptions caught the true form of that shadow.

Burst Linker. Not one—two. The deputy leader of Nega Nebulus, also known as ICBM, Sky Raker. And someone else was clinging to her, low against her back. A jet-black duel avatar with obsidian armor and long swords as limbs—the Black King, Black Lotus. The pale flames jetting out far behind Raker's Enhanced Armament, the Gale Thruster, colored the translucent black armor a beautiful sapphire.

In the instant they passed each other, Raker/Fuko and Lotus/Kuroyukihime looked at Haruyuki with eyes of madder red and of blue purple, and gently smiled. Their voices echoed directly inside his head.

Welcome back, Corvus. Leave Suzaku to us.

I'm trusting you with the future of the Legion, you know, Haruyuki. Now fly. Straight ahead without looking back.

The extended flow of time returned to normal, and Haruyuki, with Utai in his arms, and Fuko, with Kuroyukihime on her back, immediately receded from each other.

"Ah!" Unable to put the brakes on his own body as he flew ahead at full speed, Haruyuki simply let out a sound that was more like a cry as he earnestly turned his head and picked out the scene behind him in the corner of his field of view.

The single bullet that Fuko and Kuroyukihime had become grazed the right eye of Suzaku, who was even now about to spit out its lethal flame breath. Black Lotus's right arm flashed, slashing into the Enemy's eye. An ocean of flames like blood gushed out, and the monster bird howled its thunderous rage.

Suzaku stopped its breath attack and began to turn its massive frame back toward the north. It had shifted its target from Haruyuki to Kuroyukihime. Which meant—

They were planning to die.

In one sense, this was equivalent to the sacrifice of the young samurai Lead, luring away the dozen or so Enemies so that Haruyuki and Utai could make it through the gate, but in another sense, it was very different. Because unlike Lead, who would immediately be moved to a safe zone when he next regenerated and thereby avoid the unlimited EK state, Kuroyukihime and Fuko had nowhere to run. The only thing to the rear of Suzaku was the square altar—the very place where Ardor Maiden had been sealed—and if they died there, the next time they regenerated, they would only be immediately attacked by Suzaku and die once more.

Most likely, Kuroyukihime and the others had witnessed the sudden materialization of Suzaku while on standby and seen that it was an action designed to hinder Haruyuki and Utai's escape. And then they had made an instant decision: use themselves as bait to let Haruyuki and Utai get away. Even if it ended with Kuroyukihime and Fuko being sealed away themselves.

No.

That couldn't happen. That absolutely could not happen. Haruyuki's only objective as a Burst Linker was to revive Nega Nebulus and stand by Kuroyukihime's side as she reached beyond the horizon of level ten she yearned for. If his Legion Master and Submaster were sacrificed here, there would be no point in him alone surviving.

Haruyuki was seized with momentary conflict when, up ahead, a sharp voice reached him from below.

"Haru!!"

He turned with a gasp. A large, light-blue avatar with heavy armor was waving his left hand wildly about two hundred meters from the foot of the bridge. Cyan Pile. And beside him, a yellow-green lightweight avatar, Lime Bell.

"Haruuuuuu!!" Bell also shouted as loud as she could, and whirled the large bell equipped on her left hand all the way around. A faint chime rang out, and the bell was wrapped in a fresh green light effect.

"Citron Caaaaall!!"

As she shouted the technique name, she brought the hand bell straight down. The lime-green light that gushed out folded up around Haruyuki, a warm blanket of air.

Before his eyes, the damage he'd taken from the fight against the Enemy in the Castle and only moments ago from Suzaku's heat wave was healed. However, the wounds on Utai, still unconscious in his arms, remained. The target for the Citron Call effect was individual, so they couldn't both be healed at the same time. But shouldn't Lime Bell have cured the more heavily damaged Ardor Maiden first?

For a moment, Haruyuki failed to grasp what Chiyuri's intention was in recovering Silver Crow's health gauge first. But then Takumu called out to clear away his confusion.

"Haru, I'll take Maiden!"

Haruyuki opened his eyes wide and then immediately and without hesitation handed Ardor Maiden over to the outstretched arms of Cyan Pile below him. Lighter now, his body bounced upward, and he pulled into a tight U-turn.

"Haru, Lotus and Raker!" Chiyuri's voice pierced the air roaring past his ears.

"Got it! Leave it to me!!" Haruyuki shouted as he finished his turn.

His childhood friends had agonized and hesitated and decided for him that they could not let Kuroyukihime and Fuko die here.

That whatever happened, they were all going home together. With Takumu's and Chiyuri's feelings as a tailwind, Haruyuki flew north once more.

Ahead of him, Suzaku, also changing course to the north, bent its long neck into an S shape and opened its beak wide. He had only five—no, three seconds before the super-hot breath was released.

In his sights, Sky Raker and Black Lotus were carving out a parabola in the sky as they descended. The flames jetting from the Gale Thruster flickered irregularly, on the verge of dying. The thrust of the Enhanced Armament was incredible, but once its energy was used up, a long recharging period was required before it could fly again. They wouldn't be able to escape Suzaku's flames. Orange light flickered in the massive beak. The air around him shook with a heat haze.

I won't let you!!

"Unhaaaaaaaaah!!" With a force that would use up everything left in his special-attack gauge, Haruyuki vibrated the metallic fins on his back. A hazy light enveloped Silver Crow's entire body. He pierced the wall of wind pressure with the tips of his sharply outstretched hands, turning his avatar into a lance shooting forward through the sky.

Having lost its eye to Kuroyukihime's devastating blow, Suzaku didn't notice Haruyuki approaching from that side. He charged forward on a course so close to the giant bird that he nearly brushed alongside its face. Passing only a few dozen centimeters to the right of the beak, which looked like it would spit out its conflagration even now, Haruyuki sprinted out in front of the Enemy.

Behind him, a wave of overwhelming rage swelled up at this intruder. Before him, the two Burst Linkers opened their eyes wide in stunned surprise.

"Why?!"

"Haruyuki!!"

With a force that was very nearly a collision, Haruyuki grabbed in midair the two avatars groaning and crying out. He held the slender waists of Sky Raker and Black Lotus, who were basically the same size, with all his might and abruptly started flying upward.

The situation resembled the mission to rescue Ardor Maiden two days earlier, in which he had picked up Utai after she appeared in the center of the altar. However, one difference was that, unlike Utai, who had been on the ground, Kuroyukihime and Fuko were still maintaining an altitude of twenty or so meters. From here, he still had the leeway to change direction and take their sole route of escape—straight up.

Abruptly, their surroundings were dyed red. Suzaku had finally launched its flame breath. A raging river of overwhelming heat damage chased after them; one direct hit, and no matter how high-level they might be as Burst Linkers, they wouldn't be able to avoid being incinerated.

"Ngh. Aaaah!" Gritting his teeth, Haruyuki used every ounce of strength he had to fly directly upward.

Zzt! Something brushed up against the tips of his toes. His health gauge plummeted over 10 percent. He probably hadn't touched the breath itself, but rather the damage zone around it; still, he didn't look down. He simply, intently stared up at the blue-black cloudy sky of the Demon City stage and flew.

The slightest deviation in his trajectory would not be forgiven. A no-fly zone where extra gravity reigned was set up on both sides of the large bridge, and invisible barriers stretched up to infinity above the gates to the Castle and the walls of the palace. The instant he touched any of these, his flight would be over and they would fall.

The only course permitted was a completely vertical ascent. He would fly up as far as he could go and break free of Suzaku's targeting, cut out a large arc due south, and descend to escape to the south side of the bridge.

Through the roaring wind, Kuroyukihime whispered in his right ear, "Honestly. You really are…"

And then Fuko said with a smile in his left, "Hee-hee, I had a feeling it might turn out like this."

"I'm sorry. I'll apologize plenty after we get back!" Responding as he had two days earlier, Haruyuki fluttered the silver wings on his back even harder.

"Ah!" Fuko cried out.

Sensing something abnormal, Haruyuki reflexively looked down—and saw the figure of the massive bird shrouded in flames, surprisingly close. But why? They should have reached an altitude of close to three hundred meters already.

So then, it was chasing them. The guardian beast, the God Suzaku, supposedly unable to leave its territory, the large southern bridge, was also rising up into the sky, following Haruyuki and his friends.

The Enemy narrowed its remaining left eye as though it were laughing. A ponderous voice rang out in Haruyuki's mind.

Fools. I shall not allow you to escape from these wings of mine on such imitations.

At the same time, Suzaku violently flapped those wings, wings that likely spanned twenty meters. The enormous bird accelerated suddenly and began to close the distance between them.

"Ngh!" Turning his gaze straight up once more, Haruyuki tried to go even faster. But he immediately realized something terrifying.

His special-attack gauge, fully charged when they took off inside the Castle, was very quickly running out. When he thought about it, it only made sense. He had been flying continuously at top speed, first with Utai and then with Kuroyukihime and Fuko. It was no mystery that his gauge would disappear several times faster than when he was flying solo.

But if he lost thrust there, they would immediately be burned to a crisp in Suzaku's flames and die. And the place where they would regenerate was directly below—the altar in front of the south gate of the Castle. If that happened, they would all fall into a state of unlimited EK.

Staring at his special-attack gauge disappearing pixel by pixel at a frightening speed, Haruyuki investigated all their options in a brief thought.

Just Kuroyukihime and Fuko escape? Not possible. If they fell from this height, they would die instantly from the fall damage. And before that, they'd be killed by Suzaku immediately beneath them.

Do a U-turn now and escape to the south? Not possible. As long as they were targeted by Suzaku, even if he did manage the turn, they'd take a direct hit from the breath before they reached the ground.

Get them both to attack Silver Crow and recharge his gauge? Not possible. If his speed slackened even slightly while he was taking damage, they would instantly be caught in Suzaku's attack range.

His only choice was to fly.

Even if his gauge ran out. Even if the Brain Burst program announced that he would not be permitted to fly any farther. He would smash the controls of the system with the power of imagination, overwrite the phenomenon of impossible flight, and fly.

Imagine. The image of true flight.

The lone and maximum power given to the duel avatar Silver Crow. Flight was the form the scar in his heart, a scar he had carried for so long, had taken in the Accelerated World.

And that scar was the desire to escape. He wanted to break away from the ground, where nothing good ever happened, and go somewhere high up, somewhere far, far away. He wanted to go to a world where there was nothing but the speed of light, free of everything.

But...

Haruyuki hazily felt now that maybe that wasn't really flying.

No bird could fly forever. To fly, they had to eat, sleep, store up energy. To fly, they lived. To live, they flew. These two were one and the same, indivisible.

In which case, even if a person didn't have wings on their back, they could definitely fly in the real world, too. Hold the things you aim for, the things you want to overcome in your heart, imagine *that* materializing, and move forward one step at a time. Rather than looking down and passing the days with dissatisfaction, stare up at the sky—the place you want to reach someday—and actively put your feet forward. When they were doing that, people were definitely flapping invisible wings and flying.

"Fly!" Haruyuki cried briefly, staring intently at the sky of the Unlimited Neutral Field and its swirling black clouds.

Instead of vibrating the propulsive objects called metallic fins with the numerical energy known as the special-attack gauge—he had to flap the wings created by his own heart, flap them with the power of the imagination, and fly.

When she was first teaching Haruyuki the Incarnate System at the top of the old Tokyo Tower, Fuko had once said, "Perhaps you are the one who will be able to fly one day with Incarnate alone. But that will probably take a very long time."

As a Burst Linker and as an Incarnate user, Haruyuki was still just a little chick. He didn't have anywhere near enough training or experience. But if he was going to fly, now was the time. If he couldn't fly now, then for what purpose had he been born with the name Silver Crow?

The image. He had to imagine it. The meaning of flying itself. The meaning of kicking at the ground and aiming for the sky.

In Haruyuki's view, a vision of a small scops owl danced up, flapping white wings.

"Fly, Crow!!" Kuroyukihime to his right.

"Fly, Corvus!!" Fuko to his left.

He melted all this together into a single silver image, sending it racing through his body before concentrating it between his shoulder blades. And then Haruyuki saw with his mind's eye. He saw the ten metal fins extending from Silver Crow's back shine dazzlingly and change form, overwritten into real wings resembling those of a bird of prey.

"Unh...ah...aaaaaaaah!!" As Haruyuki howled, the last pixel of his special-attack gauge was consumed. But the propulsive force accelerating his whole body into the sky did not disappear.

Haruyuki flapped with all his might the wings shining a daz-zling silver and called out at the top of his lungs the name of the new Incarnate technique that came rising up from the depths of his heart.

"Light...speed!!"

Pwaan! His entire field of view was enveloped in the dazzle of silver. He approached the vision of the owl flying slightly ahead of him, touched it, became one with it. Cradling the other two duel avatars, Haruyuki flew with an incredible acceleration he had never felt before. The thick clouds of the Demon City stage drew closer in the blink of an eye, and then he was plunging through them without a hint of resistance.

His view was painted over with a thick gray. But soon, a crim-son light shone below. Suzaku was chasing after them even now. The pace of the Enemy's acceleration was clearly increasing. The two flying bodies of different sizes pierced the sky of the Acceler-ated World, carving out trajectories of silver and red.

A few seconds later, his field of view suddenly cleared.

The limitless sky, an azure so blue it almost sucked him in. A sea of snow-white clouds below, stretching out into the distance. He couldn't even imagine how many hundreds—or thousands—of meters up they were. But Haruyuki flapped his silver wings even harder.

Bompf! An enormous hole opened up in the sea of clouds beneath them. Appearing from within it was the enormous bird, shrouded in flames that burned even hotter. The God Suzaku was burning up anything and everything for the sake of the intrud-ers who had not once, but twice disturbed its territory. Its fierce will spilled out from its lone eye as it charged forward at the same speed as Haruyuki flying with the power of the Incarnate.

Exactly what I was hoping for! Come on!! Haruyuki howled in his mind and mustered every bit of his imagination to beat the silver wings.

The color of their surroundings gradually began to change. From azure to ultramarine, and then to black. Beyond them, several small points of light glittered. Stars. And far off to the right ahead of them in the sky, he noticed a thin silver thread stretching straight up, shining. That was…Hermes' Cord. The low-earth-orbit space elevator that circled the Accelerated World at a super-high altitude. It was just moving into the Tokyo area.

Finally, the speed of their ascent gradually began to falter. It wasn't that Haruyuki's Incarnate was weakening; it was that his "wings" had reached their maximum altitude. No matter how he might try to overwrite with his imagination, the propulsive mechanisms extending from Haruyuki's back were wings, and they'd had their limit. Without air, they could not fly. And he was basically in space.

The crimson light chasing them from below abruptly grew weaker. At the same time, the enormous bird's rage-filled roar shook the thin air.

Haruyuki stopped flapping and he looked down as they continued to gently ascend through momentum alone. The flames eternally blanketing the body of the God Suzaku, who had been right on their tail up until that point, had almost entirely disappeared because of the little oxygen in the air around them. The exposed, sleek red feathers began to frost at the tips.

"This is our chance!" Kuroyukihime suddenly shouted.

"Crow, let go! Raker, you can fly, right?!"

When Haruyuki reflexively opened his arms, the jet-black and sky-blue avatars drifted gently in what amounted to a zero-gravity world.

"Of course, Lotus!" Fuko nodded sharply and turned her back to Kuroyukihime.

"Good!" Black Lotus grabbed hold of Sky Raker's back with both legs. Raker whirled her body around, and blue light burned at the exhaust port of the Enhanced Armament, now recharged to some degree.

"Here we go!!" Fuko announced briefly, and without hesitation went full throttle with the booster.

Trailing a long streak of pale flames, the two avatars joined together as one charged fiercely toward the God Suzaku cruising

below them. Unlike Haruyuki's wings, Sky Raker's Gale Thruster was an energy-injection-type propulsive mechanism. Only she could fly in space where there was no air.

Left eye burning with fearsome rage, Suzaku spread its half-frozen wings to greet the two avatars with an attack. But no matter how it flapped, its massive body didn't move. It gave up on advancing and opened its beak to launch its flame breath, but it seemed that the warm-up took more effort than it had on the ground.

"Too late!!" Kuroyukihime shouted, opening wide the swords of both arms from her position on Fuko's back, and then drew them back into a downward V. Haruyuki had never seen this movement before. Both swords were enveloped in a whitish-blue light reminiscent of a distant star.

"Haaaaaaaaaah!" Fierce battle cry surging from her throat, the aura on her arms focused into several points of light. Eight on each sword for a total of sixteen.

With the collection of lights from an enormous constellation trailing her, Kuroyukihime called out in a voice so clear it threatened to echo to the ends of the universe, "Star Burst...Stream!!"

Both swords shot out so fast they became invisible to the naked eye as they alternated. With each blow, a single, pale, shining star was released, becoming a shooting star that slammed into Suzaku. Each time, the sound of the impact was enormous, shaking Haruyuki's body.

Each time a falling star, riding Sky Raker's incredible acceleration, crashed into it, the God shrieked. The massive body of the Enemy had lost its armor of flames, and any number of red feathers and damage effects flew off and scattered into the air. Displayed in Haruyuki's field of view, Suzaku's five-tier health gauge was carved away with such intensity that he almost doubted his eyes.

"Hnnngaaaaaaaah!!" Kuroyukihime's swords glittered and flashed nonstop to launch the shooting stars created by her Incarnate, a celestial machine gun. Ten shots. Eleven. Several holes had already been gouged out of Suzaku's wings, and its chest and tail were also torn up here and there. But the flames of rage burning in its left eye did not disappear. Even as it took this massive damage, it opened its beak and tried to force out its flame breath.

"Aaah!" Haruyuki reflexively howled, and drew his right arm back. The image of light collected from all over his body contracted into a single point, and then changed into a lance of light—and shot forward.

"Laser Lance!!"

The lance became a beam of light and raced through space, overtaking Kuroyukihime on the right to hit Suzaku's remaining eye precisely on target.

The God faltered on the verge of breathing out its flames, and in that single-second opening, Kuroyukihime released the last star—the sixteenth—with a roar. Drawing out a tail like a comet, the star fell from the heavens and crashed into the inside of Suzaku's mouth, causing the white-hot flame breath there to explode.

Haruyuki's view was filled with red light.

An unbelievably enormous ball of flames—a second sun—was born, and a surge of overwhelming energy expanded in all directions.

Haruyuki intently grabbed with outstretched hands the bodies of Kuroyukihime and Fuko, blown backward by the blast. He held them to his sides once more, caught the energy stream with the wings on his back, and turned the force into thrust. This phenomenon seemed like nothing other than Suzaku itself exploding, but the last bar of the Enemy's health gauge was still about half-full. They couldn't get reckless and get too close.

Haruyuki carved out a large arc as he circled the fireball and entered a downward course toward the earth's surface.

The red light gradually weakened, and the figure of the large bird on the verge of death was revealed. It had already lost the menacing air of a God; it lifelessly flapped its beaten and battered wings.

If we're going to defeat it, now's the time?! Haruyuki thought fleetingly.

But then a strange light cloaked Suzaku's massive frame—a tricolored aura of white, blue, and black. Haruyuki opened his eyes wide, wondering just what this was, and then something even more supernatural happened. Suzaku's injuries were healed from the outside in before his eyes. And its health gauge, down 90 percent, suddenly started to recover.

"Honestly. That the support of the other Gods would reach even this far into space," Kuroyukihime murmured, and he finally remembered.

The four super-level Enemies that guarded the four gates to the Castle were linked to one another. Even if one were attacked and damaged, as long as the other three were not engaged in battle, they would endlessly heal the injured one with their support abilities.

"It's pointless to chase this too far, Corvus."

Haruyuki nodded at Fuko's words. Their current objective was not to defeat Suzaku but to get out of its territory. He flapped the wings still wrapped in silver overlay to catch the thin air and move straight downward. The surrounding darkness shifted before his eyes to ultramarine and then a clear azure.

They finally approached the thick clouds and flew in headfirst. He broke through the gray veil to the sky of the Demon City stage. Far below, he could see the enormous palace surrounded by a circle of walls and the bridge stretching straight out from the south gate. He caught sight of three tiny figures waving their hands wildly at the southern end of the bridge.

A hundred meters above the bridge, he changed direction and moved into a gentle feetfirst glide. Flapping his wings carefully to avoid popping out over either side of the bridge, he headed for the ground as quickly as possible. The patterned tile of the surface of the bridge rose up, and the resolution increased.

Finally, the tips of the toes of Haruyuki, Kuroyukihime, and Fuko simultaneously touched the surface of the bridge. The place they landed was one meter from the southern end of the large bridge—the border of the territory of the God Suzaku.

Before them were the grinning faces of their three friends. The small shrine maiden standing on the right had apparently also been healed with Chiyuri's special attack; Ardor Maiden was stretching out a completely restored left arm alongside her right.

Haruyuki, Kuroyukihime, and Fuko took one step, two, and then three toward them and left the bridge.

"Welcome back!" Takumu, Chiyuri, and Utai said in unison.

"We're home." Kuroyukihime, Fuko, and Haruyuki also brought their voices together to speak as one. And then they each took a final step forward.

Haruyuki and Takumu. Kuroyukihime and Chiyuri. And Fuko and Utai. They all hugged one another hard. At the same time, a pillar of red light shot down from the sky above the altar in the distance and was sucked into the floor there, disappearing.

In that instant, the twin missions to rescue Ardor Maiden and escape the Castle, executed by all members of the Black Legion, Nega Nebulus, were completed.

11

At the same time as his overlay disappeared, Haruyuki's wings turned back into his original metal fins. These automatically folded up neatly and were tucked away in a protruding cover. After silently offering words of thanks to his own wings, Haruyuki looked again at the faces of his friends in turn.

They smiled gently, as if they could all tell he was crying beneath his mirrored visor. But, in this moment at least, he didn't feel like he had to hang his head in embarrassment. Because the presence of the grinning shrine maiden directly in front of him was the result of an indescribable success that was nearly miraculous.

Sealed away at the southern gate of the Castle in the Unlimited Neutral Field for two years, the "shrine maiden of the sacred fire," Ardor Maiden, was finally free. Once she moved a mere hundred meters to the south and slipped through the portal inside the triangular building—a police station in the real world—Utai would return normally to the real world, together with her avatar.

"You did it, Haru." It was Lime Bell—Chiyuri—who spoke, a grin spreading across her face all over again.

"Yeah," Haruyuki replied earnestly as he looked into her eye lenses, holding back translucent droplets. "Thanks, Chiyu. Thanks, guys." Instantly, the strength rushed from Haru's legs and he nearly collapsed on the spot, but he hurried to brace himself. He couldn't relax yet. He still had one—no, two more things to do.

First, the purification of the Armor of Catastrophe lodged inside himself. And once they succeeded at that, he wouldn't have to worry anymore about a bounty being placed on his head by the Seven Kings. At the same time, the repeating cycle of catastrophe would finally be broken.

And once they were done with the purification, training alongside Sky Raker's child, Ash Roller, to learn the Incarnate System awaited him. He couldn't imagine what kind of Incarnate Ash would materialize, but he was sure it would be a flashy technique to scare the wits—

"H-huh?" Haruyuki realized that the skull face of the century-end rider was not currently before his eyes. Blinking back the tears blurring his vision, he turned to Fuko. "What about Ash? You guys met up with him in front of the condo in Suginami and came here together, right? Oh, no way! He didn't get freaked out by Suzaku and make a break for it or something?"

He added this last bit 30 percent seriously, 70 percent jokingly, but Fuko didn't laugh. In fact, she bit her lip lightly as a hint of unease rose up in her eye lenses.

"Well, actually, we couldn't meet up with him."

"Huh? Wh-what do you mean?"

Ash Roller was supposed to have dived into the Unlimited Neutral Field from Fuko's car in the underground parking garage at Haruyuki's condo building in the real world. There was basically no horizontal distance between them. It should have been a simple thing to meet up in front of the building.

"The thing is, Haru," Takumu explained in a subdued voice, "in front of your condo, there were just tire tracks that looked like they had been left by Ash Roller's motorcycle. We kept waiting and waiting, but he never showed up."

"Tire tracks? So then, he couldn't wait and took off for the Castle by himself...and maybe got lost on the way or something?"

"No. That's hard to imagine." Fuko shook her head lightly. "He knows the route from Suginami to the Imperial Palace quite well. It's also easy to find the way in the Demon City stage. I can't believe he would get lost."

"And, Haruyuki, we chased after the tire tracks for as long as we could. They looked to continue on quite a ways due south of the condo," Kuroyukihime said, crossing the swords of her arms in front of her chest.

It was indeed strange. If you were going from Suginami to the Imperial Palace, even if you started out to the south, you'd have to turn to the east pretty quick.

Suddenly, an ominous feeling, strong enough to take his breath away, came over Haruyuki.

Ash Roller did have his flaky side, but he wasn't the kind of guy to blow off a promise. Especially when the person he was meeting was his master and parent, Sky Raker. Even if he had, hypothetically, seen some small Enemy that looked easy to defeat off in the distance, Haruyuki couldn't believe he would just chase off after it on his motorcycle.

In which case—something had happened. Most likely while he was on standby in the parking garage. An emergency so urgent he couldn't even wait to meet up with Fuko and the others had sent Ash racing off to the south. And then, over there, something else had happened.

Two and a half hours had already passed since Haruyuki and the others had dived into the Unlimited Neutral Field. And if Ash had dived even a single minute before seven, then he had already been in this world for over a dozen hours.

"Uh, um, I'm going to look for him!" Seized by an indescribable unease, Haruyuki spread the metal wings on his back once more. He used his special-attack gauge, recharged during the space battle with Suzaku, and floated gently upward.

"Haruyuki, it's dangerous to move alone! If you're going to search for him, we'll all—"

"It's okay!" he interrupted Kuroyukihime as she tried to stop him. "If I find anything, I'll come back and get you first! Please wait for me in front of the portal in the police station!" He hovered upward, gaining more altitude.

"Haru, if you're not back in an hour, we'll pull the cable on the other side, okay?"

"Got it! Thanks!" he shouted, grinning wryly at Chiyuri's declaration, and shot up into the sky.

If Ash Roller had gone south from Koenji, then that was southwest from the Castle. From a height of around fifty meters, he strained his eyes, but there were too many tall buildings in the Demon City stage, and he couldn't see anything. Gaining even more altitude, he began to move slowly.

Haruyuki flew in a straight line south of the Castle, first hitting Kasumigaseki and then moving into Akasaka and Aoyama. He let his eyes race intently across the landscape as he flew, but the only things moving were small- and medium-size Enemies. If he had seen a party hunting Enemies, he would have stopped to ask them if they knew anything, but perhaps because it was a weekday evening, he heard no sounds of battle.

He listened carefully, but the only sound was the hard wind of the stage blowing. The silence only further deepened his unease. Although he was flying at a speed that just barely conserved energy, his special-attack gauge was dropping bit by bit. And he definitely didn't think he could use the new Incarnate technique he had just awakened earlier, Light Speed, in this mental state.

"...Okay, then..." Haruyuki made the decision to go higher, bracing himself against the risk of being spotted by a hostile presence from the ground. Before he knew it, he had reached Harajuku. After this would be Yoyogi Park, and then Shibuya to the south.

Then.

In the center of the large intersection where Meiji and Inokashira crossed, at what was probably Meiji-jingumae Station in the real world, he felt like he saw something flash. When he looked down again, there were no Burst Linkers or Enemies there, but he decided to go down just in case.

Looking around carefully, Haruyuki landed on the blue-black

road and reached out to pick up what was probably the source of the reflected light.

At first glance, it was an unidentifiable object. A semicircle of clear orange glass set into a silver disc about four centimeters in diameter. A thin pole extended from the edge of the disc, but it seemed to be broken in half.

"...What is this..." Muttering, he turned the mysterious part over and over in his hand, the faint sunlight of the Demon City stage reflecting off it so that the object flashed orange every so often.

Instantly, Haruyuki realized what it was.

A motorcycle turn signal. He was sure this was part of the turn signal Ash Roller had made blink as a feint during the duel on Kannana that morning.

In the Unlimited Neutral Field, pieces broken off Enhanced Armament and the like stayed around for a fairly long time compared with the Normal Duel Field. Most likely, Ash Roller's motorcycle had been in some kind of accident when it passed through here, and the turn signal had been damaged. Haruyuki looked around again with this idea in mind and found several burn marks on the walls of the buildings lining the south side of the road.

So the direction of attack was from north to south. Which meant that Ash had ridden here, taking Inokashira from Kannana, been attacked from the north by someone, and turned south at this intersection?

Still clutching the turn-signal part, Haruyuki kicked at the ground and flew upward. The unease filling his chest had reached the level of his throat.

At a speed that just barely kept his gauge from decreasing too suddenly, he flew south along Meiji Street. After just twenty seconds, he spotted the next fallen object. He descended to the ground to check it out.

He didn't have to wonder about what it was here. A hub and rim with thin fixed spokes. Around it, a thick gray rubber tire. The bike's wheel. Guessing from the width, the front wheel.

On the ground, he saw a concentration of black attack marks just like the ones he had seen before. He assumed that the motorcycle had taken serious damage here; the front wheel had broken off, and the experienced rider had continued riding south, doing a wheelie. But he wouldn't have been able to keep up the trick-riding forever.

"Ash!" A hoarse voice slipped out of Haruyuki's throat, and he turned his gaze to the road stretching out to the south.

At that moment, the faint sound of a collision shook the air. On the wall of a group of buildings a hundred meters or so down the road, something flickered green. The hard noise and the light were not the explosion of an object or an attack effect. They were a duel avatar's death effect.

Reflexively, Haruyuki started to run, before remembering he could switch to flight. He took a shortcut, flying up over the roofs of the buildings along the road that gently curved to the right. The instant the road near Miyashita Park in Shibuya Ward came into sight, his entire body started shaking. His wings stiffened up, and he unconsciously hovered about twenty meters in the air.

Directly ahead, his eyes picked up an object that was once a metallic gray American motorcycle, mercilessly destroyed—tire, engine, frame, muffler, pieces of it scattered everywhere.

A little farther ahead, a group of six Burst Linkers stood in a circle. Not only was he close with none of them, he didn't even know their names. The one thing all six shared was a weak aura of darkness rising up from their bodies. Incarnate overlay. The energy source—the "eye" glittering red like blood in the center of their chests. ISS kits.

And in the center of their little circle, a single Burst Linker curled up in a ball. Shiny leather riding suit. Flashy knee and shoulder pads. And on the head, a helmet with the shield of the face mask patterned after a skull.

"Ash?" Haruyuki squeezed out a voice that was not quite a voice from his chest.

Deep cuts covered Ash Roller's body. But the damage wasn't what was keeping him from moving. He wasn't moving because he was using his avatar as a shield to protect a tiny light floating above the road.

The flickering grass-colored point of light was a marker left in the place where a Burst Linker died in the Unlimited Neutral Field. Probably the owner of the death effect Haruyuki had felt a minute or so earlier. He'd seen that color before. He was sure of it—that was Ash's "little brother," Bush Utan.

Haruyuki understood the situation in a flash of intuition. What had happened here while he and Utai were struggling to escape from the Castle.

It was probably something like this:

While waiting for the seven PM dive time in the car parked under Haruyuki's condo in the real world, he had been called to the Gallery of a duel. In that stage, he had run into Bush Utan, who had been the dueler or maybe another spectator. There, he had persuaded Utan to meet up with him in the Unlimited Neutral Field, so that he could communicate the things that he should as a big brother.

The meeting place had probably been around Shibuya. So Ash had no doubt thought he'd go and get Utan before meeting up with the four members of Nega Nebulus in front of the condo at precisely seven o'clock, and he'd dived early and headed to Shibuya.

But the time and place had, somewhere along the line— probably in the duel field where he was in the Gallery—been leaked to people in possession of ISS kits. They launched an ambush at Meiji-jingumae Station to hunt Ash and Utan as prey. Caught off guard by the dark Incarnate technique, Ash fled all the way here, even as he took damage to his motorcycle, but his beloved ride was finally destroyed. No, not only that. If Ash Roller had dived into this world a little earlier than seven o'clock, then Haruyuki assumed that more than ten hours had passed already. Which meant—together with Bush Utan, he had gone through the cycle of death and regeneration at least a few times.

In the Unlimited Neutral Field, Enhanced Armament that was completely lost once did not regenerate until you left the field and re-logged in. Ash Roller would have lost his entire health gauge and died, but when he regenerated an hour later, the American motorcycle that contained nearly all the potential of his duel avatar would not have returned with him.

So then, the Burst Linkers standing there were surrounding an Ash Roller who had lost the majority of his battle power and torturing him to death with the dark Incarnate generated by the ISS kits.

Over. And over. And over and over and over and over...

"Unh...Ah...Aah..." A moan slipped out of the hovering Haruyuki's throat.

Not seeming to notice this, one of the six stepped toward Ash Roller crouched over on the road. He had a midsize, unremarkable form, but there was a fair bit of volume to his arms. Haruyuki felt like he had seen him before but couldn't remember his name.

"Next up...is me. Wonder how many points you got left?" the avatar said, and then grabbed hold of Ash's helmet tightly with his large right hand, a black aura pouring over it.

Skrrk! A sharp sound rang out, and Ash's trademark skull face broke into pieces and crumbled.

The attacker now grabbed on to the exposed head of the duel avatar, a face that seemed delicate and boyish somehow, for all the swagger of the character he played.

The attacking avatar pulled Ash Roller—still trying to protect Utan's marker light—up off the ground forcefully. Face turned upward against his will, Ash caught sight of Haruyuki frozen on the roof of the building. His pale-green eye lenses opened wide momentarily, and then he seemed to smile weakly. In Haruyuki's mind, the usual reckless and boastful voice echoed haltingly.

Heh-heh...Messed up. Sorry, Crow...Wasted...the good vibes from you and Mast—

Krnch! A thick sound echoed in the stage, and the left arm of the attacker pierced the center of Ash's chest. A pillar of gray light shot up, and the slender rider together with his riding suit exploded into pieces.

Showered in the scattering fragments, the attacker turned his

head slightly to look at his own Instruct menu. "Oh!" he said. "One more time and I can level up. I hope he hangs on until my turn comes again."

Haruyuki's entire body shook so hard that it threatened to fly into pieces. Tensed to the limit, his limbs creaked, and his teeth chattered beneath his helmet. The voice that leaked out from his throat was low and broken, cracked in a way he himself had never heard before.

"Ah...Aaaaah...Aaaaah..."

His body felt like it had been filled with freezing liquid. Or maybe fiery hot like molten steel. At any rate, a single enormous feeling was concentrated within him, and this raced around his body instead of blood.

Rage.

Anger. A rage so overwhelming it turned his vision red. A dark hatred. And the urge to destroy.

"Ah...Aaaah, ah, aaaaaah...!"

Keee! A sharp metallic noise came from Haruyuki's hands. Silver Crow's slender fingers were tapering into the talons of a bird of prey, curving, getting larger. At the same time, the color of his armor changed. From the glittering mirror silver to a clouded chrome silver.

No! You can't give in to those feelings! You'll disappear!

Someone somewhere far, far away was shouting. But the faint voice no longer reached Haruyuki's consciousness.

Metal still shrieking, his arms were covered in additional chrome-colored armor. And then his legs. This form, with its malicious edging, was much more sinister and far more demonic than when it had materialized at Hermes' Cord.

Instead of the girl's voice, a distorted metallic voice filled his mind.

We are you. You are us. You cannot be resurrected, should even an eternity pass. I am Catastrophe. I am Demise. The one who shall sound the death knell for this world.

It was exactly the same voice he had heard after school in the yard of Umesato Junior High in the real world, but unlike that time, he didn't feel any pain at all. Which meant that this wasn't an overflow of negative Incarnate. Haruyuki himself was calling *it*, seeking to fuse with it.

Haruyuki shouted the name at the same time as the voice.

My name is…

"…Chrome Disaster!!"

The ferocious yell that gushed out was nothing other than the roar of a beast hungry for blood, seeking slaughter. Purple system font cut across the top left of his field of view like a flash of lightning. You equipped an Enhanced Armament: the Disaster.

Shrieking metallically, armor like the fangs of a demon covered him thickly from stomach to chest. A sharp tail shot out from his back and his wings were transformed into a weapon-like silhouette. His smooth, round helmet was completely swallowed up top to bottom by a visor patterned after the maw of a wild animal. His field of view was covered by another thin gray layer.

In the sky above, the black clouds of the Demon City stage formed an enormous vortex. From its center, a bolt of black lightning rained down, accompanied by booming thunder. Haruyuki reached out his right hand to greet it.

The bolt stopped in his hand, changed shape, and became an object. A one-handed long sword, hilt blackly lustrous with a sharply tapered blade. The high-level Enhanced Armament once called Star Caster in the long-distant past.

This was the strangely glittering binary star of destiny, following alongside the sixth star Kaiyou aka the Arc Destiny, the original form of the Armor of Catastrophe, the eighth star of the Big Dipper.

"*Hnggaaaaaaah!!*" Haruyuki roared, brandishing the demon sword high above his head.

The battle cry was filled with boundless rage and hatred, but it rang through the sky of the Accelerated World like a wail somehow.

To be continued.

AFTERWORD

Reki Kawahara here. Thank you so much for reading *Accel World 8: The Binary Stars of Destiny.*

In this volume, the rather vague-sounding "image power" ended up being the key word, and since I'm sure this doesn't quite click for some readers, I thought I'd take this opportunity to offer a little supplemental explanation.

I believe that image power—imagination—is the greatest ability human beings have. Because the power to imagine is the only one where the end result is output that the human mind generates from zero, rather than output from some given input.

And now it's no doubt even more confusing (lol), but the basic idea is that perhaps this thing called imagination doesn't stop with specialized fields like arts, literature, science, and sports, but rather is incredibly important and effective in the little things we do in our lives every day. For instance, everyone alive has hard times, times of struggling, in addition to the good times. I think that if we first think about these things when we confront them, we can change the amount of energy needed, and even the result, if we imagine the situation in advance and make preparations to accept it.

Every morning, after I wake up, I check my plans for the day, and if there's something unpleasant or annoying, I try to imagine how I'll get past it. Although I can't say for sure if that's actually useful or not (lol), at any rate, when I do actually get going, I feel like I'm at least a little prepared to tackle it. I'm going to the dentist after this, so I'm focused on imagining the drilling sensation!

Also, in this book, Haruyuki managed to tough it out in the basketball game using image power, and even if that might have been an exaggeration, I don't believe it was an outright lie. I'm also really terrible at sports and exercise, but when I'm riding at my maximum speed on my bicycle, there's a real difference in how long I can keep going, depending on whether I'm imagining my breathing and pedaling or not. Although, of course, I can't actually activate the Incarnate System and manage sixty kilometers per hour or anything. (Right now, anyway...) And so in the end, this turned into an explanation that really doesn't make any sense (lol), but please do try imagining all kinds of things if you get the chance! And I'm sorry for continuing the story again! I'll definitely finish it next time! Really!

To my editor, Miki (former basketball player), and my illustrator, HIMA, I'm sorry for being late with my manuscript once again and causing problems for you! And to all you readers, these are difficult times, but let's keep an image of the future in our minds and keep on fighting!

Reki Kawahara

April 14, 2011

Dive into the latest light novels from *New York Times* bestselling author REKI KAWAHARA, creator of the fan favorite *SWORD ART ONLINE* and *ACCEL WORLD* series!

©REKI KAWAHARA ILLUSTRATION:Shimeji

©REKI KAWAHARA ILLUSTRATION:abec

SWORD ART ONLINE Light Novels

©REKI KAWAHARA ILLUSTRATION.abec

And be sure your shelves are primed with Kawahara's extensive backlist selection!

SWORD ART ONLINE Manga

©REKI KAWAHARA/
TAMAKO NAKAMURA

©REKI KAWAHARA/TSUBASA HADUKI

©REKI KAWAHARA/
NEKO NEKOBYOU

©REKI KAWAHARA/KISEKI HIMURA

ACCEL WORLD Manga

©REKI KAWAHARA/HIROYUKI AIGAMO

ACCEL WORLD Light Novels

©REKI KAWAHARA ILLUSTRATION:HIMA

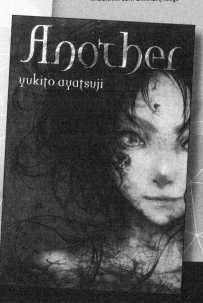

ACCEL WORLD, Volume 8
REKI KAWAHARA

Translation by Jocelyne Allen
Cover art by HIMA

ACCEL WORLD
©REKI KAWAHARA 2011
All rights reserved.
Edited by ASCII MEDIA WORKS
First published in 2011 by KADOKAWA CORPORATION, Tokyo.
English translation rights arranged with KADOKAWA CORPORATION, Tokyo, through Tuttle-Mori Agency, Inc., Tokyo.

English translation © 2016 by Yen Press, LLC

Yen On
1290 Avenue of the Americas
New York, NY 10104

Visit us at yenpress.com
facebook.com/yenpress
twitter.com/yenpress
yenpress.tumblr.com
instagram.com/yenpress

First Yen On Edition: December 2016

Yen On is an imprint of Yen Press, LLC.
The Yen On name and logo are trademarks of Yen Press, LLC.

The publisher is not responsible for websites (or their content) that are not owned by the publisher.

Library of Congress Cataloging-in-Publication Data

Names: Kawahara, Reki, author. | HIMA (Comic book artist) illustrator. | Beepee, designer. | Allen, Jocelyne, 1974– translator.
Title: The binary stars of destiny / Reki Kawahara ; illustrations, HIMA ; design, bee-pee ; translation by Jocelyne Allen.
Description: New York, NY : Yen On, 2016. | Series: Accel world ; 8
Identifiers: LCCN 2016034782 | ISBN 9780316317610 (paperback)
Subjects: | CYAC: Science fiction. | BISAC: FICTION / Science Fiction / General.
Classification: LCC PZ7.K1755 Bi 2016 | DDC [Fic]—dc23 LC record available at https://lccn.loc.gov/2016034782

ISBN: 978-0-316-31761-0

10 9 8 7 6 5 4 3 2 1

LSC-C

Printed in the United States of America